A GROTESQUE FIGURE HOVERED OVER THE INDIAN BOY.

It was the medicine man, Big Horse; and it was now clear that the "red eye" was a most peculiar medicine. For the eyes of the man were swathed in a heavy blindfold and in the center of his forehead, held in place by a single cord, appeared a great red stone, that gleamed and shimmered.

Rory Michel, in a single glance, knew that it was a ruby, and one of the true pigeon's blood, the purest color, the richest fire. He told himself that one day the jewel should be his!

"I have brought a great medicine man to heal my son," the chief told Big Horse. "His skin is white, but his heart is as red as yours. Let him try his skill."

Then he turned to Rory. "Tell me if you can save him!"

"All will be well," Rory said, and forced himself to smile. If he succeeded, he would claim the ruby. If he did not . . .

MAX BRAND

TAMER OF THE WILD

WARNER BOOKS

A Warner Communications Company

Chapter 1

Two months before the tragedy of Santa Anna, Rory
Michel came to the Ware mine. There was then no
token of disaster in the air. The stages had been going
through uninterruptedly for months; and the Apaches
were as quiet as mice. Up to that time, in fact, they had
not formed a taste for white meat. A Mexican diet
suited their palates better.

The mine promised well, too. It was more than a
promise, because forty thousand dollars in bar silver
was waiting to be hauled, and that forty thousand was
the clear profit of the past six months. Dean Ware
promised himself and his family two more years in
Arizona before he went back to the "States" with a
comfortable fortune—a quarter of a million was big
money in those days. Or he might find a purchaser. At
any rate, fortune was at the prime when Rory Michel
came in.

He appeared from among the scattered live oaks and
the bean-bearing mesquite of the valley and, like a
snail, he crawled up the slope toward the mine, leading
a stumbling horse behind him. Some of the Mexican
laborers were about, for they had knocked off work for
the day, and when they saw the man on foot, leading a
horse, they began to laugh and slap their legs, for they
said that he was drunk. He was swaying like a tree in
the wind; and once he dropped to his knees.

Some of them ran out to torment him though Dean
Ware called to them to leave the fellow alone. They
went on anyway, but when they came to the wanderer,
they drew back; and they kept on drawing back to give
him a larger amount of elbowroom.

"Look, Dean," said his wife. "They're crossing
themselves."

"Maybe it's Satan," said Dean Ware.

At this their daughter, Nancy, lean and brown as an Indian herself, stood up suddenly and looked down the slope.

It might have been a caricature of Satan, for a fact, that now came up to the house. He needs describing, and the horse comes first. For it was a tall wreck of an animal and seemed about to fall to pieces every moment. It should have been black, but it was sunburned and weather-faded to a dismal, dark, rusty color. The ribs stood out clear to the points where they hitched onto the spinal column, in which every vertebra was a separate lump. It had no muscles in the legs, just withering tendons and bones. Its chin hung down below its knees; it had been trailing its feet so far that the hoofs were beveled off in front.

That was the look of the horse; except, it must be added, that the stallion had a fine sweep of mane and tail that looked totally incongruous, like young wigs on octogenarian heads.

That was the horse, but the man was a great deal worse.

He was dressed in what looked like the rags of a coyote skin. A coyote skin is not very large but this one was big enough to swathe Rory Michel twice around, for he was a picture of all the famines that ever were; he was famine itself. He was hands and feet, elbows and knees. One could have picked him up by the projecting collar bone like a vase by the ears, and not a heavy vase, at that.

There was not much to his face except the rags of beard that hung from it. It seemed as though his eyes had been put out; they were like the hollows in a museum skull. When he came nearer, one could see the gleam, deeply buried in the shadows. His head hung forward, like the head of a trailing hound; he looked like a sleepwalker, as though he would try to walk right through the solid wall of the house. But, almost worse than all else, was the shower of wind-entangled black hair that fell down to his shoulders and over his face. Like the horse, he was wind-burned and sunfaded.

8

As this ghost came staggering up the slope, Dean Ware saw finally that he left a red mark on the grass with every step he made.

Then Ware jumped up.

"Go into the house—Nancy! Harriet!" he commanded with a military precision, for he had always wanted to join the army, when his ship came in.

Neither of the women paid the slightest attention to him.

"It's a Negro!" said Mrs. Ware, for Michel was weather-blackened and tarnished more than even a Mexican's hide.

"He's dying!" said Nancy, and ran straight out to the stranger.

Her father was a step or two behind her. She already had Rory by the grimy knobs of his elbows, supporting some of his weight.

"Brandy!" said Rory, looking vaguely straight before him.

Mrs. Ware vanished into the house, with a gasp, and got a bottle of Mexican brandy, almost colorless and stronger than a buffalo bull. When she came out, she found that her husband and daughter had got the stranger as far as the steps of the veranda, but there he stuck and shook his head.

"Let him have the brandy, first," said Mrs. Ware. "He's half out of his head, poor thing!"

They gave Rory the bottle. It seemed that there could not be strength in his pipe-stem arms to lift it, but I suppose that Michel, at the point of death, would still have been the master of either bottle or jug. He did not lift it to his own lips, however, but he turned around and pressed up the sagging head of the stallion, thrusting it high. He put his hand inside the mouth of the horse, where the lead rope was knotted around the lower jaw, and when the mouth opened, he poured half the contents of the bottle down the throat of the nag.

"Now, God bless you all!" said Rory, handing the bottle back to Mrs. Ware. "That shot in the locker will do him good?"

Ware called some of the Mexicans to get the horse to

9

the stables; he himself tried to persuade Rory into the house but, half-dead as he was, Rory was not to be moved. He clung to the lead rope and drew the black after him toward the barn.

Mrs. Ware said he was obviously more than half mad or entirely so; and Rory was permitted to do as he chose. What he chose was to get the black into a stall, tether him there, make a thick, deep bed for the rickety brute, and then give him oats and hay. Rory sat in the manger: the exhausted horse would not eat until his master held out oats in the cup of his double hands. Bit by bit, he fed the animal for an hour. Then the stallion slumped down upon its bed in a state of collapse.

Even then, Michel would not touch the food that had been brought to him from the house until he first had counted the breathings of his horse and listened to the beat of the heart.

After that, refusing all other nutriment, he ate some porridge with salt, drank a little tea, tied the leadrope around his arm, and lay down in the manger in front of his horse.

He slept for twenty-four hours, nearly; and so did the horse. He slept so profoundly that when Nancy Ware came out to dress those incredible feet—they were worn to the bone—the washing and the bandaging only roused him to confused muttering. Straightway he began to snore again.

For a week, Rory hardly exchanged a word with a soul. He ate and slept and, when he awakened, it was to labor over the starved skeleton of the stallion.

"He ought to die. So ought the horse," said Dean Ware. "I've seen starvation before, but never anything like that. There was no stomach to the man. It was all gone."

"I knew they wouldn't die, either of 'em," declared Nancy.

"Bright child!" said her father. "And how did you know, pray?"

"By the look in their eyes," said she.

"Knowledge after the event," began Mr. Ware. "Harriet, I have some old clothes that might do for him. He's a white man, by his manner of talk."

That was at the end of the week. On this day, Rory shaved, got one of the Mexicans to clip his hair, took a thorough scrubbing, and led his horse out into the sunshine of the corral. There they walked up and down, and Rory sang in a language which no one understood.

It was not Spanish or French; it was no Indian dialect, some of the half-breeds were willing to swear. He sang as he strolled with the black, looking toward it from time to time, and noting how it lifted its head.

That same night, dressed in the cast-off clothes of Ware—"Colonel" Ware most people called him, for no better reason that his military manner of speech and carriage—Mr. Michel sat with the Mexicans at dice and risked the battered boots, retained them and won, in the course of an evening of charmed play, fifty dollars, a saddle, a good bridle plated with silver, and a pair of spurs, together with an excellent new blanket.

He tried the equipment on the stallion the next day; and when the horse was led out into the corral again, the saddle covering the wreck of its middle piece, Nancy Ware saw it and cried out: "Look, dad! That old black nag was a beauty once upon a time!"

"That old black nag is a five-year-old," said her father. "I've looked at his teeth! There's a story behind that couple. Can you make him talk, Nan?"

"All I know is that his name is Rory Michel, and that you pronounce the last name like 'Mickle.' He's particular about that, it seems. He said it several times over. But he won't talk about anything."

"He's a refugee from California," declared her father, who was a man of sudden and violent opinions. "He's one of the rascals who have been driven out by the vigilantes."

"What makes you think that?" asked the girl.

"He has a wild eye. And he doesn't talk. Silence is generally guilt," replied the colonel.

"Why should he have dragged that wreck of a horse with him all the way from California, then?"

"Freak of the fancy. Never can tell about the 'bad men.' They're like children—superstitious, you know! He may have attached his luck to the stallion, and so he kept it with him."

"And how did he lose his clothes? And would his hair have grown that long just on a journey from California?"

"You know my dear, that it is always easy to ask a list of baffling questions," said the colonel. "How can I answer everything that may be asked about this desert waif? He's a bad one. That's all I'm sure of."

"Just from the look in his eye?"

"He's a gambler. He wins at dice from the Mexicans every night."

"That's not any proof of villainy, so far as I can see."

"In addition," concluded Colonel Ware, "there's the horrible condition in which he reached this place. Out of my experience I've drawn the conclusion that suffering comes where suffering is due!" Poor Ware! He could not look into the days which lay ahead!

"I don't believe a word of it," said his daughter. "Some day I'll have the story from him."

"Never," said the colonel. "Guilt is the tightest gag in the world!"

Chapter 2

Nevertheless, Rory did talk, though it was some weeks later. He was a different man by that time. Little by little, he had seemed younger, passing from middle age almost to boyhood through the stages of his convalescence. He looked forty, if a day, in the beginning, then thirty-five and thirty. He was hardly more than his early twenties, when his recovery was completed.

He was a cheerful one, with hair sleek and shining, blue-black eyes, and always a touch of healthy color in his cheeks. He was about middle height, with a good-natured face. He was a little heavy in the shoulders and in the jaw.

Now that his recovery was perfected, however, he hardly won so much as a glance, compared with the stallion he had brought in. For the black, it appeared, had been aged by starvation, only, and when it was smoothed out by a good feeding, it was the loveliest picture of a horse that ever had filled the eye of Ware, though he knew thoroughbreds as he knew a book. Sixteen hands of him, jet black without the flaw of a single white hair, ebony even in his hoofs, he danced in the corral like a colt or skimmed over the valley as fleet as a bird, with his master in the saddle.

"Not even a very good rider!" said Ware.

"He's good enough to handle that big black flash," said the girl, "and he's the only one who can."

"Nobody else has tried," said Ware.

"Every Mexican horse-tamer on the place has tried," said she. "They've stolen their chances and slipped saddles onto him. He doesn't mind that, but when they get onto his back he sheds them with one snap of himself. He's as supple as a whip and just about as fast moving."

"Well, look at Michel's seat," observed her father. "There he comes now, up the valley road. Is that a horseman's seat?"

"No," she admitted. "But that's a horseman's horse."

"Nancy," said her father, irritated, "you're like all your sex. You have an answer, and it pleases you just as much to answer with nonsense as with real understanding. I say, that boy is one of the strangest people I've ever known, and I don't trust him!"

"You think that he's an outlaw, driven all the way from California," said the girl.

"I don't know. He may be an outlaw, but he hardly knows one end of a rifle from the other. I saw him shooting at marks with the Mexicans yesterday. He couldn't hit a thing. But whatever he is, he's a useless addition around here. I hope he'll drift on soon."

"Not till I have the story," said the girl.

"You'll never have it," replied the colonel. "And I've already told you why."

She ran down from the veranda into the road. As she waved her arms, Rory Michel drew up the stallion.

"Whoa, Doc," said he.

"That's no name for that sort of a horse," she objected.

"Any name is good that's short," he answered.

"Rory, I want you to tell me the story of yourself and that stallion," said Nancy.

"Of course, I'll tell you," replied he.

"You will?"

"Yes. I'll tell you. Why not?"

"Because you've dodged every time I've asked. I asked you where you got it, for instance."

"And I told you—in the West."

"That's no answer. Tell me the name of the man."

"What man?" he asked.

"The man who bred him."

"No man bred him," replied Rory.

He turned the big black into the corral and stripped off saddle and bridle. Doc turned about and hung his head over the fence, while his master rubbed his nose.

"No man bred him?" the girl was asking.

"No. No man bred him. He was running wild."

"Ah, and you ran him and caught him! Was that it? Come in and let father hear the yarn."

They went up to the veranda where Colonel Ware greeted the boy with a nod.

"He was running wild. And Rory caught him, and tamed him!" exclaimed Nancy. "Isn't that wonderful, dad?"

The colonel muttered something politely indistinct.

"How long did you run him?" she asked Rory Michel.

"I didn't run him. I walked him."

"Hold on!" said Ware, bending heavy brows upon the youth.

"Oh, start at the beginning, Rory," said the girl. "I want to hear every step of it."

"I was with a caravan, heading west. I wanted to dig up a few millions in California. We were heading straight down the Mormon trail and I rode out on my saddle mule one day, and had a glimpse of this big black thunderbolt breezing along the edge of the sky.

"I trotted up to a hilltop, and had a better look at

him, and he seemed to me something I'd seen before, something right out of my own mind. That's how badly I wanted him."

"I know," murmured Nancy Ware.

She let her eyes shine at him. The colonel folded his hands and raised his head. He looked somewhat down his nose toward the speaker, for he was a big man, with a leonine head.

"When Doc saw me," went on Rory, but the girl interrupted to say: "I wish you had another name for him. You ought to call him Thunder or Midnight, or something splendid."

Rory grinned.

"You know," he said, "I don't run to fancy names, Nan."

The colonel stirred. Two things displeased him in this speech. One was the grin and one was the familiar nickname. He would speak to Nancy about discouraging this attitude in a nameless man. In his heart he was very sorry that some small portion of his own dignity had not descended upon his daughter.

"Well, go on," said she. "Then you went back to the caravan and got some of them to come out and help you run the black? The beauty!"

He looked into the corral, where Doc was drinking from the watering trough.

"When Doc saw me," he resumed, "he went off on wings and dipped into the next valley. I galloped my mule to the divide, and just as I reached it, that fool of a mule put his forefoot in a hole and broke his leg."

"That's bad luck," said she. "Were you hurt?"

"Gave my head a knock," said he. "I had to get up and shoot the mule. But I lost my temper; that was the bad part of it!"

"Well?" she encouraged, as he fell into a dreaming silence.

He smiled toward the mesas far down the valley on which the sun was pouring torrents, and the bluest sky in the world walled up the end of the ravine.

"You know," said he, "I made up my mind that I'd have a closer look at that black beauty, anyway. So I went on across the next ridge, missed him and trailed

15

him over the next beyond, and there I saw him on the rim of the sky. Then the sun went down. But a moon came up, and I kept on walking. I hadn't brought a rope with me, but somehow I couldn't resist trying to get a hand on him. D'you know what I mean?"

"Entirely illogical, I should say," said the colonel.

"I know," answered the girl, "but then I can feel the human nature in that. I've done the same thing, just to get an antelope, though I knew it was like trying to tag the wind."

"Well," said he. "That's all there is to it."

"All there is to it?" exclaimed the colonel.

"Yes. I just kept on walking after him, and finally I got him. I made a rope on the way."

"Wait a minute," said the colonel. "You forgot the caravan. I suppose that you returned—"

"No, I didn't return."

The girl, her lips parted, stared at Rory as though she were suddenly frightened by something she heard him say, or saw in his face.

"And your property in the caravan?" asked the colonel sharply.

"I didn't have much. I had the mule, chiefly. And the mule was dead. So I just went on."

"This, you say," pursued the colonel in his most judicial tone, "was near the Great Salt Lake?"

"Yes."

"Humph," said the colonel. "And you walked all the distance from there to—just a moment—where did you catch the horse?"

"Two days from here," said Rory. "I don't know how many miles. A million, I thought, in those last two days."

"Ah!" said the colonel, politely and coldly. "You walked, from the Salt Lake to—this place?"

"Yes."

The colonel cleared his throat.

"How long ago did you begin the trail of the horse, may I ask?" said the colonel.

"How long? About six months," said Rory.

"Six—" began the colonel.

And suddenly his jaw fell and he gaped like a child.

16

He never could explain it, afterwards, but the naked simplicity of that remark convinced him at a single stroke that he was hearing the truth.

He saw, too, the picture of Rory as he had come in on the first day, the skeleton clad in the tattered skin of a coyote. Pain and wonder flooded slowly through the heart of the colonel.

"My boy," he said gently, "you walked through an inferno, a great part of the way, I have no doubt."

"It was just misery to watch Doc grow so thin and weak," said Rory.

"That's what made me lose sleep, mostly. When my clothes wore out, and we crossed high passes, that was pretty bad; the cold, I mean to say. But the worst thing was watching Doc wear down. I knew it was that or I'd lose him and all my work. But I was afraid he'd die before I got to him. Well, I had a stroke of luck, at last!"

"Luck?"

"He stood with his legs braced wide apart. Right in the middle of the day, with the sun blazing. Asleep, I think. Asleep with his eyes open. I got up and landed the noose around his neck."

"And there you had him?" cried the girl.

"Yes. He dragged me for awhile, but I managed to hold on till he was tired. Two days later we landed here. That brandy saved him, I think."

He looked at Colonel Ware.

"I've never thanked you for that," he said. "It's because I haven't any words that fit!"

Chapter 3

Rory slept in the mow of the barn just before the manger of his horse, and in that stable occurred the next act in the chain which was to bring the tragedy upon Santa Anna.

17

He slept no longer the leaden sleep of exhaustion, but as lightly as a cat. For he had seen the greedy looks of the Mexicans as they stared at the stallion, and he knew that more than one of them would gladly cut his throat to win the chance of leading the black away.

It was not a Mexican that he found on this night, however. Sounds came faintly into his sleep, and he wakened when someone entered the stall of Doc. Raising his head, he saw the dim silhouettes of loosed horses passing by the window in the side of the barn. Every stall had already been emptied, up to that in which his horse stood, and against the same background he now saw a head which was topped by two feathers like two raised fingers.

There was a good revolver at the side of Michel, but he did not use it either to shoot with or as a club. In fact, he forgot all about it and remembered his fist alone. The head of the Indian was turned sidewise, and Rory landed the stone-hard weight of his right fist fairly upon the side of the chin.

The Indian dropped from sight and Rory went after him in a flash. As he dropped over the side of the manger, he saw a form twisting in the darkness in front of the feet of Doc, and then the brighter gleam of a knife. He had barely time to jerk up a knee; the knife stroke gleamed idly past his throat as the knee went home in the face of the red man. And he lay still.

"Hai! Hai!" Rory heard a voice calling softly, and the silhouette of another befeathered head appeared at the entrance to the stall. Then, in Spanish, a voice said: "Is it well, brother? Has the horse struck you? This is the one—this is the great black which will make you a chief and—"

Rory picked the knife from the nerveless hand of his first opponent and went for the second, but the latter, with a grunt, side-stepped the lunge and fled. He went out the door of the stable into the open moonlight bounding like a rabbit.

Rory sent out a single shrill whistle to sound the alarm and went back to his first man.

A tethering rope secured the hands and feet of the man and when Ware and the cook and the bookkeeper

18

came rushing out, half clothed and armed to the teeth, they found their best saddle stock loose in the corral and Rory walking from the barn with a senseless figure in his arms.

He told them briefly what had happened, and the cook, still panting with excitement, bawled out:

"That's what I call pretty good investin', Colonel Ware. You give a man a suit of old clothes and a month's keep, and he saves you a thousand dollars worth of hossflesh from the Apache dogs. Let's have a look at this thing!"

They brought the captive into the kitchen and set him on his feet. Everyone was present now, including the two women, and several of the Mexicans, their eyes like the eyes of cats in the night.

What Rory Michel saw in the lamplight was a squatty built youth with a face that looked more apt for biting than for thought. His nose was flat, with flaring nostrils. His long, braided hair streamed down in front of his shoulders. His legs were bowed into the outline of a cipher. There was a big, swelling bruise upon one cheek, where the knee of Rory had gone home. But the protuberance was not a disfiguring thing; alteration could hardly have spoiled that hideous countenance.

He was almost redeemed by his poise, however.

"He's like a dignified nightmare," said Nancy Ware. "What's to be done with him?"

"Hang him," said Ware. "Hang him, of course!"

There was no law, no semblance of law in Arizona, at that time. Where the military posts could be found, military rule held, but only within the boundaries of the forts. Outside, there was a waste ocean of lawlessness. The population of the territory was made up very largely of scoundrels who had made California too hot to hold them; renegade Mexicans from Sonora, and all manner of desperate scum from the Eastern cities.

A few honest men were trying to work the mines or to establish themselves in the cattle industry. And their methods with transgressors were likely to be short and

19

severe. For one thing, they had little time. For another, hanging was generally deserved for crimes either of the present or of the past. It was not strange, therefore, that the colonel suggested death at once for the Indian.

"Poor rascal!" said Nancy. "Does he deserve—"

"Harriet!" commanded the colonel, sternly, "take your daughter away. This is a matter for men only."

Neither of the women stirred. They were enjoying the dreadful picture of the marauder and his brutal face.

And their glances shifted from him toward Rory, who stood in the background.

"We'll find out who he is, first," said the colonel. "Here, Juan," he added in Spanish, "you can speak Apache, and that's exactly what he looks like to me. Ask him who he is."

Juan, a round-faced peon, stepped forward importantly and put several questions in gutteral dialect to the captive. But the face of the latter was like a stone.

Juan turned to his master.

"He won't talk," he said. "But he's Apache. Those are Apache moccasins. That's the Apache way of dyeing feathers too. He's killed men before this. Likely enough, whites. Those feathers wouldn't be in his hair otherwise. Not with that dye on them."

"An Apache and a murderer," said the colonel. "A horse thief he's been proved already. I don't think there's any reason to hesitate. Tod," he went on, to the bookkeeper, "do you think there's any reason to hesitate?"

Tod Merritt was one of those waspish little men who love more trouble than they can make. He looked fiercely at the Apache now.

"Hanging's too good for him," he said. "I'd roast the red wretch first. That's what I'd do. Roast him?"

"Hush, Tod!" said Nancy. "He understands English."

"English? What makes you think so?"

"He looked straight into the fire, when you talked of burning him. What a horrid idea, Tod! Don't say it again!"

The Apache did not turn his head, but his glance slowly shifted to the face of the girl and dwelt upon it for an instant. There could hardly be a doubt that she was right; he knew what had been said.

"The more shame to the villain," said the colonel. "If he understands English, it's a proof that he's had a chance to enjoy the benefits of our civilization. And he's refused to use 'em. Hanging is the only trick to suit him. I hope he understands what I'm saying. Tod and Blucher"—this to the cook—"come out with me and we'll rig a rope over that cottonwood. It has a branch that's made for our purpose. Rory, you've handled him before with his hands free, so I suppose that you can handle them when they're tied. Harriet, you and Nancy get to bed."

The men, the Mexicans following, hastened out from the room. Their voices sounded raucously loud and jubilant outdoors. But the women still had not moved.

Rory turned to them.

"I think I can get something out of this man," he said, "if you'll leave me alone with him."

"He'll never talk," said Mrs. Ware. "That's the nature of the brutes. Death is nothing to them. They're raised for horrible lives and frightful deaths. Murder is all that they can understand."

But she and Nancy left the kitchen, nevertheless, and Rory instantly cut the ropes that tied the hands and feet of the Indian. Then he pointed to the open window.

He was amazed to see that the Apache did not stir. For a moment, his breast enlarging and his head high, he stared at the white man; there was in his eyes a fire like the light of hatred.

"You know," said Rory, quietly, "that I can understand a little. To you fellows, stealing isn't a crime, it's a virtue. I'm glad that I still have my black horse. I'm glad that you're not to be throttled. There's the open window; dive through it!"

The Indian stepped swiftly to the window, then turned about as if to speak, but words seemed to have deserted him and, whirling about, he leaped through

21

the window and dropped soundlessly to the ground.

Rory Michel dropped the ropes into the fire that burned in the stove and only when he had replaced the lid did he shout out: "Help! Murder! He's gone!"

There was a rush of men and women back into the room, and they arrivel in time to find Rory picking himself up from the floor.

"What happened?" shouted the colonel.

"I don't know. Broke his ropes or slipped out of 'em, I guess. All I know is that I got a whang that floored me, and he shot through that window like an arrow."

"After him!" bellowed the colonel. "Get horses. After him!"

And he led the way with a cursing crowd at his heels. Mrs. Ware followed him, entreating him to beware of ambuscades, begging him not to ride out into the treacherous dark.

Only Rory and the girl remained alone in the kitchen.

"Thank God that he didn't have a knife!" said Nancy. "You'd be dead if he had."

"Of course," said Rory, "but I'm the lucky one, you know."

"Anyway," she went on, "I'm glad that he's not to be hanged. And if—"

She stopped talking; she glanced suddenly at Michel and then, crossing the room, she lifted the lid of the stove.

Slowly she replaced it and turned again toward him.

"That's the coolest Apache I ever heard of," said she.

"Oh, he's the cool one, all right," nodded Rory, watching her carefully.

"He even stopped," said she, "to burn his ropes. That's what I call an instinct for tidiness. Civilization hasn't been entirely wasted on him, Rory!"

He said nothing. And for a moment they looked at one another until each began to smile, very faintly.

"You know something, Rory?" said she at last.

"I'm ready to learn," he answered.

"It's only this—I'm not as silent as that Apache, but I can keep still, too, at times."

"Thanks," said he. "But how did you guess?"

"Through my nose," said Nancy. "D' you think that rope burns like wood?"

Chapter 4

Ware and his men rode frantically through the night, here and there, for the greater part of an hour. But they discovered nothing and came back in ill humor to find Rory Michel singing Gaelic songs to an accompaniment which he picked out on a guitar. He did not have a very musical voice, but he threw into his rendering a good deal of spirit, and at appropriate moments he uttered whoops and yells of glee or simulated battle rage. And Mrs. Ware and her daughter appeared to enjoy the performance.

But Mr. Ware was not pleased. He sat down on the veranda and delivered a half-hour pamphlet on the importance of being wary in one's dealings with the red man who was, he said, as slippery as a serpent. He congratulated the boy on the capture of the Apache, but he stated that this was worse than useless, because the Indians would despise the inhabitants of that post and most certainly would make them free to attack again at the earliest opportunity.

When the half-hour was ended, perhaps Ware would have continued his discourse, but his daughter pointed out to him that young Rory was sound asleep, his back against one of the narrow pillars that supported the veranda roof, while still, from time to time, he managed to nod his head as though acquiescing in the wise points which the colonel was making.

Mr. Ware was indignant. He said that it betrayed a criminal levity in Rory, this ability to sleep through sound advice. He hoped that his daughter would take warning, and Nancy said that she would, so the colonel went stalking off to bed, and Rory strolled, yawning, toward the barn.

Said Mrs. Ware: "You know, Nancy, some day your father will find out that you've been laughing at him all these years."

"He'll never find out," declared Nancy. "He wouldn't believe the ears that heard such a thing or the eyes that saw it. No, no, he'll never find out!"

"Rory didn't seem to care a whit about the Apache's getting away," said Mrs. Ware. "He's a strange child!"

"He cut the Apache's ropes," answered Nancy. "That's a secret I have to tell you, but not to another soul. Only, I want you to see that he's not half as innocent as he seems."

"I never thought that he was particularly innocent," said Mrs. Ware. "He turned that Indian loose, did he? Well, Nan, I'm glad of it. Murder's a horrible thing, legal or illegal!"

They went to bed. And Rory stretched in the hay mow, slept soundly until awakened by the morning sun.

He wakened to find that he had come into a new place of prominence in the eyes of the Mexicans. They had seen him come out of the desert as a ghost, they had watched him transformed into a sleek and active youth, while his skeleton of a horse became a silken beauty, fleet as the wind. They had seen his lucky hands shaking the dice and winning their money. But none of these things seemed conclusive to their minds.

Now, however, he had routed two Apaches, single-handed, and he had captured one of them. The escape of the latter meant nothing. The original achievement was the main thing.

For untold generations, the Apaches and the Comanches had been in the habit of following the Mexican moon southward along a trail marked as with white chalk by the skeletons of beasts and men. During that time the Mexicans had learned to look with an almost superstitious horror upon the Indians. Ten of the Apaches would drive thirty Mexicans like dead leaves in battle. So great was the dread that Chihuahua offered bounties; a hundred dollars for the scalp of every grown male Apache, fifty for every grown female,

24

twenty-five for every girl or boy baby! That horrible offer was withdrawn, but not without protest.

And now the Mexicans who worked in the Ware mine suddenly found in the character of the careless boy something in the nature of a hero and, beyond that, a mystery.

His origin was remembered. The change in himself and in his horse was pointed out. Finally, what man, with bare hands, would attack two murdering Apaches?

Rory Michel was made aware of the change in the attitude of the brown men the next day. Then an elderly peon, tough as rawhide, ugly as a monkey, came to him bearing a small flask of mescal. He sat on his heels and smoked a cornucopia-shaped cigarette and presented his offering. Rory, amazed, accepted it. He could not remember having put the other under any obligation to him; in fact, he had merely won quite a few dollars from the old fellow.

Finally the Mexican drew attention to a mule he had with him that looked almost as old as his master. It was more than gray. It was white to the fetlocks, white to the lips.

"Father," said Jose to young Rory, "it would not be a great thing for you to do. If you would look closely, you would see that it is a very old mule. His joints creak. He groans when he carries a load uphill. Some day, very soon, he will fall down and die and leave me to walk many miles and carry the weight of the saddle. If you were to touch him, and tell him to become young—hai! That would be a thing!"

Rory laughed. And then, stopping his laughter, he looked narrowly at Jose, for he saw that the elder was taking the thing seriously. So he leaned a little forward and said: "Tell me, Jose, what makes you think that I can do such a thing?"

Jose slowly shook his head, closed his eyes, and made the sign of the cross.

"I, father," he said, "am not a fool. If I see a little, it is not because I am prying into the secrets of the great men and the wise men. No, no, I am only looking around the corner, and what I see, I keep to myself."

He opened his eyes. He nodded and winked at young Rory. Then he added, in a whisper:

"You know, father, that it will cost you no more than a touch of the hand!"

Rory stood up and went to the mule, so that he could turn his back to the Mexican and smile without being seen. He knew that there was still, among the Mexicans, a guilty belief in witchcraft. He, it appeared, was a wizard. He could not doubt the sincerity of the grave face of Jose.

"All right, Jose," said he. "One of these days, I'll turn your mule into a young one, a regular colt, as sleek as a deer!"

Jose thanked him as though that trifling service were already ended and went off singing, leading the stumbling brute behind him. Rory Michel laughed and thought no more of the matter until, in the middle of the night that followed, he was wakened in his bed in the hay mow by the pleading voice of a woman and the whimpering of the child.

He got up and looked at a pitiful group in an empty stall of the barn. The father, a peon with a stupid face, held the lantern. The swarthy mother carried a child with a face swollen by crying.

"Oh, father," said the woman to Rory Michel, "will you look at this little one with a kind eye? See how weak he is? Look at his little, withered neck! This is his leg, like the leg of a tiny old man, all bones and skin. There is no flesh on him. He is dying; he is dying! Father, be merciful to me!"

Rory Michel jumped down into the stall, half in anger and in pity, for the child seemed at the point of death. The weakness of its crying was not from want of effort to make noise, for its mouth opened wide, but from the throat came only a husky, whining sound. It was exhausted.

"What is your name?" asked Rory of the woman.

"I am Maria," she said, "and this is my man, Pedro Gonzales, by the blessing of God! And this is our only son, Juan. And the daughters grow like weeds, but there is a curse on our luck.

26

"See—Juan! Poor little fellow!"

The tears began to roll down her face.

"Who told you," demanded Rory, "that I'm a doctor?"

"Not a doctor, father," said Maria, "but more than a doctor. Far, far more! Did we not talk to Jose? Yes, he himself came into our house this evening. He was going by and heard the crying of Juan and pity came over him and he came in and told us about you and your power."

"He did?" said Rory, wishing to break the neck of the foolish Jose.

"He told us, father. But, for that matter, we have eyes of our own. When old men grow young and horses turn into colts, ah, there is a meaning behind such things. But we never thought of coming to you with Juan and begging you on our knees."

"I really can't do a thing," said Rory.

The woman shrank as though he had struck her. She turned to her husband with an imploring glance, and he nodded. From inside his shirt he took a leather bag and opened it, and poured out a small shower of golden coins. This he offered to Rory.

"I am one of the wretched and poor ones of the earth," said Pedro Gonzales, "but I have saved my money as it was paid. Here is seventy dollars in gold. We thought it would take us back to Chihuahua one day. But it is yours. There is no use making a journey that leaves flesh and blood dead behind and under the ground. Father, have mercy on us!"

"Did Jose tell you," asked Rory, "that I could heal the boy?"

"Did you not turn the mule into a young colt, as you promised?" asked Gonzales.

"Is the mule now a young colt?" asked the astonished Rory.

"At least," said Maria, "this very evening Jose won at dice, and got four dollars and Fernando Garcia's beautiful young four-year-old mule. Is not that turning the old into the young? Jose is not a fool, father. He understood very well that you had granted his prayer. He, also, is praying for you. Tomorrow he will come and make you a present, have no doubt. Now, we know that this little handful of money is no great price for the life of our son. This is only an advance payment. We will give you more, hereafter."

"Put up the money," said Rory, harshly. "What have you been doing for your son?"

The peon remained with his hand mutely extended. He looked to the superior wit of his wife for guidance.

"Put away the money," she whispered quickly. "He is not at all pleased."

Then, in answer to Rory's question, she went on: "I have done everything that wit could think of. I have asked all the old women. They have helped me with advice. I have not let the harsh outer air come against his delicate skin. This is the first time in a month that I have dared to take him out of the house, and tonight, only so that your kind eye should see him, father! Every day, every night, he has been safely sheltered."

Rory closed his eyes.

He could see the picture well enough—the crowded little hovel, turned into an oven by the summer heat of the sun and the fire of the stove, the fumes of cookery and tobacco smoking, the dust, the uproar of the other playing children.

He opened his eyes. The woman was continuing:

"Three times a day, I give him a little oil and some bread soaked in it. Three times a day, too, I give him tea and crusts softened in it. More than this, I dare not offer him. His stomach will not keep even this much!"

She paused, drew a sobbing breath, and continued: "He is well covered and no cold comes to him, you see? But the spirit is weak in him. That is why I have come to you, father! In the name of God, look kindly on us both!"

He examined the clothing. The poor youngster was swathed in four of five layers of heavy cotton cloth.

Rory went to the window of the barn and leaned there, breathing deeply of the pure air which blew against his face. He felt stifled and sick at heart. The close heat of centuries of ignorance oppressed him.

"His face is turned from us," he heard the woman murmuring behind him in a broken voice. "Let us go,

Pedro Gonzales. Our hope has already gone away before us!"

Rory forced himself to turn around.

"Maria," said he, "please listen to me!"

"And to the voice of the father God!" said the woman, stopping and clutching the child closer to her breast.

"You know, Maria," said Rory, "that sometimes evil spirits come into the body."

"Aye," said she, shaking from head to foot and striving to cover her child still more with her spreading hands.

"And sometimes," said Rory, "they need to be given a chance to drift away. But you have kept the bad spirit warmly housed and comfortable and that is why it will not leave your son."

"Ha!" cried Pedro Gonzales, a thought crossing his foolish face like light. "I have said something like that."

"You are a fool, and the son of a fool," said his wife, fiercely. "Keep your tongue. Let us listen and say nothing. Father, I take your words into my heart like a sacrament."

"Now, then," said Rory, setting his jaw a little and nerving himself, "I will tell you what I will do."

"I listen, father!" said Maria submissively.

"I will send away the bad spirit that is killing little Juan."

"Oh, God be praised, and you are praised also, Padre Rory!"

"Hush," said Rory Michel. "I can only do this thing if you have perfect faith in me. If you believe that I can do this thing and follow all my directions, it will be accomplished."

"We have seen the old mule turned into a young colt," said Pedro Gonzales nodding his head.

"Well," went on Rory, "the first thing is: keep the child all day long in the open air, under the shade of the oak trees, where it is cool and a wind blows. One of your neighbors can look after the girls."

"Ha! They can look after themselves!" said Maria,

fiercely. "It shall be done. Our father knows that the strong, harsh wind will not harm Juan?"

"I know perfectly well," lied Rory. "Besides, take three of these wrappings away. One will be enough. In the night, leave open the door and the windows of your house."

The woman gasped.

"The terrible, damp, dark night air, father!" she protested.

Pedro was mute, but shuddered at the thought. "It is for the life of your son," Rory reminded them.

"True! Everything shall be done as you say," said Maria.

"Instead of oil," said Rory, "give him a little gruel or porridge thinned with milk, three times a day. And when he is in the house at night, let there be no sound. Let no one even cough or sneeze. Ask your neighbors kindly to be quiet. I tell you, this is a sort of magic that has to be worked in silence."

"Ha!" cried Maria. "Now I begin to be sure that the spirit will be cast out."

"Be sure of it. Never doubt it," said Rory. "I shall be working night and day to help you."

"God bless you!" said the parents in unison.

"And," said Rory, remembering, "when the child is in the house, never light a fire in the stove, that would be a terrible mistake. Do you hear?"

"We hear everything and we believe, and it shall be done as you say," said the mother.

"Look, Maria," whispered the husband, amazed. "He has stopped crying. Do you see? He cries no longer. All the saints look and take wonder! He smiles into the face of Padre Rory!"

"It is true," said Maria. "The evil begins to depart."

"Go home quickly and quietly," said Rory Michel. "Put out the fire in the stove, open the doors and the windows, and take three of the wrappings from the child. Then give it a little porridge and milk. If you have none, get it at once from the neighbors. You will see. Before the morning, it will fall into a good sleep."

They were already departing. Blessing came tremulously from their lips, and Rory looked after them with an oddly twisting smile.

"Blessing from me!" he murmured, and then laughed silently and mirthlessly there in the dark of the barn.

Chapter 5

The way of a magician, he discovered, if not holy was at least very busy. Before three more days had passed, he dreaded the sight of a Mexican. For, by the time the three days had ended, his blind prescriptions had begun to work well upon little Juan. It appeared that he could digest the simple food. It appeared that he actually breathed better in fresh air than in the crowded fumes and vapors of a house hermetically sealed all night and most of the day.

And he prospered in the open air under the oak trees, where presently he was rolling in sun and shadow. Maria swore that he was beginning to fill out and that the wrinkles in his poor neck were less deep. There was color in his cheeks—look for yourselves, you who doubt! And he cried little, very little. Last night he slept the whole night through. He awakened in the morning with a shout, an angry shout, demanding food.

Poor simple Maria! Now she laughed all day long. The gossips came out in groups or one by one and sat with her under the oak trees, and wondered over the miracle. They were not quite sure that the soul of Juan had not been sold to the evil one, but they envied the fortune of the happy parents, nevertheless.

And the worker of the magic?

Everyone of those peons crossed himself, covertly, when he came near the boy. Nevertheless, they beamed and smiled upon Rory. One who could turn old mules

31

into young and restore by miracle even more profound, though more slowly working, the actually faded life of a child—that was a man to be admired, almost worshipped, even if he had received his power from Satan.

It was all the more wonderful because it was so simple. There were no drugs, no herbs, no charms to wear. He simply gave good fortune, when he chose. The children used to come and stand at the corral fence and press their faces against the closely ranged bars to stare at the great man, walking up and down with that tigerish beauty, the Doctor.

"What have you done to the Mexicans?" asked Nancy Ware of him.

"Nothing," said he. "But they think that I've done something. You know how it is. They've got an idea in their heads. That's all. It's useless to try to get it out again."

"I went down to that poor old woman, the mother of those two surly brothers, Alonzo and Miguel; I never knew their last name. I've been going to see her two or three times a week, because she's bedridden. It used to be a dreadful thing to see her lying there, wasting away, clasping her rosary, mumbling prayers for the sake of her soul. I went down this morning and found her up cooking for her boys. She says that you raised her from the bed!"

Rory laughed.

"There was nothing to that," he answered. "The fact is, she thought she wanted to die. Life wasn't much to her. But when she heard of the baby—" He stopped short.

"I know," nodded Nancy. "Maria's baby. All the peons are talking about that miracle. Are you a doctor, Rory?"

"Not a bit," said he. "But old Alicia had heard of that. She sent for me and asked me to make her younger. I didn't laugh. I can't laugh at them now. They expect me to do queer things for 'em. Those two half-breeds, Miguel and Alonzo, were standing by, scowling at me, defying me to do anything. So I didn't laugh, for fear of a knife between the ribs. Well, I looked at her eyes. They were clear. She said that she

32

had no strength though and hadn't been out of bed for a month. So I told her that I'd make her young again."

"You did!" exclaimed Nancy.

"Well, I told her to get up every day, and drag herself to the door and sit there in the sun till her head turned dizzy. Soon she would feel much stronger and better. And that's the way it worked out. Her own belief has taken charge of her. The last time I saw her, she was sitting cross-legged on the floor, admiring her ugly face. She said that she was already three years younger. She's a full-blooded Apache, isn't she?"

"She looks it."

He pulled out a knife, beautifully mounted with silver.

"Miguel and Alonzo brought me this before they went to work this morning. They said that they brought their hearts, too, the cutthroats!"

He laughed as he ended, but the girl was serious.

"You could do something with those people," she said. "And they need handling."

"There's somebody coming who looks as though he'd need handling of another sort," said Rory. "Look there!"

Up the road along the valley, a fast traveling spot of dust dissolved into a rider who was urging his horse to top speed. As it came nearer, they could see the exhausted staggering of the animal.

"A soldier!" said the girl. "See the gleam of the buttons? That's to show the Indian arrows to the mark, I suppose, those shining buttons."

"He's killing his horse, the fool!" said Rory, angrily.

"An officer, too!" said the girl, peering more closely.

Full upon them came the rider, drew up his mount and flung himself to the ground.

"Where's Ware?" he cried. "Apache! Give the warning. Get into the house. Grab rifles, every man!"

Chapter 6

He was a splendid, big, young man, a captain of cavalry. Rory, looking up in admiration at the stranger, decided that two such as himself could be carved from the Herculean frame of the other. He had shoulders as wide as a door; he bore himself rigidly erect. He was handsome and everything about him promised admirable manliness, from the shining boots to the good, clean cut of his jaw.

Nancy, therefore, did not laugh as she pointed down the valley.

"There aren't any Apaches in sight, captain," said she.

He turned about and stared. It was true that the valley was empty, so far as could be seen, except for a good number of cattle, spotted about on the bleached grass. He muttered to himself a moment and then he said. "Well, it seems that I've been a fool. But I never thought that I'd get by that mound—there, that one with the flat head. When I was a distance from it, those red men were already whooping close behind me. I promised myself that I'd turn and make a last stand with my back against that wall of rock."

He shrugged those wide shoulders of his.

"Instead of that, this shaky old horse managed to pull me away from them. I'll think the better of him the rest of his days. I thought he was tottering like a rocking horse, but he shook off those tireless Indian ponies."

"If you think a lot of the gelding," said Rory, "you'd better look out for him. He's going to be a dead horse before long, unless you give him a hand."

The captain looked suddenly at Rory and frowned. Then he smiled.

"I'm making an ass of myself," he said. "I come in bringing an Indian alarm, and it turns out that all I've done is half kill my own horse. You're right, my friend. The old horse is shaking in the knees. I'll have to give him some help."

Nancy sent a Mexican to scout down the valley and report any sign of actual trouble. Then she and Rory went into the corral with the captain to help him walk his horse about and rub it down. Slowly it was cooled off. It would be days before it recovered from its great effort. In the meantime, however, it promised to recover from the immediate danger of dying of exhaustion. Rory supervised the giving of a dram of brandy and the final blanketing of the gelding, and at last he said that the good horse, well bedded down, might safely be left alone.

They came out into the sun again and the captain paused to admire the shining beauty of the black stallion in the little adjoining run.

"There's a beauty," said he. "There's a horse and a half! Does that belong to Mr. Ware?"

"That belongs to me," said Rory.

"Aye," said the appreciative captain. "You'd know what horse to invest money in. I never saw a handsomer stallion. He could move now, that one. That's an eight-foot fence around him. Does he try to climb out?"

"He'd jump anything lower. He'd break through anything weaker than those heavy bars," declared Rory. "And I'm cramping him in there while I teach him to be savage to anything in the shape of a man who tries to sneak through the bars."

"Savage?" exclaimed the captain. "Teach him to be savage to a man. You don't mean that!"

"Look, then!" said Rory.

And he threw in a loosely stuffed contraption made of stout sacks, sewed together with rawhide thongs. The stallion caught it while it was in the air with driving hind hoofs and it flattened against the bars. But, before it could fall, the great black brute was at it again, tearing with forehoofs and ripping with its teeth.

35

Its flattened ears, its distended, red-rimmed nostrils, its flashing eyes gave it the look of a dragon.

Rory whistled, and the monster leaped back across the width of the corral, while Rory extracted the badly battered dummy. Tufts of straw were sticking through the many rents.

The captain shook his head.

"A man would be dead ten times over before that expert in murder had finished so much time on him," he declared. "Stallions are savage enough, man. Why do you want to turn this one into a trained demon?"

"Because this is Apache and Mexican land," said Rory. "If he won't protect himself, I'll lose him fast enough. I make him an expert murderer to discourage the expert horse thieves. And they're the most expert in the world, the ones in this neck of the woods, I'm thinking."

The captain sighed and shook his head.

"Fifty picked mules and horses have been snatched out of my hands!" he told them. "Don't ask me to admire their thieving. I don't wonder that you've trained the stallion this way. I hope he eats a few red demons before he's through!"

They asked him what had happened. By this time, Ware had come in from the mine and his arrival interrupted the narrative. It seemed to Rory that he never had seen two finer-looking men together than this statuesque pair. They were of an equal height and they were equally imposing in bulk and in erect carriage. When they shook hands, they measured one another gravely, and each seemed to be saying silently that he never had encountered so real a man. From the first glance they became friends.

"Colonel Ware," said Rory, introducing them. "And this is Captain Burn."

"Have you been in the service, sir?" said Burn.

"I have not," said Ware, who had listened to that question more than once before. "I have not been in the service, and I'm sorry for it. Inclination would have put me there, but I've never had the opportunity. A lit-

36

tle dabbling in the militia—well, it amounted to nothing."

Captain Burn pointed out that irregular troops often performed fine service for the country. Colonel Ware modestly doubted this. Captain Burn, it appeared, came from West Point. He was only two years out of it, in fact.

And Colonel Ware was so delighted to have a real regular—"a scientific regular," as he expressed it—that he could hardly keep himself from shaking hands all over again. Rory and Nancy were left on the side, in the backwash of the conversation, as it were, until the others chose to draw them in. But when the introductions were ended, supper time had come and it was not until supper was over that the captain would tell his story.

He was not proud of it. He was ashamed enough to blush, but he was man enough to laugh also, and young Rory liked him better and better.

It needs a resolute fool to stay a fool; and the captain was hardly that type. He was the kind to take fortune by the forelock, even when fortune was a bull. But he accepted fortune's bufferings without a whimper.

He said that he had been sent out by Colonel Sellers from Fort Rankin to pick up some extra mounts for the troopers and a few good mules for the transport work. He had taken with him none of the soldiers, but only half a dozen Mexicans from the service of the fort, trusted men who were to act as guides, help in the bargaining for the sake of a small commission, and herd in the animals after they were purchased.

He was successful in picking up some good material. In a ten-day round, he secured twenty horses, more or less, and thirty excellent mules, small, to be sure, but as tough as jackrabbits. With these he started home toward the fort, when trouble came at him one evening.

They had camped, and the herd was scattering to graze, when a body of wild horses, or so they seemed, came cantering over the hills. To the amazement of the captain, they came straight on. He noted that the wind was blowing toward them, but they seemed to have no fear of the scent of man. Perhaps, he told himself, this was a herd which had descended from the intricate and ultimate fastnesses of the higher mountains and, therefore, not a one of them had ever crossed the trail of man before!

It seemed a likely theory to the captain. And why not, when one had arrived at the end of the world? Plainly that was what Arizona was to Captain Thomas Burn!

He conceived on the spot an excellent plan, which was to send out his men quietly and run the whole wild herd into the tame and bring in the lot straight to the fort. He would then have a hundred animals, instead of fifty, and only half of them would have cost government money. He could imagine himself receiving favorable mention for the exploit. He could almost see the terms in which the mention would be made, for zeal, intelligence and ready wit.

"And then," said the captain, "what do you think happened to that approaching herd of wild horses?"

He looked around the table, his blond mustache fairly prickling with embarrassed amusement.

"I'll tell you," said Nancy.

"You will?" said he.

"I think I can."

"Never in a thousand years!" exclaimed the captain. "But you may try!"

"Well, then it was this way, I suppose," said the girl. "On the rearward mustangs, on the back of every one, suddenly an Apache Indian appeared, yelling his head off and waving his arms and driving the front of the herd, crash, right through your own horses!"

The captain stared, agape.

"Great heavens, Miss Ware," said he, "where could you have heard that?"

Even Colonel Ware forgot his respect for a regularly commissioned officer in the United States Army long enough to indulge in a faint smile.

"Those red rascals have done it before," said the girl. "Didn't the Mexicans smell a rat? They should have!"

"I didn't have a chance to ask the Mexicans what

38

they had suspected," said the captain. "I luckily had the reins of my own gelding over my arm, and I jumped into the saddle and called on the Mexicans to join me in a charge."

"You're a lucky fellow that they didn't," said the girl.

"How did you guess that they didn't?" said the captain.

"It isn't a favorite Mexican sport, charging Apaches," said she. "And if they had, you wouldn't be wearing your scalp just now, and neither would they be wearing theirs. Apaches know how to shoot in these days."

"They scattered, at any rate," said the captain, naively. "And I saw that one man against so many was a foolish thing, so I rode for my life. And a few times I thought that I was a goner. Twice, I give you my word, the men behind me threw spears that whistled past my head by inches. And any number of bullets cut up the air around me. But—this is the happy ending of the story!"

And he both blushed and laughed as he looked around the table.

Chapter 7

Everyone except Mrs. Ware joined the captain in his laughter. But Harriet Ware shielded her eyes from the picture of the handsome captain so hemmed in with dangers. Then Colonel Ware grew angry. He thumped the table with his fist.

"I tell you, man," said he, "that there's no peace or hope of peace and order in this country until the Apaches are put down."

"I dare say that you're right," said the captain, "but it seems a tidy job to undertake."

"When I say put down," went on the colonel, expanding on his favorite theme, "I really mean exterminated!"

"Hello!" murmured the captain. "Exterminated?"

"Exactly," said Colonel Ware. "That's the only hope, the only hope for the whole great Territory of Arizona. A rich country, sir. Rich in grazing lands, incredibly rich in minerals. But cursed by the Apaches; murderers, traitors, thieves, scoundrels. They must be hunted as wolves are hunted, with a price on their heads, and traps laid for them. Let them be snared with flags of truce, promises, baits of any sort and then ruthlessly cut down in cold blood."

The table was silent, somewhat appalled, and particularly the captain. He looked to Rory Michel for some interpretation of this terrible gospel, but Rory was calmly proceeding with his supper as though nothing untoward had been said.

The colonel saw that he had created a sensation, and he enjoyed the feeling. He continued:

"You're surprised, Burn, at what I say, but that's chiefly because you haven't lived among the rascals as long as I have, I dare say. You don't know the history of their raids, their butcheries, their barbarous cruelties."

"I've heard a good deal at the fort," admitted the captain. "Still, I thought that they were human beings."

"Not a bit of it. Vermin. Sheer vermin!" said Ware.

"I found them pretty good fellows," said Young Rory Michel, unexpectedly.

"Hello!" said the colonel.

He looked down his nose toward Rory. His feelings about that young man had been for a long time of the most mixed variety. In spite of his bloodthirsty talk about the Apaches, the colonel was reasonably warm-hearted and he was glad enough that the desert waif had been rescued and brought back to health in his house. But he was highly suspicious concerning the dealings of Rory with the Mexicans. In the first place, he could not understand the lack of dignity that led a white man to converse familiarly and shake dice with Mexican laborers.

In the second place he had no use for "medicine

40

men," or other shams, red, white, or black. Finally, he wondered why Rory remained loafing so long at the Ware mine. It was true that the saving of the livestock represented many times the value of the food that Rory could consume in a stay twentyfold as long as he made. Still, the colonel felt that a man of pride would not have continued to linger on in this manner, doing nothing but play about with a black horse, and chatter with ignorant Mexican laborers.

Now he said, severely, and in his best manner: "And pray, Mr. Michel, what do you know, intimately, about the Apaches?"

"Why," said Rory, "when I was meandering along on the trail of the Doctor—that's the stallion's name," he explained to Burn, "a party of Apaches met up with me on the trail."

"And they didn't scalp you?" asked the colonel.

"They didn't even try to. They didn't even discuss it," said Rory. "But when they saw what I was after—that shambling skelton of a horse—they said that there must be medicine in the thing. They talked Spanish to me, you see, so I could understand what they said. They offered to catch the horse for me."

"The mischief they did!" exclaimed the colonel. "However, you have a way with the dark-skinned people!"

He hardly concealed his sneer and Rory looked him in the face with a very odd smile.

"Perhaps I have," said he. "I told 'em that if they touched the stallion their right arms would wither at the root. They seemed to believe me. Anyway, they didn't try the experiment."

He laughed a little.

"Why didn't you let them catch the horse for you?" asked Nancy, leaning forward.

"Well, you know how it is," said the boy. "When you've plugged away for a certain time at a job, you begin to feel that it's your particular business, and you want to finish it with your own hands. So the Apaches just took me in and offered me food and everything that they had."

"They fed you, eh?" said the colonel.

"They wanted to," said the boy, "but I wouldn't let 'em."

"You wouldn't let them?" exclaimed Nancy. "And why not?"

He frowned down at the table.

"Well, Nancy," said he, "by that time I was hardly right in the head, perhaps. And it seemed to me that it was a fair fight between me and the Doctor. A finish fight. One of us had to win or drop. It was that way in my thoughts."

"Singular fantasy," murmured the colonel.

"Yes, it was singular, all right," said Rory. "But by that time. I had calluses on my soul, if you'll follow me. I was stubborn, like a child. Just winning didn't matter so much. How I won seemed to be the chief point. The Doctor had had to live off the country and from the first I had done the same thing."

"A horse can eat grass," observed the colonel, intelligently.

"And a man," said the boy, "can knock over a mountain grouse or a prairie hen, and cook and eat a sound meal in a tenth of the time that it takes a horse to graze his insides full. Altogether, after I was out of ammunition I had to depend on the berries, bark, roots, stupid grouse that I could knock over with a stone or a stick, or rabbits that I could trap along the way—after that, I mean, it was a fairly even fight between us. We were both starving. And it didn't seem right to let the Indians step in and spoil—"

He paused, his eyes fixed upon distant space. "Your glory?" asked the girl. He stared at her. "Yes," he said. "You understand me. My glory! That's what I had in my mind. So I refused the Apaches. And they followed on, half a mile behind me, for three more days. At that, they were a help. I had to win, with such an audience watching. And on the third day I got the horse, all right. Then they put on a little show for me. They rode around me in a circle, and they threw up their spears and caught them again, and they yelled and whooped. They did me honor. And afterwards they rode off."

"They didn't offer to feed you, then?" asked the girl.

"Well," he answered, "they said I was a medicine

man and, therefore, I could pick out of the empty air all the food that I wanted, now that my work was done."

He ended with a smile.

Captain Burn, his eyes riveted on the face of the boy, finally said: "That's the most remarkable story that I've ever heard!"

"Rory's not like other people," said Nancy.

Both her father and her mother looked sharply at her, but she merely shrugged her shoulders a little, as though she wished to say that she stuck by her point of view.

"You worked a little hocus-pocus, and managed to escape with your scalp," said the colonel to Rory, "but you've just heard the captain tell how he barely escaped from the marauders with his skin whole."

Rory smiled.

"I've heard the captain tell how they barely missed him with their spears," he said. "And it struck me as a strange thing that if they were in reaching distance with their spears they couldn't hit him with any of their bullets."

"Hold on!" exclaimed the captain. "You mean to suggest that they could have had me if they had wanted, but they simply let me off?"

"They played a game with you. That was all," said Rory.

"A game to the tune of fifty mules and horses!" said the colonel with bitterness.

"Stealing isn't an Indian fault," said Rory Michel. "It's a virtue. They learn it. They pray to get better at it. A good thief's as much as a good warrior, almost, in their belief."

"In their belief!" snorted the colonel. "The scoundrels always believe whatever is to their own advantage. Opportunists, just like all criminals. Wasters, murders, brutes in human form—talk to any of the old mountain men and ask their opinion of the red-skinned vermin!"

"I'd rather talk to the Apaches themselves," said the boy. "How many times have you talked to Apaches, Colonel Ware?"

The colonel had struck a stump.

He could only glare at Rory Michel.

"How many times do I need to talk to them?" he cried, loudly. "By their acts I know them well enough. Words are cheap!"

"That's what I've always felt," said Rory.

His voice was gentle, but his eye held steadily upon the colonel in a way that made the latter wince. Yet he hardly knew why.

"And by the acts of the Apaches," said the colonel, "they've made themselves into bywords!"

"I'd rather know them better before I judge them," answered Rory Michel.

The whole table suddenly realized that the talk had passed beyond the bounds of calm discussion. There was lightning in the air, and the colonel was the very first to understand this.

Therefore, he gathered himself, and like a Jove he darkened his brow and prepared to cast thunderbolts.

He was interrupted by the voice of his daughter, who said, as she leaned forward: "Father, don't move! There are two rifles leveled at your back through the window behind you!"

Rory Michel looked in that direction, and there he saw the barrels of the weapons and, behind them, dimly, like washed-out pencil drawings, in the darkness he distinguished the ugly features of two Indians who held the guns.

"Steady, everyone!" said the girl, in the same wonderfully quiet voice. "If they wanted to kill, they would have fired before I even saw them. There's something behind it all!"

And then the door to the veranda opened and into the room stepped an Apache chief, his long hair falling down past his shoulders and his feathered headdress sweeping to the floor. There was no weapon in his hands. There was no need for him to carry a weapon, for behind him they could see a dark huddle of warriors and the faint light struck repeatedly upon naked steel.

Chapter 8

Mrs. Ware gave the intruder one frightened glance. Then, securely closing her eyes, she began to pray in a rapid whisper. But no one listened to her. All were frozen in their places, with the exception of Rory Michel. He looked from the leveled rifles at the windows, so effectually commanding the people in the room, to the stalwart form of the chief in the doorway.

He thought of reaching for the lamp which stood in the center of the table and hurling it at the chief. But he realized that before he could complete half of such a gesture, he would have a rifle bullet through his brain. Men firing from a rest, and at such a distance, could not very well miss their mark.

The chief now spoke, in perfectly good Spanish.

He said: "To all of you, I come as a friend. To the great chief who lost fifty mules and horses, my young men are bringing in the herd. They are a little behind us. All that I ask is that my father should return with me to my people."

And here he looked straight at Rory.

"He means you, Rory," said Nancy Ware quietly. "What is it all about?"

"I don't know," answered Rory. "I have a queer suspicion, because he's calling me 'father.' At any rate, I have to go."

"By heaven, Michel," said the brave captain, thrusting out that fighting jaw of his, "you shall not go. We'll fight it out to the last drop of our blood!"

"If you lift so much as a finger," answered Rory, "you're a dead man, and cold dead at that. These fellows mean business. I don't think they mean murder. I'm going with them."

45

He stood up.

"Well, my friend," said he to the chief, "if you tell me why you want me, I will go."

"My son," said the chief, "was as happy as a foal in spring and as strong as the north wind. Now he is a weak old man. That is why I have come for you, padre."

"I'm not a doctor," said Rory. "I don't know how to heal people. But if you're returning the horses and mules to the captain, he'll make it safe for you to send your son to the fort. They have a doctor there."

"Your son will be perfectly welcome," said the captain, "and perfectly safe."

The chief did not answer. But his nostrils flared a little.

"A white man," said he, "talks very smoothly. It is wonderfully pleasant to hear that talk. But my son is dying. I have come to a wise man who has cured others. I am not like the Mexicans, father," he went on. "And after you have cured my boy, I shall make you happy with a great many things. There are many horses and mules which men say walk in the herds of Rising Bull. There is feather work. There is also gold, which all white men love. Whatever your eye sees, that shall be yours."

"Whether you argue or not," said Nancy Ware calmly, "you'll have to go, Rory."

"I see that," he answered. "This is good-by to the rest of you. Colonel, I'll come back to tell you what the Apaches are like in their own camps. Good-by, Mrs. Ware. Captain Burn, I'm glad that you're getting the horses and mules back."

"A curse on the lot of them," said the captain, with an honest heat, "if you're to be the price of 'em."

Nancy Ware stood up and came around the table. She took Rory's hand in both of hers.

"I don't think that you're much afraid," said she.

"I'm trusting to luck," said Rory. "I don't think that they're animals either. They're men even if they have red skins. Good-by, Nancy."

"Good-by," she replied. "I only wish that I'd come to know you better, Rory."

46

"Time wouldn't work that way, for you and me," he answered oddly. "But I'm coming back to see you again. Tell old Alicia that she has to walk an hour in the open air every day. And Maria must carry on with the baby exactly as she's been doing. Good-by again to everyone."

He turned to the chief.

"I'm ready, Rising Bull," said he. "You can send your men with me while I saddle my horse."

Not a voice stirred behind him, as he went through the doorway past the chief.

Stepping onto the veranda, he half expected to be seized upon either side by the warriors who stood there, a dozen of them, but at a few gutteral words from Rising Bull, they separated and let him through. Only three men remained with him, two behind and one at his right shoulder as he went through the corral gate to the barn.

The stallion knew his step and whinnied for him, and he called in answer. "Also the horses know your speech, father!" said the warrior who walked beside him.

Young Rory did not answer. But he went on to the stallion and warned the braves to keep a little distance, for the Doctor had learned to fight like a desperado if strangers approached too near. So he saddled the great horse and led it out into the corral, where he mounted. At the same time, he saw that twenty Indians were in their saddles and waiting beyond the corral fence. When he had passed the gate, he was among them, and the whole party started off at a furious gallop down the valley road.

He gave one glance behind him and saw the light of Ware's house blink and disappear behind a knoll. Then there was only the glimmering of the stars in a stainless sky, and the rough-shouldered mountain forms on either side of his trail.

Suddenly an Apache youth, naked except for a breechclout, gleaming like coppery water even under the stars, drew up beside him on a little flash of a gray mare whose mouth was opened by the pull of a Spanish bit.

"I race you to the trees, father!" he shouted in Spanish.

He pointed ahead to a cluster of oaks near the second winding of the road.

Rory laughed, for all his other life, his wild, incredible life, swept over him. He was in the middle of the storm again, and he loved it.

"To the trees!" he called in answer, and the gray mare leaped away and left the black stallion standing, as it were.

The heart of Rory sank, for as he dug a heel into the ribs of the Doctor, the big horse merely turned his head, questioning, without increasing his speed a whit.

And were there not picture horses, had not all men heard of them, that fill the eye, but never the pocket of him who bets on them? Perhaps the beautiful stallion was another of these.

He called to the Doctor. He leaned forward. In his ears rasped the harsh, mocking laughter of the Apaches; and the gray mare was sweeping well ahead.

Then the black started. Leaning as he was, with the horse already at a strong canter, the sudden impulse almost unseated Rory Michel. The stars streamed back above his head, blurring. The wind cut into his eyes, until he had to squint as though he was reading fine print.

Beyond the nearest of the Apaches he darted. Off to the right he was vaguely aware of a herd of horses and mules being driven in toward Ware's place. That was the work of Rising Bull to redeem his plighted word.

But Rory had small time to think of this. The little flash of a gray mare was standing still, was it not? No, it was streaking away with all its might, the tail drawn out in a straight line by the speed of its racing, and the mane flying up into the face of the rider. Yet the gigantic bounds of the black overtook her momentarily with an incredible ease.

Now his nose was level with her tail. The next jump put him at her haunch, at her middle, at her shoulder. There were the oaks, at the right, a black blur. And the stallion went past them a full length in the lead.

He called to the Doctor again. It would be easy,

48

would it not, to ride straight away from this war party? No, for he could see the rifle in its scabbard under the knee of the boy who was racing against him. So he called to the Doctor, and the big horse answered his voice and rein and came down swiftly to a long, rocking lope.

He knew that stride well enough. It was like the flight of a swallow as it dips through the sky from horizon to horizon. It was as smooth as the way of wings in the air. Even this gait kept the Indian ponies pounding along at a full gallop. And young Rory Michel, lifting his head to the stars, began to laugh.

There was no pretty Nancy Ware out here under the night, but there was something better, the long trail, the unknown trail, which never had ended for him before and which now promised to unravel new wonders to his eyes.

The Apaches came hurtling about him again.

There was the boy who had challenged him to the race and the lad was laughing, also. So were they all, these wild Indians.

Where was the dignity, the stiff reserve of which people talked when they mentioned the red men? This party chuckled and chattered like so many magpies.

"A medicine horse! A medicine horse!" shouted the lad of the race. "He was behind me, with me, and before, all in one moment. And this mare is not tied to a tree, either. A medicine horse!"

He heard the deep voice of the chief answering: "Would he ride on a common horse? This is a stallion from the sky, a chief of horses, that can leap along the clouds. Hai! We have found good fortune. My son is already well!"

And he laughed, and shouted, and threw up one brawny hand above his head and brandished the spear which he was grasping. Fourteen feet of stalwart wood, shod with steel, it trembled in his grip.

Rory Michel looked and admired. He felt that he would like to be as these others, on wild horses, half naked, stripped of foolish laws, free as the wind.

And might he not be?

All things will come to him whose heart is strong!

49

He had heard it in his childhood, out of lips old and wise. He could not remember the face, but only the broken voice of the man who had spoken. And the words were registered in his heart—all things to him whose heart is strong!

Chapter 9

They rode three hours only, straight down the valley to a ravine that cut to the north, then climbing steadily into the hills. And before midnight they came onto high, rolling ground starred with camp fires and glistening with tents. From a distance the noise of their approach was heard, and braves and young boys galloped out to meet them and whirled like leaves in the wind around them, escorting them into the camp.

What shouting, what brandishing of weapons! Rory Michel found it exciting enough. It would have been childish braggadocio in white men. But these were Apaches. These were the riders down the red trail of the Mexican moon. And if they chose to act more like wild spirits than men, they had proved their right to do so!

Rory Michel, therefore, came into that noisy camp with pleasure in his heart.

He saw a flock of big, wolfish dogs come leaping about the feet of the wild ponies. He saw little children come darting out from the lodges, flashing naked in the light of the fires that shone behind them. He saw women laboring. Night or day, they seemed always occupied.

And then he was conducted to a lodge somewhat larger than the others, with a great red sun with blue rays projecting from it painted upon the face of the tepee. He dismounted, at the word from the chief, and at the same time the entrance flap of the lodge was raised and a tall woman stepped out, almost as tall as Rising Bull, and far more stately. Her features and her graceful bearing were not like those of the true Apache.

Rising Bull pointed Rory out to her, and he said in Spanish, a courtesy which Rory could appreciate:

"This is the man. All is true that we have heard of him. All is true. For we have seen the speed of his horse, and it is not like the speed of any other horse that runs. It has wings, though we see them not. Let him come quickly to our son."

"He may not come now," she answered in the same tongue. "Big Horse is inside the lodge. He is making medicine. He is purifying the place with sweet grass, and he is smoking to the four corners of the sky."

"Tell Big Horse to be quick," said the chief. "I must come in!"

"He will be very angry!" said the squaw.

"Let him be angry, but let our son live!" said the chief.

She passed back into the tepee, her head obediently bowed. In the meantime, a swarm of people had pressed around the stranger, and Rory had turned to face them. Braves, old men, youths, boys, and girls, infants in arms, dogs, even a stray burro, caught in the jam and patiently enduring it, thronged in closer toward him. An open fire burned nearby, and the wild, shaking light of it played over the faces of the crowd. Gaping, chattering, staring at Rory, they pressed closer and closer, until the chief took note of what was happening.

He roared out a few loud words, and instantly the crowd gave back, and Rory saw a number of men and women drop their faces suddenly. Rising Bull then explained pleasantly to his guest:

"I told them that they were foolish, and that my father would wither their right hands for them all if they shouldered him too closely. That will give you much room while you are in this place. However, I know that you are kind. You will not do the thing that I have said."

Rory was about to say that the threat was as far as a star from his real powers. But he remembered, in time,

51

that no disclaimers on his part were of any use. They had failed to impress the Mexicans. They had failed to impress the war chief of the Apaches. All he could do, apparently, was to let them make up their own minds about him. Words would not serve him at all; actions alone would speak.

The squaw now appeared through the entrance flap of the tepee, and in a low voice she spoke to the chief. He seemed troubled.

"Father," he explained to Rory, "Big Horse is looking now at my son with the red eye. Do you know what that is?"

"No," said Rory. "I never heard of that."

"'The red eye,' said the chief, very seriously, "is used by our great medicine man, Big Horse, only for wonderful things. It may be that he will have more luck with it. But I don't think that his medicine will be strong enough to make my son well again. With the red eye, it is true that Big Horse has looked into many things for the Apaches. He has pointed lucky trails for our war parties. We have taken many scalps and counted many victories when we rode where he told us to go. But everything that he has done, has failed until this time. Can we go in and see him work with the red eye?" he asked of the squaw.

"Go if you dare," said she. "I am afraid. I shall stay out here in the darkness and wait. I have seen the thing once, and it makes my stomach feel empty and my bones as light as the bones of a bird!"

"Do you fear, father?" asked the chief anxiously, of young Rory.

"I'm not at all afraid," said Rory Michel.

"Step first, then," said the chief. "If bad fortune flies out of the red eye toward us, you will meet it with your strong medicine and throw it away again, will you not?"

"I'll do what I can," said the boy. "But sometimes," he added calmly, "bad medicine spoils good medicine. We'll see, very soon. First tell me what is wrong with your son?"

"If you had seen him only a little distance of three moons ago," said the chief, "he was still the tallest

52

among the Apaches, for his age. He was the strongest, he ran the fastest, he rode with the surest seat. His play bow could strike birds dead. With a rifle he had learned to shoot, because his eye was clear and his hand was steady. He was so cheerful and happy that my people called him South Wind, because the south wind means a clear moon for riding on the trail, and warm weather in the winter, and happiness in the lodges.

"But then South Wind began to grow sick. It came to him like a fever. He lay down. His skin was hot and dry. He would not eat. His eyes stared. He understood nothing that was said to him. He grew worse and worse.

"Then I called for Big Horse. He came. He is a great medicine man, and has cured many people. He has cured people who were about to die, and who already knew that they had one foot upon the trail that goes through the darkness. But Big Horse has saved them, and brought them back. Well, I sent for Big Horse, and he worked very hard over my son. He worked, and has worked, for three moons!"

"How did he work?" asked Rory.

"He worked so hard, day after day, that the sweat ran down from his body like rain. Big Horse worked so hard that he grew thin. He danced, and shook the rattles, and tried to drive out the bad spirit. And he purified South Wind with sweet grass, burning it constantly, and gave him the sweat bath every day, and a plunge into cold water and, for a time—"

"A sweat bath and a cold plunge every day?" asked Rory sharply.

"Yes," said the chief. "All of the Apaches know that that is a very good way to make a sick man well. And for a time it was very easily seen that Big Horse was winning. The bad spirit in my son was growing weak and beginning to leave. For many days, my boy had clear eyes and was very well. But after that he slowly got weak again."

"And still he took the sweat bath and the cold plunge every day?" asked Rory.

"Almost every day," said the father. "But sometimes we were not camped near water. Then that was too

53

bad. He could only have a little cold water thrown over his body after the sweating. Perhaps I have been very wrong not to stay with him near cold, running water. Perhaps that is the great trouble, father?"

He asked it with great anxiety. Rory, shivering at the thought of the three months' torment which the patient had endured, replied: "You know, Rising Bull, that a man cannot tell everything from hearing another man talk. I must have a look at your son. Perhaps I can do something. But three months is a long time to have a bad spirit in the body."

"It is a very long time," agreed the father, with a sigh. "The evil spirit has eaten away almost all his flesh. There are bones left, merely. His face is like the face of a skull. There is very little life left in him!"

He approached the flap of the lodge.

"Is there anything more that you wish to tell you, father?" he asked.

"No," said Rory. "We'll go in, now."

The flap of the tepee was lifted, and he was motioned to enter first.

Chapter 10

What he saw inside was the symmetrical circle of the tepee, marked off in sections where the tent poles pressed against the hides that made the sloping walls. Several back rests were ranged about, and there were two posts from which hung weapons, bridles, saddles and other equipment of the warrior. By this, it was plain that not only the father, but the son, also, had achieved at least in part the status of a man and a full fighting member of the tribe.

Whatever the wealth of Rising Bull, he was not displaying it. In two parts of the tent, to be sure, there were well-wrapped packages which might contain goods of almost any sort, from gold to lacework, but he had little in view that the commonest warrior might not have exhibited, except, to be sure, that there were four rifles leaning in place against the posts.

In the center of the tent was a fire, smoldering low, its smoke rising to the top of the tepee, where the mist gathered thickly and seemed to compress before it gradually rolled out at the vent-hole. Over the fire stood an iron tripod, from which hung, on a movable arm of clumsily worked iron, a heavy pot, crusted and blotted with masses of soot. Plainly it stood all day over the flames, with meat simmering inside. The smell of the stale cookery filled the room, soaked into the walls and mingled with the acrid, eye-stinging wood smoke.

Just opposite to the door lay the invalid on a deep bed, and it seemed to Rory that he was seeing the starved child of Maria, grown older and larger. Two highlights rested upon the prominent cheek bones; the cheeks themselves were so sunken that a ghastly smile pulled at the corners of the lips. The eyes were lost in pools of black shadow.

Opposite to the boy stood a grotesque figure wrapped in a clumsy bearskin, with the grinning head of the bear surmounting him, and the skin of the feet, armed with claws, dangling. It was the medicine man, Big Horse; and it was now clear that "red eye" was a most peculiar medicine. For the eyes of the man were swathed in a heavy blindfold and in the center of his forehead, held in place by a single cord, appeared a great red stone, that gleamed and shimmered in even the dull firelight.

Rory Michel, in a single glance, knew that it was a ruby, and one of the true pigeon's blood, the purest color, the richest fire. Knowing that, the size of the gem bewildered him, until he recalled that a favorite diversion of the Apaches had been the robbing of the wealthy churches of old Mexico, many of them heaped with the accumulated treasures of centuries.

Well did Rory know the rarity of that gem.

And with his second breath he told himself that one day the jewel should be his!

From the ruby, he passed to a consideration of the medicine man in person. The latter was a squat figure, of the true Apache type, with legs fitter to waddle than to run, a deep chest, a big throat, and bulging, brutal jaws. He looked as if his face had been trampled upon in his childhood and permanently deformed; it was the characteristic appearance of his tribe!

He was weaving himself from side to side, taking dancing steps, but they were short, never more than a few inches. His body swayed, bent slightly forward and back, and kept rhythm with a strange, almost wordless crooning that arose from his throat.

The chief, in the meantime, with a raised hand as though to warn the white man from any interruption, remained motionless by the entrance during the ten or fifteen minutes this chant endured. When it ended, he still waited for a little, and then he said, speaking again in Spanish, no doubt for the sake of his guest: "Big Horse, tell me what the red eye has seen?"

The medicine man, after the completion of his chant, had remained for a moment with his head raised, his body rigid, his arms as stiff as though they had been lashed against his sides. He retained that position while he answered, in a sepulchral voice:

"There is a very great spirit, Rising Bull, which is fighting to capture the soul of your son. Red eye has surely seen this demon. Red eye has told my heart that we must be brave and fight hard. But no doubt we may win. It is a terrible spirit. It is worse than ten Cheyennes, all painted for the warpath. Only because your son is the son of Rising Bull has it failed to kill the boy long ago; also, I have helped to keep it from winning. Keep a brave heart. Tell South Wind to be brave, also. Every day I shall fight."

He turned, saw the white man for the first time, and his attitude changed at once.

"Who is this?" he demanded, glaring at the boy.

"Big Horse," said the chief, in the most conciliatory tones, "you have done many great things for the Apaches. You have given us victories and many scalps, many horses and mules. A mule is better than a horse, and you are stronger and better than most medicine men. You have fought hard since three moons to save my son. But it seems to me that he needs a new medicine. So I have brought a great medicine man. His skin is white, but his heart is red as yours. He, also, is a father to the sick. Let him try his skill. Let him try to cast out the evil spirit!"

The Apache doctor gathered his dignity about him like a visible mantle of darkness. He looked for a long moment, fixedly, at Rory Michel. Then he turned his head toward the chief of the tribe.

He had removed the blindfold at the same time that he took the cord and the ruby from his brow.

Now he held up the stone, and it caught the shining of the fire in its facets and was red as blood and fire combined.

"By the light of the red eye," said he hoarsely, "I tell you that no good will come to the tribe from a strange medicine man. Who has seen a white Apache? Now I give you a great warning. He cannot save your son. And if he remains in your lodge, Rising Bull, I will never come back to it. I give up the work that I have done. Answer me now. Choose between us!"

The chief glanced at Rory, and Rory, irritated by the manner of the doctor, could not help shrugging his shoulders and smiling, as though he put little faith in what they had just heard. Yet, in his heart, he had little faith in the ability of even a real physician to restore the wasted life of the sick boy.

It was a skin-clad skeleton that he saw before him, not the real semblance of flesh and blood.

Yet the Irish in his heart rose up and made him smile and shrug at the chief.

The latter was so desperately put to it, that the sweat shone on his forehead. He looked at Rory, seemed to mark afresh his youth and his white skin, and shook his head. Plainly he was about to dismiss his new doctor, but just then the boy uttered a faint, rattling moan, as though every muscle in his throat were already relaxed in death.

The chief, at this, groaned aloud, and started violently.

"Big Horse," he said hastily, "you are a man with a

very strong medicine. That I know. I have seen the thing. Still, sometimes there are two trails to reach the home tepee. We have tried one trail and have been riding on it a very long time. Therefore, I shall try the other way."

"You have said enough," said Big Horse furiously. "I pray that the Sky People may not strike you. But I see the evil spirits crowding to come into the entrance of your lodge. Only because they see me here they delay! Farewell!"

He stalked out.

The chief, still uncertain, overawed by the manner and the harsh voice of the medicine man, made a pace after Big Horse and was about to speak to entreat him back, no doubt, but Rory took him by the arm. Big Horse left the lodge uninterrupted.

Said the chief: "Now, father, you see that I am a desperate man. I have one wife, and I have one son. Such a son as no man ever had a better. Tell me if you can save him!"

"That," said Rory calmly, "I cannot tell you."

"Ha?" exclaimed the Apache, glancing anxiously toward the entrance, as though about to run out after the other doctor.

"No," said Rory Michel, "I only know one thing, to begin with."

"What is that?"

"That Big Horse has been wrong. He has been trying hard. But a fool may work blindly all day to climb up a steep cliff, and a blind man who keeps his wits about him, may fumble for the proper trail and find it."

This pictorial mode of speech seemed to impress the chief. He stared at the boy, sighed profoundly, and then he said anxiously: "Begin, father. Must I go from the lodge? Do you speak to the spirit in secret?"

Said Rory, suppressing a smile: "No. I want to have you here. You will see the difference between us, between me and Big Horse. He meets the spirits in the dark. I meet them either in the dark or the day."

He added: "Call in your squaw, also. Let me see the boy's mother, too."

The chief, amazed but apparently delighted, stepped

to the entrance flap, but the woman was already hurrying in, her eyes on fire with hope.

Rory measured her anew, and more clearly with the firelight upon her face. She was plainly of an outlander tribe. Not only was she made tall and straight, but her features were beautifully cut. She resembled the boy, who was almost handsome, in spite of the extreme emaciation of his face.

"Now," said Rory Michel, "Big Horse has discovered only one thing: that there is a very powerful spirit attacking the body of your son. We are going to try to drive that spirit away. Perhaps we won't succeed. You have left him too long in the hands of Big Horse, who knows nothing about the matter. I am going to work with all my might, however."

The mother looked sadly and anxiously toward the boy.

"Begin, then, father!" she murmured. "Begin the dance, the purifying smoke, the chant! See, he is dying now!"

Poor South Wind was slowly turning his head from side to side, gibbering through soundless lips.

The heart of Rory sank as he watched, but he forced himself to assume a cheerful manner.

"I do not work, usually, with chants and dances and purifying smokes," said he. "This time I shall not, either. I can do those things, but not now."

"Is it only to wait, then, and do nothing?" asked the chief desperately.

Rory half closed his eyes.

As far as medicine was concerned, he knew something about first aid and bandaging. He could even sew up a superficial cut. He had sewed them on his own body, in his time! But for the rest, he only understood that rest, light, nourishing food and plenty of fresh air help a sick man.

He opened his eyes again.

"Do as I say," said he.

"In everything!" answered the chief. "Now I vow a new saddle with silver—"

"Vow nothing," answered Rory. "Wait till I ask you to make a sacrifice. But now help me and your squaw to roll up the flaps of the tent. Open the entrance, first."

"The night air!" cried the chief.

Rory was reminded of the Mexicans so that he almost smiled in the faces of the others.

"I shall make the night air friendly. I shall fill it with kind spirits," said he.

And straightway, the chief and his wife hurried to help him do up the side flaps of the tent. A pure current of the air instantly swept through. The smoke drew down from the top of the lodge and passed away.

Then Rory came in and sat by the side of the boy.

He felt the pusle.

It was very feeble, uncertain, wavering between fast and slow. The breathing was slow, shallow. The skin was cold and dry to the touch. He felt as though he were handling one already more than half dead. And a wave of gloomy despair rose like darkness over the heart of Rory. He looked up and saw the keen, doubtful eye of the mother.

"All will be well," said Rory, and forced himself to smile.

Instantly he himself felt better and more assured.

Chapter 11

He set himself to the serious work of nursing the boy. All that he knew to do was to keep the lad warm without crushing him with the extreme weight of the clothes. He arranged the robes in this manner, therefore, and critically tested pulse and breathing. They became a little steadier. The head no longer turned so desperately, so feebly from side to side, as though looking for an opportunity to escape.

But, every now and again, a chorus of dog-barking roared through the camp or a caterwauling of youths.

With each of these explosions of sound, the boy shuddered and stiffened slightly. Rory, considering all things, began to make up his mind to an important step.

The chief and the squaw, in the meantime, seated near the boy and pretending to be perfectly at ease, were watching every gesture of his with the utmost attention.

Once the boy overheard the chief whispering: "You see, the new medicine begins to work. It must be in the touch of the hands."

"Hush, hush!" murmured the wife.

Even in her whisper there was a pulse of sobbing pain.

Hours went by. Again and again, as the sufferer was about to sleep, his eyes jerked open for a fluttering instant as a fresh outbreak of noise crashed through the camp. And each time he muttered.

"What is it that he says?" asked Rory Michel.

"He begs to have the evil spirits sent away," said the mother.

"Aye, the evil spirits. That is the only word on his tongue," said the chief. "He has seen them in his sleep."

"He has seen the truth," moaned the mother.

Rory said nothing. He knew where the boy had seen the evil spirits of which he complained—in the language of the lugubrious medicine man. And the uproar of the camp called the words to mind.

It was hardly a wonder that the invalid was dying, for a sea of noise filled the camp. The howling of dogs hardly ever ended. As one fight died down, another was sure to begin in a distant quarter and rush across the village, gathering recruits as other dogs poured into the fray, and finally passing the lodge in pandemonium. Then there would be more young serenaders, with caterwaulings sufficient to raise the lofty roof of the inferno itself. In between, accompanying and surpassing all else, there were needlelike pulsations of lament— the wailing, shrill voices of babies.

The Apaches seemed to take this hubbub as a mere nothing, but the sick boy was continually trembling with the sounds. Before morning, young Rory had quite made up his mind.

He said: "The bad spirits are used to this place. We must go to another one. They will not know how to find him so well there. We must go away from here. Make a litter. Put him on it. Carry him after me."

They did not answer a word. They simply rose and followed his orders. The litter was made. The mother took the head and the father took the feet. And young Rory Michel walked before them, straight through the camp.

As they approached the confines of the camp, the chief asked anxiously if they had gone far enouth. "Not yet," said the boy. And they passed on beyond the outermost circle of the tents. The outer darkness received them with what seemed a kindly silence to Rory.

Behind him he felt the bearers of the litter walking more slowly.

"Father," said the chief, at last," We have many enemies. They stalk the camp. They wait for a chance to steal horses or scalps!"

"I," said Rory presumptuously, "will ward the enemies away. Keep on."

He added, for he knew that Indians were very likely to make their camps near a stream: "I feel running water not far away."

"Our father knows all things," said the chief's voice, very humbly.

"It is this way, the right."

So Rory turned to the right and presently heard the water, and next saw the dim stars dropping into it. He walked along the bank until the clamorings of the village were in the distance, muffled. Then he paused.

A snug little grove of trees went down to the bank of the creek. Wood, water, shelter from the sun, fresh air, quiet, all were here. He himself could do little more. He must trust in nature, the true healer.

So he said: "This is the place."

And he stamped.

He could have laughed at his own ceremonial manner, but the Apaches took it very seriously. Twice they shifted the litter before they made sure of setting it down over the very spot where he had struck his heel into the turf! And, in the darkness, the boy smiled.

The dawn was beginning. Light was still hardly perceptible, but the stars receded, and the mountain arose a deeper black against the sky.

Rory was cross-legged on the ground beside the sick lad. He felt the pulse. It wavered more than ever. The mouth sagged open. He leaned his ear and heard the faint fluttering of the breath.

Plainly the removal of the invalid had taxed the frail remnants of his strength, and as the day gradually deepened to rose and amber, and the glory of the naked mountains lifted from the night, Rory studied the changes in the boy.

He had strengthened, even in the few moments. Once he began to shiver, but this tremor ended when the robe was drawn closer about him.

"Father," whispered the mother, "it is stern battle, is it not?"

"It is a great battle," said Rory truthfully.

"And you fight," said she gently, "almost as a mother fights for the life of her child. So I should fight, if only I knew the wise heart of the medicine man and the skill of his touch."

And Rory felt greatly humbled. He would have liked to tell her that she herself would be able to do these things as well and better than he, but he knew that his great grip upon these people was through their own false imaginings, and he dared not betray his real ignorance. Instead, he fortified himself to a more impudent imposture, for the sake of the parents and of the child, also.

When the day, therefore, was losing its color, growing more radiant, more yellow-bright, he said: "Now, Rising Bull, speak quickly to your son and tell him to waken."

Rising Bull spoke sharply, but in Spanish. And the eyes of the sufferer opened looking bewildered, straight upward toward the zenith.

"It is the green and golden happy hunting fields!" he murmured. "I am already dead!"

"You are not dead," said Rory loudly. "Look at me.

63

I have come to save you. I sit at your right hand. I have driven away all of the evil spirits. Now you are only weak because they have been in you. They wish to come back into you again but, when you feel them coming and when your heart sinks with fear, grip my right hand, and you will feel the evil ones rush with a tingling out of the tips of your fingers!"

The boy looked at him with wonder and with belief filling his eyes.

"Everything is strange," he said. "I believe! All is as you say!"

"Now close your eyes," said Rory. "You are going to sleep. Do you hear? Answer if you hear me!"

"I hear you," said the boy.

"You are soon to hear me no more. You are to sink into a great sleep. All your fears are gone. You are safe. You are falling as if into a great, dark pit of softness and slumber."

"I fall, I sink to sleep!" whispered the boy.

And, almost instantly thereafter, his breathing became regular and his body relaxed in a perfect sleep.

Then Rory looked up, and for the first time he felt that the battle might be won. He wondered how much magic in the dead ages was based upon the sheerest common sense, and so miracles were accomplished.

He looked up and saw the great, waiting eyes of the chief and his wife.

Suddenly the woman smiled and tears rushed into her eyes, overflowed them, rolled down her face. She was like the Mexican woman, Maria.

"You have conquered. You are the conqueror!" she kept whispering.

He held up a hand for silence, and they were still. He made another gesture to signify that they might lie down, but they preferred to sit up all through the lonely night, patiently, beside him.

And he almost literally felt the life wax and wane in the boy.

Twice South Wind stirred suddenly in his sleep and wakened with a groan. Twice he reached out his right hand, obedient to what he had been told to do. And twice the firm grip and the reassuring voice of Rory almost instantly threw the youngster again in a sound sleep.

These moments were not wasted upon the parents. Rory was aware that they exchanged looks and whispers. But he began to care very little about their applause that he was to receive. He was too concerned in the progress of the boy.

For a week he was never certain. Day and night he hardly left the side of South Wind for a moment. He did the cooking. He made broths and thickened them, after the first day, with ground corn, sifted in. And then he added a thicker soup, and so, gradually, built up the careful diet of the invalid.

But seven days had passed before he was certain that South Wind was definitely on the road to recovery. The proof of it came to him with a start when, rousing on the seventh night of Rory's vigil, his patient suddenly thrust himself up at arm's length.

Rory Michel called to the mother.

"You come here and stay beside him," he said. "For my part, I shall go to sleep. All the bad spirits are out of him now. All that he needs is time. Tomorrow, we may go back to the village. Now, I must rest."

Neither did he need to leave that spot. He simply stretched out on the ground, threw out his arms, crosswise, and was instantly lost in the most profound and dreamless sleep. The accumulated weariness of the seven days weighted him down, but the profound slumber began to carry that fatigue away, little by little, as a running water washes away sand.

Chapter 12

Young Rory Michel was a month with the Apaches, and it was almost the gayest month of his gay career. For he had all of the pleasures of the free life and few of the displeasures. For the sake of South Wind, he induced the chief to maintain a lodge well away from the main camp, and two or three young warriors were generally assigned to keep guard over this outpost; they watched from a distance to see that dangerous enemies did not draw too near. Rory Michel could hunt all day long or run horse races against the Apaches, or foot races in which he beat their bowlegged fleetest shamefully. Or else he would roll dice with them with a religious fervor.

One day he was rich in horses and robes; the next day he was a beggar whom the great chief, Rising Bull, staked anew. Rising Bull always had his stake returned within twenty-four hours. And there was a regular caravan movement flowing between the isolated lodge and the main camp to cart the gains and the losses of the white youth to and fro.

The heart of Rory was filled with content; above all, because he did not have to sleep in the roaring maelstrom of the big camp at night. The pure open air, the silence, the breathing of the pine trees surrounded them.

But he remained a stern tyrant in a sense. He would not allow the daughters to come back to their parents as yet. Rising Bull and the mother might be there to rejoice in the recovery of their son. But young Rory Michel had decided that three Apaches were quite enough to occupy his attention without new recruits.

Besides, it was better for the sick lad.

He could no longer be called sick, however.

On the seventh day, as has been said, he had sudden strength enough to sit up among the blankets. A week later he was walking, and a few days after that he was practicing with weapons again. Not that he could manage a war bow, but he worked away at a child's play bow, disciplining the muscles of his arms and shoulders. In that short fortnight, he had turned from a dying skeleton into a magnificent youngster.

He had his mother's tall body and excellently regular features. She was a Navajo, with all the good looks of that most handsome of Indian peoples, and the boy took after her. He was fifteen. He was straight as a pole, limber as a whip stalk, tough as well-seasoned rawhide.

Three weeks after the coming of the white medicine man, young South Wind was riding ponies over the hills at a breakneck speed. And he was demanding that the party return to the village where he could join the feastings of the rest of the youths and meet them in lying and boasting.

But Rory Michel did not consent. He declared that the time still had not come when young South Wind could go safely back into the camp, where the spirits of evil might have a better chance to get at him. South Wind used to plead.

So he said, on a day: "You are strong, father. You can snap your fingers at the evil spirits. See what you did with me. I was a dead man. I can still feel an ache in my back, where my hip bones used to break through the skin. Well, you yanked the bad spirits out of me and put me on a horse in three weeks. Hai! That is medicine. You could keep the spirits away from me. You could drive them, no matter where. And it is a lot happier in the camp with all the rest of the people."

Rory shook his head.

"You don't understand spirits and their ways, South Wind," he declared. "You see, they know that I'm at home out here in this place. Therefore, they don't come near. The first few days, yes, but after a few dozen of them had been mauled—I made some of them groan, I can tell you, when they tried to pounce on you—after that, South Wind, they began to be afraid of this place, just the way coyotes are afraid of the den of a mountain lion or a grizzly bear. They don't bother us out here. You can tell the difference. You feel better here."

"I feel," said the boy, "as though I could jump off that rim rock and fly like that hawk, in three strokes swim through the air and kick my heels over the black mountain there; in three more be back again, and chase the eagles and pull out their tail feathers while they scream with fear of me and try to drop down the curve of the sky and get home to their nests. That is how I am feeling, father!"

He was sitting cross-legged. Now he leaped to his

feet with a yell, catching up a fourteen-foot war lance as he rose. He hurled the weapon a prodigious distance into the air and maintained his whoop unbroken as he waited for it to descend again. Rory Michel pretended that he did not know that there was anything impending in the air above his head and continued to puff away at a pipe.

Down came the lance and was caught by the expert hand of the lad.

"Look, father!" cried the boy. "I could almost take the scalp of a spirit with my own hands. Only show me how to see the sneaking things, father!"

Rory Michel grinned.

"Close your eyes," said he, "spin around ten times as fast as you can, and then look. You'll see a spirit!"

"Shall I, really?"

"Try!"

The boy obeyed. He closed his eyes, revolved with sudden speed, almost like a top, and then came to a pause and looked about him. That is to say, he tried to pause, but now he was staggering dizzily. And he cried out: "I see the mountain spirits, father. And they are carrying the mountains away. They are making the mountains blow away like smoke in a wind!"

"Sit down!" commanded Rory.

The boy sat down.

He held his head in his hands for a moment, but then he said: "You have made a fool of me again, father. But I don't mind that, because there are no other people nearby to see us! However, I was really frightened for a moment. I forgot that it was simply dizziness. I was expecting to see a spirit, and therefore it seemed as thought the spirits were really dissolving the mountains as mud dissolves in water. Well, you are never more than half serious. There is always a smile in what you say and what you do. But tell me, father, how long you will stay with my people?"

"Forever, perhaps," said Rory. "I'm happy here."

"As long as there is meat in the camp, it is for you," said the boy gravely. "But you will not stay very long."

"Why not?"

"My mother has told me about white men. She has

seen them. She has seen them with the Apaches, and among the Navajos it was the same thing. They do not stay very long. Only two possible things keep them."

"What two things?" asked Rory.

"No, you would be angry."

"I'm never angry with you, South Wind," said Michel truthfully. "What are the two things that keep a white man among the Indians?"

"A wife or gold," said the boy. Rory nodded.

"I'm not looking for a wife," he said.

"Why not?" asked South Wind. "Very soon I myself shall marry. And you are older than I and very much wiser. Why don't you have a wife to cook for you and make clothes, do bead work, and set up the lodge, scrape the hides and make them into good soft leather? A wife costs very little and she works all her life. She is always contented—when she is the property of a medicine man or a great chief. And you are both!"

"You have a lot of good reasons," said Rory, thinking of the squat, broad-mouthed Apache girls, but without a smile. "However, this is not my time to marry. I have made medicine and the medicine was bad. It told me not to marry."

There was no answer to this remark from the viewpoint of South Wind. But he shook his head.

"And there is not much gold in our tribe," he said. "However, I have one great hope about your staying. My father told me!"

"What did he tell you, South Wind?"

"That when you saw the red eye, you looked at it as though it were a very old friend, and you were glad in your heart to see it again."

Rory looked narrowly at the boy.

"It is worth looking at," said he. "You admit that, South Wind?"

"Any man would be glad enough to have it and to wear it," said the Apache. "But even Big Horse cannot wear it often. It is altogether too strong!"

"What does it do?" asked Rory.

The boy answered quite seriously. "It burns. You can see the fire in it. That is not a cold fire. It burns inward. It burns the blood and then the bones, Big Horse

69

says. He has to make big medicine before he can put it on. He is afraid of his life every time."

"Is he? Well, South Wind, I don't think that I would be afraid of my life."

"No," said the boy, "perhaps you wouldn't be afraid. You know all the spirits, and I suppose that you know the red one that lives in that stone, also. My father says that some day you may have the stone and thereby you will become the chief medicine man in the place of Big Horse. He has made some very strong medicine but, of course, you would make still stronger."

"Is the owner of that red eye always the medicine man of the tribe?" asked Rory.

"Yes, of course."

"How long has that been true?"

"The stone has always been with this tribe of Apaches," said the lad. "Thunder once ran all the way down from heaven and dropped it among my people. The man who caught it in his hands became the great medicine man of the tribe. When he grew old, he gave it to the next medicine man. That has always been the way. So you see what we hope, father?"

"Tell me exactly what you hope," answered the other.

"Why, we hope, of course, that you will not leave us until you have red eye. And after you have it, of course, you will have to stay with us forever as our medicine man."

He rocked back a little on his heels and laughed.

"Look long at it, father! It may keep you with us all the days of your life."

"I've looked at it long enough already," said Rory, muttering.

And he fell into a grim thought and gripped his jaws together.

Chapter 13

There was much truth in what South Wind had said. At least, it was the attraction of the great ruby that kept Rory in the Apache camp long after he knew that South Wind was thoroughly on the road to recovery. The stone burned in his daydreams and in his thoughts at night. His fingers itched for it. He wanted to hold it in the hollow of his palm and see the red fire welter back and forth as he shifted it. He wanted to see it by candlelight and firelight and in the full, intolerable blaze of the sun.

What made him so grim was that it appeared the tribe itself looked on the gem as communal property. What would the tribe have in mind, therefore, if the stone were carried away from them?

His eyes narrowed, as he thought of this.

However, his intention was fixed upon the jewel firmly.

If he could win the ruby from the great medicine man, that ruby would be his. At least, so it seemed to him. As for the tribal right in it, the tribe would be hanged, for all of him.

The moral sense of Rory was not, perhaps, the most acute in the world, but he was determined to have the ruby. The itch for it was not only in his palm, but in his very soul also.

That day, leaving South Wind, he rode straight into the camp and sought out the lodge of Big Horse. A squaw came out and gave him a broad smile of welcome, and held back the flap, so that he might enter. Once he was inside, Big Horse favored him with the expression of a stone image, and not a pleasantly cut image at that. He had been at some of his foolery and solemn rites. His face was still daubed with black and red and green stripes, and he was smoking a pipe in the most ceremonial manner.

He put out this pipe, filled another, lighted it and passed it to his guest. Rory took one whiff, almost choked on the foulness of the fumes, and opened his business.

"Big Horse," said he, "the young men say that among your powers there is a magic that enables you to read the minds of the dice as they roll. Is it true?"

At the mention of dice, the expression of the medicine man altered completely. His brows drew down over his eyes, and from the eyes themselves came a gleam of intense cunning and pleasure.

He had no love for the white man; he had no reason for love. It was true that the coming of the stranger had meant life to the son of Rising Bull, but Big Horse felt that the cure had not been a holy one. He had, himself, done all that was in the lawful powers of man to do in order to heal the lad. For there was little of the charlatan in Big Horse, when it came to his profession.

He was convinced that he had, more than once, filled the sky with clouds, and then brought down the rain from them. He was convinced that he had effected various cures, that charms of his had procured invulnerability for more than one of the Apache warriors, and that medicine of his making could and did bestow fortune upon the warriors when they departed for a raid.

Therefore, he was only in part jealous of the success of the young white man; his chief emotion was one of religious fury. The rightful gods had been impugned.

However, he forgot everything except the core of this hatred of Rory, when he heard the magic word, dice!

"The hearts of nations grow old, brother," said Big Horse.

"In what way?" asked the boy.

"When I was young," said the medicine man, "the youths and the chiefs were glad to gamble with me. But now it is ten years since I have shaken dice. They say that the dice understand my wishes, and come for me as I would have them. But you, brother, no doubt have a greater medicine than mine. You could make the dice roll better to suit yourself?"

He actually canted his head a little upon one side, as he said this, and Rory could hardly keep from laughing in the face of the painted rascal.

It was, however, a rather naive challenge. It was the equivalent of admitting that the medicine man's dice were crooked.

"Suppose that I return to my camp and bring my own dice," suggested the boy. "And then we can play, and each roll his own dice?"

The medicine man listened with a clouded brow.

He shook his head.

"Two sets of dice make two games, and I can only play in one," he said ambiguously. "Here are my dice. Here is a robe to throw them on. Here is a cup to shake them in. What is better, brother? And what is needed except something to stake?"

He picked up the wooden cup of which he had spoken, clapped three dice into it, and rattled them loudly together.

"One cast?" asked Rory, eyeing the other narrowly.

The very veins in the throat and the forehead of Big Horse were swelling with eagerness.

"One cast!" he exclaimed.

"Here," said Rory, pulling out a long string of beads from his pocket.

It was a magnificent string. Red and blue and yellow alternated. They glimmered with polish. And the squaw cried out, suddenly, in an ecstasy.

Big Horse looked up at her with a significant nod of his head.

"I have there," he said, "a good spear, new, and well made. It has a braided handle. It is well balanced. It is all that a spear should be."

"That is a match," nodded the boy. "Cast!"

The dice were straightaway given a swirling movement in the bowl by the medicine man, and out he flung, in a long, swift, but easily flowing motion, the three dice from the bowl.

"Good!" said the boy.

And he gathered the dice for his own cast. The first

glance at them had told him nothing. The first lifting of them, however, revealed the mystery. They were cunningly weighted, every one of them, and, furthermore, he could feel that the corners had been beveled. They were not worn down merely by long usage. Instead, they were cut off at angles along the edges, and this was, no doubt, a system well known to cunning Big Horse.

No wonder that the dice knew the mind of the master! No wonder, also, that he was willing to allow any stranger to use his dice, for according to the manner in which they were shaken and cast out, so would the throw be.

In the pocket of Michel there was, at that moment, an excellent set of dice ready for use. There had been no need for him to return to his lodge for them. But he did not intend to introduce his own dice—at least, not now.

He cast, and he lost the beads. The squaw snatched them up and made a choking sound of delight.

But that was not all.

A hunting knife, an ammunition belt, a real treasure for any Apache, and then a pair of excellent Colt revolvers over which even the medicine man almost lost his composure, followed the beads.

An then young Rory sat back and shook his head, with a sigh, while that natural pirate, Mr. Big Horse, began to eye the very clothes of Rory Michel, as though he expected confidently to have his hands on them next!

"Brother," said Big Horse, "you have buttons on your coat that are worth a casting of the dice. You have had bad luck. But good luck will come."

"If I make another cast," said Rory, "it will have to be alone with you. I see that I can have no good luck at all until I play with you alone."

A ghost of a smile troubled the mouth of the medicine man; but he controlled himself gravely.

"We shall be alone," promised Big Horse. "I send away my squaw, now."

He waved his hand, and the squaw went shuffling from the lodge. Rory looked after her with a qualm that was almost regret in his heart. But, after all, the medicine man and his crooked dice deserved an even worse fall than that which Rory planned for him.

"What shall we cast for?" asked the Apache, rolling the dice in a bowl. "Name it, brother, because I am sorry that you have lost so much. You see that I am not a poor man. I have a great many things, and I shall be glad to lose some to you. You see the parcels which are wrapped in the robes. Every one contains something that is worth having. You see how they are piled up, parcel on parcel? If the luck turns to you, you may win them all, brother!"

So spoke the medicine man, soothing and encouraging his companion; but Rory answered simply: "I'll play with you for one cast, for a greater thing than whatever you show here. The red eye, brother!"

Big Horse grunted as the word struck home.

"The red eye!" said he. "It is medicine, but you are a medicine man!" He sneered his disbelief as he spoke. "But even though you're a medicine man, what have you to offer against the red eye?"

"This," said Rory.

He whistled, and the gleaming, beautiful head of the black horse was instantly thrust through the entrance flap. Big Horse stared at the Doctor as though he were seeing a ghost.

"This is something! That is a horse!" said he. "But still, it's not worth the red eye."

"When you ride that horse you catch the birds out of the air," replied Rory Michel. "You can catch them before they can jump from the earth into the clouds. Your enemies turn to dust behind you and blow away. Or else you leap over the mountains; the warrior tries to run away, but your breath is instantly hot on his neck. That is what this stallion means to a brave."

Big Horse drew in his breath with a groaning sound.

Twice he shook his head, and twice he glanced back at the shining, brave eyes of the stallion and changed his mind yet again.

"I cast, then!" said he.

"Let us see the red eye, first," said Rory.

The medicine man groaned again but, rising, he went to a corner of the lodge and, after fumbling in a pile of his household goods, he returned with a twist of leather in his hands, and from the leather he exposed the red eye itself.

The first crimson gleam of it darted through the very soul of young Rory Michel.

"Now!" cried Big Horse.

His face was coppery, corrugated with the violence of his concern, as he spun the dice like mad in the wooden cup and cast them out on the blanket. He had done almost as well as could be hoped. They did not count combinations but simply gave the victory to the man who showed the highest number of spots. And the counting crookedness of the medicine man had turned up a six and two fives—almost the highest possible score!

Chapter 14

No matter how crooked the methods of Big Horse, he seemed surprised and delighted by the excellent result of his cast. It even wrung a low grunt of pleasure from him as he passed the wooden cup and the dice to his guest.

"Good luck," said Big Horse.

And he grinned with an offensive confidence at Rory.

The latter took the cup in his left hand, shook it, and instantly the three dice were securely palmed. He passed the cup to his right hand, and from the palm of that hand he allowed his own three dice to rattle into the bowl. The originals he put back into his pocket.

Once, twice and again, he whirled the wooden cup with its rattling contents; then out flashed the spinning cubes, ran half the length of the robe and flipped to a halt like three well-drilled soldiers, side by side.

Two sixes and a five looked up into the horror-stricken face of the medicine man.

"I have lost!" he groaned.

"The luck changed, for a cast," said Rory smoothly, and swept up the dice. He changed them instantly and offered Big Horse the cup.

"That is enough for today," said Rory. "Tomorrow perhaps we try the dice again."

And he picked up the leather and the ruby on it. He held it in the cup of his doubled hands, and it seemed to fill and overflow that bowl with rosy light.

Big Horse attempted to laugh, but his facial convulsion was a ghastly caricature of mirth.

"You know, brother," said he, "that you have won a useless thing. It is better for you to keep live fire in your pocket than that red stone. For it is cold, and still it burns to the marrow of the bone or the brain. I, brother, am a medicine man. I have many spells so strong that even the clouds stop on their way across the sky when I call them. But even I dare not wear the red eye, until I have made special charms. And the charms will last only for a little while. However, there are many other things in this lodge. There are guns. There are packages of bright clothes, painted robes, bead work. Take as much as will fill your arms. Leave the little red stone here with me. It would be no better than death for you!"

He tried to speak casually; but his glance burned with apprehension as he stared at the boy.

Young Rory Michel already had dropped the jewel into his pocket. Another picture than that of the chief was already in his mind, for he was seeing, in his fancy, a counter, and a man behind it with a microscope screwed into his eye while he bent above the blaze of the jewel. He was seeing the weighing of the gem, watching the head of the jeweler wag with amazement and delight.

And Rory began to laugh. He waved his hand jauntily to the medicine man and, stepping through the entrance, he swung into the saddle upon the stallion. The squaw hurried past him into the lodge, favoring him with a black look as she went, and, as Rory rode off, he heard behind him the wild and dismayed outcry of the woman.

He wanted to be off at once, but it was not a cheerful prospect to look forward to a long journey through the mountains without a weapon, and his revolvers, his very hunting knife had been left in the tepee of Big Horse.

So he set out for the lodge of the chief, Rising Bull. There were plenty of weapons to be had there, and eleven of the best. Neither would questions be asked, for everything that the chief owned was his for the taking.

He was in haste, but he did not race back; the Apaches must not see that he was burning with eagerness to be gone with his prize. But the enormous stride of the black horse whipped him rapidly over the ground, and so he came back once more to the stream, the trees, and the pleasant lodge of Rising Bull.

South Wind was amusing himself on the sunburned field nearby. His aim was to shoot with a war bow a war arrow as high into the air as he could send it, so that it diminished and went almost out of view in the pale shimmer of the sky; so that perhaps it was no more than a glitter of the sun upon the steel arrowhead. Then, as it turned and dropped down, the boy raced off at full speed to be under it in its descent.

A dangerous business and one needing wonderful skill to pick from the air that down-flashing arrow before it struck the stones and was shattered. But South Wind managed it again and again.

He laughed and leaped, when he saw his healer in the distance. With a run and a bound, he planted himself behind the saddle of Rory, and so they came galloping home together.

There the squaw sat in the sun, beading moccasins; she looked up to smile on them. And a strange smile she had in these days when she looked on the boy, for it faded toward the end and her eyes grew fixed as she saw, at the side of her son, the ghostly image of what he had been.

As usual, she wanted them to try the contents of the

meat pot that simmered all day in the lodge. But young Rory Michel had something better than meat to think of.

"I am going to hunt," said he. "Where is the strongest rifle and a good revolver?"

She got them in haste, though it meant patiently waiting until the rawhide strings and leather that wrapped the rifle had been done off it. Then the ammunition belt had to be filled by young South Wind. He wanted to know where the hunting was to be, and if he might not go along, and bitter was his disappointment when he learned that Rory would go alone on this day.

However, the guns were ready at last, the belt filled and buckled about the hips of Rory Michel, and, as he drew up the thongs, he heard what to him was worse than the roll and rattling of a war drum—the beating of many hoofs of strongly galloping horses which approached the lodge.

"Who is that?" he asked.

South Wind looked with a scowl from the entrance flap.

"It is not my father," he said. "But it is not an enemy, either. It is only Big Horse and a dozen warriors. They come fast. They are bringing some news for my father!"

"I can tell the news," said Rory. "They've come to say that I have won the red eye from Big Horse. That's all. And now I change my mind about hunting. Big Horse makes me sleepy. I'm going to lie down and rest. South Wind, you keep the entrance!"

The squaw and her son, when they heard of the treasure that their doctor carried, looked steadily on him and seemed almost turned to stone with surprise and with fear. But when the boy understood what was expected of him, he gripped the knife at his girdle, half bared it, and drove it home again into the leather sheath.

"No one shall trouble your sleep, father," said he calmly, and stepped outside the flap of the tent.

At the same time, the roar of the hoofbeats swept up to the lodge. The huge, rather hoarse voice of the medicine man shouted; and there was a rumbling chorus

79

from his companions. Not even a fool could have failed to detect the open hostility in the tones of these men.

South Wind responded calmly, and in Spanish: "Speak in Spanish, Big Horse. I can understand you better, then. I am too tired to speak our own tongue today."

At this insolence, there was an exclamation of rage from Big Horse, but he obediently said in Spanish:

"Where is the white man?"

"He is here," said the boy.

"Call him out to me quickly."

"He is asleep," said South Wind.

"Wake him. Call him out to me!" exclaimed the medicine man.

"Hai!" South Wind said. "That is an easy thing to say, but you would not be very happy if I did it. He might come, but if he did, he would be likely to wither you into an old man with a glance. And the rest of the warriors, too. He is not a man to be awakened lightly, this one who has cured me!"

"Let him be what he may," said Big Horse. "I have no fear of him. I have made the rain fall, I have brought winter into the middle of summer and taken it away again. Do you talk to me about being afraid of a boy, and a white boy at that?"

"Well," said young South Wind, "I shall not waken him. But if you want, I'll remember any message that you have to give him, when he has finished resting."

"Give him this message," said the medicine man. "Tell him that he has stolen the red eye. Tell him that I know very well how he stole it. I wait, now, with my friends. We smoke our pipes and think of what should be done to a man as bad as that. When we have finished smoking, we may let him give back the red eye. Perhaps that will not be enough, however. We are going to talk together and see what should be done. Tell that to him, when he has wakened. And if he is still not awake when we have ended our talk, I, Big Horse, will come in and take him by the hair of the head and waken him in that manner!"

The noise of the horses receded a little; young South Wind came back inside the tepee. He still was wearing the half contemptuous smile with which he had been defying the other warriors. But that smile disappeared when he was face to face with Rory Michel. He looked curiously and intently at the white man.

"Father," said he. "I was never half so much a foolish child as I am now. I spend my day shooting arrows into the sky, though I can't hurt the sky. But you, father, stay with the Apaches until you can steal a red stone! Hai!"

He uttered the exclamation of wonder softly, shaking his head so that the long, dark hair swung about his face.

The boy went on: "There is a fire in that stone which will burn your brain to dust. Do you know that, father?"

"You know, South Wind," said the white man, "that I didn't steal the red eye. I won it shaking dice, in the same game where I lost the revolvers, and my hunting knife, even! Where else did they go? But finally I won this. As for the fire that burns the marrow in the middle of bones, well, I have said a charm over that stone, and the fire in it heard me at once, and it will never even scorch my skin, let alone my brain."

The boy regarded him with the most obvious disbelief.

"No other man knew that charm!" said he.

"No," answered Rory Michel.

"Then the red stone with the fire has been waiting for you to come and take it?"

"I suppose so," answered Rory.

The boy shrugged his shoulders.

"Well," said he, "no matter what they decide when they've smoked their pipes, my father, my mother, and South Wind will all fight you till we die!"

Chapter 15

Through the flap of the lodge, Rory Michel looked out upon the council which was in progress under the shade of the trees. The warriors were at a sufficient distance so that the exact articulation of their syllables was lost, but there was no mistaking the sound of the high-pitched, angry voices, and the undercurrent of rage and hate in the tones of the medicine man.

The Navajo mother of South Wind had left the lodge the instant she learned what trouble was in the air. Now she returned, brought at a gallop by her husband, who had caught her up behind his saddle.

In front of the tent, the two jumped down, then came inside.

"Now," said Rising Bull, "what has happened? Tell me, South Wind, for I have only a woman's words to explain this thing."

He spoke to his son, but his grim eye was fixed upon the white man as he talked.

"South Wind can tell you as well as I can," answered Rory.

He lay down on a thick soft pile of robes, extended his shoulders and one arm comfortably against a back rest, and began to puff slowly at a pipe, watching the blue-brown clouds rising slowly up toward the wind vent at the top of the lodge.

He knew that the eye of the chief was fixed angrily upon him, but he regarded this very little. He knew that the greatest danger lay ahead of him, but still he was determined to die rather than give up the ruby.

He almost wondered, as he stared up through the curling mists of the smoke, if there were not something in the legend that the red eye burned up the brain?

Perhaps its singular fascination was the fire with which it destroyed men; perhaps he would himself be destroyed before that day was much older.

He heard South Wind saying: "You know what my mother always has said, that a white man stays among Indians only while he has a good reason."

"A woman is like a waterfall," said the chief. "She makes a great noise, but the only thing that goes walking through the air is her voice. If you listen to women all your life, South Wind, you will become very wise and never take a scalp or count a victory! Tell me what has happened, not what the Navajo woman has said to you!"

South Wind was as calm as could be under this pressure. He looked at his father full in the eyes and answered: "My mother says that a white man must have a reason. And our father, here, had one. Because he was kind, he saved me. He gave me a life, and I am willing to give it back into his hand whenever he asks for it. Also, he saw the red eye. And now the stone is with him. He won it from Big Horse at dice."

"Big Horse is a fool, and the son of a fool," said the chief. "I always thought it. I know it now. He is a man to talk, because he has a great voice. But he could not lose the red eye. It was not his to lose. It belongs to the tribe, to you, to me, to every man of the Apaches, like the brave deeds of our fathers, long ago. Big Horse could not gamble for it!"

"Nevertheless, Big Horse did gamble for it," said the boy.

The chief scowled darkly at him.

"What is this that you say, father?" asked Rising Bull.

"I risked the black stallion," said Rory, "on one throw of the dice. And how often does Big Horse lose? Already he had my two guns and the knife from my belt. He wanted to play for the buttons on my coat."

He grinned.

"We played for the red eye, instead. Now it is mine. Now I intend to keep it!"

The chief was so shocked and so outraged by this

83

calm remark that he could not answer at once and had to take a stride or two through the tepee. Then he paused again in front of Rory.

"This is a thing that you have tied with a rope, and it will not move in your mind again, father?" said he.

Rory nodded, and he saw the deep chest of the Apache slowly heave as the chief drew a great breath.

"Very well," said Rising Bull. "I have heard a man speak, and I know what he has said. I shall go and talk to Big Horse."

He left the lodge, striding rapidly. The squaw, the boy, and Rory Michel remained alone inside it. As for Rory, he did not stir from his position of comfort. The squaw picked up her beading and, with her head bowed, began to work again. Young South Wind, sitting down cross-legged near his white friend, caught up an old knife whose blade was already blunted from fleshing hides, and this he struck into the tough earthen floor of the lodge, raised again to arm's length above his head and hit again at the first mark which he had made.

"The days comes! The day comes!" said he. "The day comes, father!"

With each of these phrases, he struck the knife deep into the earth and, from the corner of his eye, Rory saw that the point was sinking into the ground always within a radius of a quarter of an inch. It was very accurate work; it filled him with admiration.

"The days come for what, South Wind?" he asked.

"For the fight," said the boy. "There will be a fight, I know. I could feel it in the cut of the wind today. I ought to be a medicine man. I can smell a fight when it is a month away. I could feel the fight coming when I first looked up into your face—that time when I was lying between sleep and dying."

"You remember," said Rory Michel.

He puckered his brow and began to think back to that moment.

Said the squaw, in her deep, soft voice: "Words are like bullets, are they not? If you send out too many words, South Wind, one of them may hurt you. Words are heavier than stones. They strike on the heart."

"Well, I've heard you say that before," answered the boy. "But what I've said, I feel. Big Horse had his face twisted up like a starved wolf, when he talked to me. He wanted to put his big hands on me. The day comes! The day comes!"

And twice more he drove the knife into the ground with a thud.

"There is always time to hope a little," said the squaw. "Your father is a great man in the tribe."

"He's great on the warpath," answered South Wind. "But this is a talking time, and that is where Big Horse is the greatest. You'll see. My father will do nothing with him. There are no talkers like Big Horse. He had twelve great warriors out there with him. Each of them would be very glad to have counted all my father's victories. They would be glad to have that, too, in the smoke of the lodge fire!"

He pointed above his head where, from a thin string of rawhide near the smoke vent of the tepee, hung several dark objects that looked like black rags, twisting slowly from side to side in the draft which the fire maintained.

The boy bent his head far back to regard the trophies of the war. In the silence, only the fire spoke, crackling cheerfully and busily.

"They may be jealous of him," admitted Rory. "I hadn't thought of that."

"Also, you have a white skin," remarked South Wind, with his usual bluntness. "How much good has come to my people from those who have white skins?"

Rory could not help nodding. "Well," said the boy, "we'll see before long. My father has a temper shorter than a winter day. He will come back here like a storm before very long."

He had hardly finished speaking, when the chief came hurrying into the tent.

Inside, he paused, collected himself a little, glaring about with a terrible eye, and then crossed to his own place.

He sat down, taking hold of the shaft of his war spear that was fixed upright, and still as he sat there he continued to finger the weapon as though the feel of it were a great comfort to him.

No one addressed a question to him, because it was too plain that everything had gone wrong for Rory at the conference.

"Oh, father!" he said suddenly, hoarsely.

"Aye," murmured Rory.

"They will have the red stone or, else, they will have your scalp."

"Well," said Rory, "I hope that their knives are sharp. I wouldn't want them to have to saw and tear."

He sat up on one elbow. The three Indians were looking fixedly at him, for this was a touch of humor for which they were not prepared. Neither did they understand it.

"Do they want the red eye—or me—at once?" asked Rory.

"They wait till the darkness," said the chief. "They wait until the little stars have come out in the sky. Then they will ask for you."

He lifted his head, and added: "I shall be ready to answer them, father. South Wind, also, will whisper a word to them!"

"Aye, the day comes," said the boy, and he set his teeth as he drove his knife into the ground.

Rory, looking from one man to the other, suddenly shifted his glance to the woman. It was plain that Rising Bull and his son intended to fight to the death for their guest, so long as he resisted.

Now he saw that even the squaw was slowly nodding her head. And the dignity of these people struck a chill into the heart of Rory. He felt that he had never before known anything so simple or so great.

The rose of the evening was beginning; in another hour the "little stars" would appear, and with them the Apache braves were sure to come.

"You know, Rising Bull," said he to the chief, "that a fire in a tepee throws the shadows of men against the walls."

"That is true," nodded the warrior.

He made a gesture to the squaw. Instantly she rose

and began to cover the embers of the fire with earth, stamping it down so that little or no smoke and steam arose.

With this, the tepee grew quite dark, but, through the cracks around the entrance flap, Rory could see that the sky outside was quiet, within and without. There was not even a whisper of wind, but all was as hushed as the grave.

Chapter 16

What puzzled Rory was the attitude of the squaw. He could understand that gratitude, for what he had done might convince the two men that their duty was to lay down their lives for him. But for the squaw, it meant the destruction of husband and son, worse than the end of life for her. Yet she remained placid, making no protest, calm and deliberate, her fingers until dark, as accurate and rapid and neat in their work as before.

Suddenly his heart warmed to these people. Their skins were red, but under the skin he felt a kinship with them all. If they were wild, he was wild, also. All their distinctions were skin-deep, and only that.

From the first, he had not intended to imperil them on his account. He wanted to meet the emergency for himself and make his own last reckoning with whatever dangers existed. That was in his mind, but he had wished to see how far they would come with him, unurged, unimpelled by any persuasion on his part. He was amazed at what they proffered him. Two would lay down their lives; one, a chieftain; the other, to whom life itself had hardly been restored, with the sweet taste of it still fresh and novel. The woman would give up more than both of them. And all this done without questioning!

He stood up.

"Go with him, South Wind," commanded the chief quietly.

"Stay here," answered Rory Michel. "I want to walk out there alone and look at them."

"You have some plan in your mind. I see the shadow of it in your eye," said the wise chief, staring at him.

"I am taking no weapons," answered Rory, showing his empty hands.

Rising Bull looked at those hands before he nodded.

"Very well," said he. "But do not stay long and do not speak many words to them, if they come near. You know, father, that the hand is quick when it sees fresh meat, and the sight of deer makes even women turn into hunters."

Rory smiled at these aphorisms and, with a most reassuring nod to his three copper-hued friends, he stepped outside into the open.

It was not yet the full twilight, for the horizon was still banded with radiant color, against which the mountains stood up black in the west, and purple bloomed in the east where the sunset struck against their faces. The evening wind was just beginning to stir, and touched his cheek with a cool, damp hand. Peace was showering out of the very sky upon the world. And yonder were the watchers for his life!

They were no longer drawn into a close circle, counseling. Instead, they had parted into groups of two; six groups, posted advantageously around the central point, the lodge of Rising Bull.

Rory looked toward them, and their rifles and nodded, and he said to himself that he was no better than a dead man. He had seen death before. He had rubbed elbows with it far nearer. But he never had had it so inescapably before him.

Then he shrugged his shoulders. There were two ways of looking at a problem. One is as a mathematician, and the other is as an optimist. Rory Michel remained an optimist.

He could mathematically deduce that there was no possible hope; but hope he blindly retained and closed his eyes upon the precise calculation of chance.

Far off, he could see the smoke from the tepees of the Indian village rising through the dusk. The wind laying in that quarter, he could hear the distant chiming of the voices. He heard the whinny of a horse, the louder braying of a mule, and the sounds seemed to fill the mountains with a sort of farmyard peace.

But here, so close at hand, the watchers were ready to kill.

The big man stepped closer from among the others. It was the medicine man, walking up with his horse, a long-maned, cream-colored pony, with gay ribbons worked into the tail and the saddle loaded with enough silverwork to satisfy even the heart of a Mexican.

Said Big Horse:

"Now, brother, where is your magic? Where is your skill? You can bring the dying back from the edge of death. But you are closer to dying than the boy was. There is only one possible way for you to escape!"

"By giving back the stone?"

"Yes!"

"And what do I get for that, Big Horse?"

"Your life," said the rascal.

"But I won the stone."

"You get your life," said the medicine man. "You took my dice from me and used your own, and yours were not honest. It must have been that."

"Ah, Big Horse," smiled the boy, "do you think that I didn't see your own dice and that I didn't feel the cuts on the edges? You knew those dice better than you know the face of your ugly squaw."

"Whatever you think," said Big Horse, grinning, "there is only one way for you to save your life. You must give back the stone. Come! That is why I am here. I am ready for it now. Then everything will be well."

"Look, Big Horse," said the boy. "I risked the stallion, and I won. If I give back the red stone, will you pay me the value of the stallion? We can ask other chiefs of the tribe to say what the value would be!"

"You won with dice that were not honest," repeated Big Horse. "Give back the red eye, and keep your life. Is the stone worth more to you than your life?"

His complacent superiority, the assurance of his position, showed in his voice, in his gesture, and it struck a heat through all the body of Rory Michel.

"Well," he said, controlling himself under a severe rein, "you see that I came out with no weapons. That shows that I wish to talk to you."

"That is what I saw," said the other.

"This is a hard thing. This morning, I had good guns, a knife, and other things," said Rory. "They are gone. Only the black horse remains, and even that your men keep yonder!"

"You see," said the medicine man, "that there is no escape for you. Even if you were to dodge away from me and catch a horse and fly, there would be no chance to escape from the great black stallion. Your own horse brings up the warrior to recapture you!"

Suddenly he laughed. The final thought had brimmed his cup with joy. And the youth, listening to the harshness of that laughter, felt his teeth brought to an edge. Through the gathering dusk, he still managed to smile at Big Horse.

"Well, then, Big Horse," said he, "I suppose that a wise man pays the only price that will be taken and then he forgets."

"That is the wise man's act always," said Big Horse.

"I look at it for the last time," said the boy.

He spread open in his hand the leather that contained the ruby and stared down at it. The thing burned like a fragment of the setting sun, shining by its own light, as it were, the rays striking up faintly from the heart of the stone.

"Do I see it, then, for the last time?" said Rory.

"Give it to me," broke in Big Horse greedily. "You have only a little time. Before long, the small stars will be shining, and then it will be too late for you to change your mind."

"Here it is, then," said Rory Michel.

He held out his hand with the treasure in it, but his eye was not upon the stone; it was fixed upon the heavy, craglike jaw of the medicine man, as the latter stepped eagerly forward. In his left hand Rory held the

90

gem; the right he whipped over with all his might and a prayer that was a whisper on his lips.

The blow landed fairly upon the bony, outthrusting ridge of the jaw, near the point. It struck home with a solid shock that turned the arm of the striker numb to the shoulder, while Big Horse swayed slowly back upon his heels, and the avid fire left his eyes. He was too stunned to raise a hand to avoid the second stroke. It was jerked home to the same spot, and the medicine man gradually sank down.

He grasped at the dangling leather of the stirrup, missed it, and settled with a tired, slouching movement all along one side upon the grass.

Michel was already at the cream-colored horse. He went for it like a cat, leaping, catching with feet and hands, and so scrambling into place, while the pony veered away with a grunt and a swerve.

It settled, bolting at full speed straight back toward the camp.

That was as good a direction as any for Rory Michel. The straightest line away from the lodge of the chief, and through the circle of the watchers, was the proper avenue for him.

Behind him, he heard yelling voices. Two rifles cracked, and the bullets kissed the air beside his head —good shots, these chosen men from among the Apaches.

But he had two closer perils. To the right and the left stood the nearest guards—four men, four rifle shots, and all at close range! He could hardly hope to escape from them all. Yet the light was very bad. It was the most treacherous moment, when the full night and the full day are both gone. Besides, might not the sudden act, the surprise, unsteady the hands of even such expert and experienced warriors as these?

He could hope for it. He could hope for little else.

He saw two guns raised. The hat jerked from his head the next instant; and one warrior was casting down in a fury the weapon which had clogged and failed him in the crisis.

Two more shots to come, at the least!

He flattened himself, along the neck of the flying pony. He shouted. Somehow, that seemed to make the peril less. He saw the red flash of fire from the muzzle of one gun that seemed thrusting almost at his face. Then it was gone. The double report was ringing in his ear; the pony still ran true, and the thickening shadows of the evening were soaking up the space behind him!

Other bullets followed, but they were not near enough to hum in his ears.

Still a danger was hurtling toward him through the dusk. He turned, and saw what seemed a winged horse skimming over the surface of the ground.

That was the chosen warrior to whom the keeping of the stallion had been entrusted, and he might be sure that a more accurate shot was not among the Apaches.

Still, the game was not lost unless the stallion had forgotten all the lessons that had been taught him at the Ware corral. A shrill whistle rose from the lips of the fugitive and, in answer to it, he saw the stallion leap high up from the ground, as though to clear an invisible obstacle. In mid-air, the whole body of the animal knotted, contorted, straightened suddenly again with the shock of landing and, with an empty saddle, the big horse raced on to find its master!

Chapter 17

At the Ware house, the night was running pleasantly. The day had ended without trouble among the Mexican laborers; the heat of it was slowly soaking out of minds and bodies in the night wind that blew gently up the valley. And, above all, on the veranda of the house there was a genial conversation.

The colonel himself had gone to collect, from some of the other mines, sums of money which were owing to him—in hard times he had made advances here and there—and he was not expected back until the next day.

But, to take his place, two troops of cavalry had arrived. They were quartered down the valley; the white of their tents, lighted by camp fires here and there gleamed through the darkness. Now and again, horses neighed from the picket line; and even individual voices raised in laughter or argument, drifted up along the wind and gave the listeners a sense of companionship and a security which was odd in Arizona in those days.

The commander of the detachment, Major Arthur Talmadge, sat on the porch with Mrs. Ware and her daughter; and the fourth in the group was the same genial captain who had both lost and found his herd, Captain Thomas Burn. It was an expedition which was aiming at the heart of the Apache country that the major was leading.

"Apaches," Nancy Ware was saying, "can be handled pretty well by people who know how to use diplomacy."

The major loved an aphorism better than whisky, and whisky better than anything else in the world.

"Today's diplomat is tomorrow's traitor," he said.

"Now, what in the world do you mean by that, major?" asked Mrs. Ware.

There was no lamp on the porch. But from the nearest room a yellow shaft struck out through the windows and gleamed in yellow obscurity over the hands of Mrs. Ware, folded in her lap.

"A soft speech today needs a hard fist tomorrow to back it up," exclaimed the major.

"But after all," said Nancy, "if what you're after is only a stolen mare and her mule foal—"

"I am not after merely a mule and a mare," said the major. "They merely offer the breach by which I hope to be able to dig into the heart of the trouble."

"It's never hard to find trouble with the Apaches," answered Nancy Ware.

"No," sighed the captain. "One can generally get enough of that, I dare say."

"One experience," said the major, snapping out the words, "doesn't make a lifetime."

"One experience with the Apaches is mighty apt to make a death, though," replied Nancy Ware. "It has more than once. But the captain was the lucky man."

"The stolen herd came back to me, well enough," nodded Captain Burn. "I still can't believe it. And d'you know that the rascals actually made a mistake and gave me back a few more than they'd taken away?"

"They gave back horses, and they took men in exchange!" said the major.

"They only took one man," said the captain.

"Men for horses!" exclaimed Major Talmadge. "The redskins, no doubt, are willing enough to make such exchanges. I'm only glad to hear that the man was only a harum-scarum sort of a vagrant."

"Did you call him that, Captain Burn?" challenged Nancy, her voice suddenly raised.

"Not a bit, not a bit," protested the captain. "I was merely trying to point out that he was different from other people, a careless sort of youth; never met anyone exactly like him. Why, he didn't seem to care very much about going off with the wild Indians. Acted as though it were rather a lark!"

"Because he's a brave man!" said the girl. "I never saw finer courage than he showed that night!"

"Hush, my dear," said Mrs. Ware. "When people have very little to lose—"

"Great heavens, mother," said the girl. "He had his life, didn't he? As for what else he had to lose, how do we know?"

"Nancy, you know perfectly well," argued Mrs. Ware, "that he was naked and starving when he came in off the desert."

"Any other man in the world would have been dead!" said Nancy. "I know that, too!"

"Extraordinary thing," murmured the captain uncomfortably.

"What did the Apaches want with him?" he added.

"His scalp!" declared the major.

"What?" cried Nancy.

"What else do they want from white men?" asked the major.

Nancy sighed.

"If they'd wanted his scalp, they would have taken it here, and ours along with it," she replied firmly. "They didn't want his scalp. I can't imagine what they really were after!"

"Perhaps I'll find out when I get among 'em," said the major. "And if I find the boy harmed, I'll have some of their best blood to pay for him!"

"If they've harmed him, they've already paid with some of their best blood for the harm they've done," said Nancy Ware.

"You're a champion of his," suggested Captain Burn.

"Oh," said the girl, "one learns to know a wild cat at a glance after living out here for a year or so. And he's all tooth and claw, I'd take it. Two Apaches jumped him in the dark, out in that very barn, Major Talmadge. And he handled them both and brought one of them in a prisoner."

"And let the scoundrel escape afterward!" said Mrs. Ware.

"Well," said the girl, "I don't know anything about that. I only know what he did with the pair of 'em. It would have kept another man talking for a month. But Rory Michel never even referred to that night afterward!"

"A hero, then," said the major, in a tone of a practical man adding up results. "And for that very reason we must bring the Apaches to a full accounting for him, and that is exactly what I intend to do."

"I wish that you had artillery and ten more troops, then," said Nancy Ware with a sigh.

"I wouldn't have 'em," said the major.

"And why not, please?"

"The fewer the men, the more the glory!" said he.

"Or the nearer the grave," suggested Nancy sternly.

"Nancy, how can you say such things?" exclaimed her mother.

"I've seen Apaches. I know 'em. And the major doesn't," said the girl. "The Apaches are fighters, too. Everybody knows that they're fighters."

"Irregular armed forces," asserted the major, "cannot stand against disciplined troops."

"You've got regular troops," said Nancy, with spirit, "but you haven't got a parade ground to march 'em over. I'd rather have irregular troops in irregular ground."

"Tut, tut!" said the major, and laughed gently at such a thought.

"You'll lose a man for every Apache you get," declared Nancy.

"When two bodies are drawn up for battle—" began the major.

"There'll only be one drawn up for battle," said the girl, "and that will be your lot. They'll be drawn up in good order, won't they?"

"I hope so, I hope so," said Major Talmadge.

"Then they'll make a more perfect target for the Apaches to shoot at," said the girl.

"A good brisk charge—" began the Major.

"Will capture thin air for you," she insisted. "They'll run all around you. They drive with them five times as many mules and horses as they need. They sweep along cattle to eat. If a pinch comes, they eat their own horses, their mules, their dogs. They know the country like a book, and they're the only people who do. Not even the white scouts and mountain men ever knew the country as the Indians do. They'll jump at you in the dark and claw you, and then run away. They won't care how long the warfare lasts.

"They have no cities that you can capture. They have no forts that they want to defend. They have no treasures that you can get at. Every man is able to live on the country. Every woman and child can be turned into a warrior if the big pinch comes. I tell you, Major Talmadge, when you tackle the Apaches, you're tackling a people who will prove to be all buffalo and wolves—just hide, bones, sinews, claws, and teeth. Nobody will ever get fat from hunting 'em or from eating 'em!"

The major, rather swamped by this storm of words, determined to laugh the matter off.

"I never recommended an Indian diet; I never have

expected to live off redskins. However, Miss Ware, you may be surprised at the outcome of this little campaign. Not a big thing, I know. But a small war may be modeled as carefully as a great one, and good precepts may be followed even in—"

A loud, wailing cry broke out down the valley road, which wound, dim and pale, before the house.

"What is that?" demanded the startled captain. "What unearthly cry—"

"Mexicans down the road, celebrating something," said Mrs. Ware. "Listen! That's their idea of laughter!"

Again came the wailing cry, but this time with a pronounced vibration in it.

"Yelling and laughing—they've got some good news!" said Nancy Ware. "I'm glad of that. They've been a sulky lot of brutes recently. I've been thinking that they had robbing the mine in mind. Listen again!"

Then, over the next hump in the road, they could see a group of riders sweeping on, one loftier than the rest, mounted upon a tall horse, and the others flocking back and forth about him like sheep about the sheep dog.

"They've found somebody who means a lot to them," said Mrs. Ware. "But who could it be, Nancy?"

Nancy ran down the steps of the veranda to the ground and paused there, straining into the night.

"Do you hear? They're calling him 'father.' It can't be anyone else! It's that mad Rory Michel come back to us!"

Chapter 18

There was a series of exclamations. Mrs. Ware cried out softly: "Great goodness, what will become of us now!"

The captain grunted that he was glad and wondered

if the boy had dropped through the sky to come back home. But Nancy, turning joyously, said: "He's our luck, mother. And I've an idea that we may need a lot of luck before long. See him come ripping up the road! It's Rory on the black, right enough."

It was Rory Michel, indeed. He stopped to shout a greeting and then went to the barn, where he put up the black stallion; after that he came toward the house, not trailing clouds of glory, but crowds of Mexican laborers. They blessed him and greeted him with the one hand, as it were; with the other, they begged for help. There was one with a dislocated shoulder; he would be happy to have the thing instantly made strong and fit for work. Another was shaking with ague; would the worker of magic heal him? A third must wear splints for a month on a broken leg; by magic, might he not be enabled to walk without them the next morning?

Two stockily built men remained the last of all, pressing close to his side. He recognized their growling voices; they were Miguel and Alonzo, and Miguel was explaining:

"If we had known, father, the cursed Apaches should have taken us before they took you. But we did not know. We were not here. Another time you will see what we can do, if there is fighting."

Rory Michel thanked them; there was a surly honesty in their manner of speech, that assured him they were ready to cut throats for his sake.

So he went onto the veranda and was there presented to Major Talmadge, and greeted the Wares and the captain. A shower of questions then fell upon him.

He simply said: "It was only a little case of magic. They had a dying boy. So I mixed up some fresh air and quiet and simple food and that magic nearly always works on Mexicans and Indians, it appears. It was a slow pull, but he got well. After that, they wanted me to stay on. I had to collect a gambling debt from Big Horse, their chief medicine man, and it was a tight pinch. They chased me for a few days through the mountains, but then I gave 'em the slip and got back here. That's all there is to it. The black horse is a little thin, but otherwise we're both all right. What's been happening here?"

They told him, in brief, about the absence of Ware to collect debts. The smelting of the silver was going on at a handsome rate, so handsomely that they began to suspect that the Mexicans were casting eyes upon the metal. It was by no means uncommon for the Mexican workers in a Southwestern mine to rise up, slaughter the white owners, and escape with the entire body of the loot which had been taken from the ore.

Then there was talk about the operations of Major Talmadge, who had many questions to ask concerning the particular body of Indians with whom the boy had been. They were, he had no doubt, the very men he was seeking, for it was said that the chief of the tribe of Apaches whom he wanted was named Rising Bull.

Then Rory retired to the barn, to sleep in his old corner in the haymow.

He was sleeping hard when a quavering voice aroused him. "It is I, father. It is Alicia, she whom you made young again. Twenty years have been lifted off my back. I have come to show you that there is gratitude in my heart, father."

"What is it, Alicia?" he asked, yawning with fatigue.

"It is this: do not be here tomorrow night. All day long, it will be well enough. But after the sun goes down tomorrow, do not be near this place!"

He sat up in the hay, sleep already far from him.

"What is it, Alicia?" he asked her. "What is wrong with this place?"

"You know, father," said the old woman, stealing closer, "that there are things done by night that cannot be told by day."

"I know that," said Rory. "But what is this? Indians, or your own people?"

"I have said too much," said Alicia. "I cannot say any more. Already, if it were known that I have spoken —even to you, father—I would have my throat cut from ear to ear. Father, farewell. Look to yourself. There will be a need of a fast horse if you stay too long."

99

"Wait a moment, Alicia," said he.

"I dare not wait," said she.

But he knew that she was lingering.

"This danger," he said, "comes on all of the white people here, does it not?"

"It comes on them all!" said the woman, a fierceness breaking into her voice.

"But there are soldiers here," said the boy. "There are a great many men with rifles, and they are ready to fight because fighting is their business."

At this, he was amazed to hear a soft, whispering laughter come hissing toward him through the darkness.

"Is that you, Alicia?" said he.

"Yes, it is I."

"Why do you laugh?"

"I laugh because I think of the soldiers," said she. "The soldiers "

And she laughed again.

"Well, then," said Rory, "I could smile a bit at some of them, myself, but still there are enough of them to make a good deal of trouble, I suppose."

Rory heard the click of her teeth between the words as she spoke. "Father, all of those soldiers, they will be scattered. You will see! All of them will be scattered like dead grass blowing on the wind. Remember what I say, because it is the truth."

"Tell me one thing more, Alicia."

"I dare not wait to tell you anything more, father."

"Tell me only this. Do you speak as an Indian or as a Mexican?"

"I am both, am I not?" was the ambiguous answer, and he heard the sound of her steps, retreating, rustling over the hay upon the floor.

Rory Michel sat for a time, blinking at the darkness, seeing sparks of fire, out of his own mind. He might go in and waken everyone and give them the warning, exactly as it had come to him. But the thought of a yawning midnight parley made him more tired than ever. So he stretched out in the hay once more and yawned, throwing out his arms into comfortable positions, so that he was presently asleep.

And he slept through without a break until the morning came, bright and strong, through the stable.

Then he stood up, climbed over the manger after throwing in feed for the stallion, and ran down to the brook that tumbled not far from the house and made a pool among cottonwoods, small and thick-growning. There he stripped, plunged in, and had a brisk swim. When he came out, he began to whip the water from his body with the edge of his hand. The cool morning air cut at him, laid icy hands between his shoulders.

"Hai, father," said a soft voice.

He turned and saw there the young Apache, South Wind. Never had he seen the boy so magnificently dressed. His deerskin clothes were incrusted with the brightest, the finest bead work. From his shoulders flowed a robe, painted in an intricate pattern. He wore about his neck one of the most honorable decorations that an Indian could aspire to, a necklace of the great polished claws of a grizzly bear. And, in his hand, he carried a spear. It was not the usual fourteen-foot war lance, but one with a shorter truncheon, of hardly more than six feet. This he grasped and leaned upon.

He was smiling broadly at the white man.

"Hai, South Wind," said Rory Michel. And he peered keenly past the lad and among the trees.

"I have come alone, here," said South Wind.

"Good," said Rory.

He grinned at the boy, and the Indian grinned back.

"Although," went on South Wind, "a good many of the warriors would be glad to see you!"

"I thought they would be," said Rory. "Too bad that they didn't come up with me, when we had the three-day race through the mountains."

"Because of the medicine horse, you won that race," said the boy, "but perhaps you'll not win the last race of all."

He whipped a forefinger across his throat.

"Perhaps not," said Rory, calmly nodding. "Everyone is likely to trip and tumble, now and then, while making good speed. Is Big Horse a very happy man since he lost his red eye?"

"He does not sleep or eat," answered young South

Wind. "But he walks all night, and makes medicine. We can hear him groaning as he talks to the spirits. They have promised him your death before long."

"He lies," said Rory.

The face of the boy clouded. "Why do you say that?" he asked. "But, even if you are to die, father, there will be time for you to do some great deeds before the end. We all know that. We all expect that."

"Do you believe what Big Horse says about the spirits he says he talks to?" asked Rory Michel.

"Why, of course, I believe it. He has always been able to talk to the spirits. He always was able to, even when he was a boy; so the braves have told me."

Rory nodded. He saw that there was no possible use in arguing with the young savage. In the mind of South Wind was fixed firmly the belief that Big Horse could actually speak with the unsubstantial Sky People. It would be the height of folly to attempt to unconvince him; easier by far to pull out clinched nails through a thick oak plank.

"He has made all of the warriors very eager to take your scalp, father," went on the boy. "He has offered them a medicine shirt if they bring the red eye and the scalp to him."

"What is a medicine shirt?"

"One that no knife or spear or bullet can possibly pierce when it is worn."

"Put that shirt against a tree and you'll be able to drive a knife straight through it, South Wind. Do you believe that?"

"Oh, yes. I believe that. It will not work except after Big Horse has purified it and put it on the right man. But after that, it turns the edge of steel and throws back flying lead."

Chapter 19

The absurdity of the thing was not the only or even the chief point of interest in this news. What was really important was that some scores of man-eating Apaches really believed that they would win permanent invulnerability by getting rid of Rory Michel. What price was that to be laid upon the head of a man! Hundreds of thousands of dollars would not have won equal exertion from whites. To be invulnerable in battle, to charge home against the enemy fearlessly, to count victories, to become the most distinguished warrior of the entire nation——these were the rewards which the medicine man offered for the killing of the white.

It did not matter in the slightest that, the first time the medicine shirt was worn, its wearer would probably be filled with arrows and slashed to pieces with lance thrusts, as he ventured rashly forward in the battle. If that happened would Big Horse be discredited? No, not even then, perhaps, for he would have a convenient explanation, saying that the unlucky warrior had neglected some necessary part of the "medicine" ceremonial in putting on the magic shirt.

"Well, South Wind," said Rory Michel, "I'm glad that you don't want that medicine shirt, because, otherwise, I would have had a spear in my back."

The boy smiled.

"You have had spears there before," said he. "Or so it looks to me."

"In the back?" said Michel.

"Yes, I see a half a dozen great white scars there."

"When I was a youngster," answered Rory, "I was scratched by a cat."

South Wind allowed his usual smile to steal over his face. "And in front, too," said he, "one your arms and on your breast, there are scars."

103

"They amount to nothing," said Rory.

"They are the sort of thing that the great warriors of my people like to show when they are dancing around the fire after the long war trial," remarked South Wind.

"Well, I'll tell you how they happened," said Rory. "Once when I was a youngster, I tumbled into a patch of cactus."

"So!" said the Indian.

"That was what happened."

"When you were a youngster, you had a tender skin," said the boy.

"A very thin skin," said Rory. "It's grown thicker, in the meantime. Where did you borrow that necklace of claws, South Wind?"

"I borrowed it from a bear," said South Wind.

Rory began to dress rapidly.

"A good-natured bear," suggested Rory.

"He grew sleepy," said the boy, "After I sent an arrow deep behind his shoulder."

"Were you alone?"

"Yes. I was alone."

"How long ago was that?"

"Two summers."

Michel nodded. The youngster could not have been more than thirteen or fourteen, then, when he had fought this hand-to-hand battle with a giant grizzly, for no small one of the species could have had such claws.

"After that, they called you a man, South Wind?"

He lifted his head.

"Tell me, father," said he, "what do you mean to do?"

"What should I do?" asked Rory.

"There are many great warriors ready to hunt for you."

"Where are they now?"

"They are coming in the wind, I suppose," said the boy. "They are everywhere. They are east and west of you."

"Your father," said Rory, "where is he?"

"He is going to talk to the white chief of the braves who have come out here from the fort."

104

Rory could easily understand this to mean the soldiers of Major Talmadge.

"Why is Rising Bull going to talk to the white chief?" asked Rory Michel.

"Well, I'll tell you. They say that some people in our tribe stole a mare and a mule foal."

"Did they?" asked Rory.

"I don't know," said the boy. "But the Apaches are very great thieves, of course."

He said it with pride.

"I have stolen a horse and two colts, myself, with a war party," said South Wind, boasting.

Rory did not argue the point of morals. For he knew that there was no use in that. Just as an Indian could believe in the efficacy of a medicine shirt, so he could readily believe in the honorable nature of theft.

"To steal from an enemy," said Rory, "that's one thing. But the whites are not at war with the Apaches, South Wind."

"That is true," answered the boy. "And that is why Rising Bull is willing to ride in and talk to the white chiefs about the mare and the foal."

"Where are they to meet?"

"In the tent of the white chief."

Rory shook his head.

"Better if they met in the open," said he.

"And why? They sent us a white flag. They have promised that it is only for talk."

"Is there any other chief with Rising Bull?"

"There is another. He is a young man, but a great fighter, and his name is Black Arrow."

"I've heard of Black Arrow. A good war chief, South Wind?"

"He has taken many scalps," said South Wind complacently.

"The rest of the warriors are not to be near the place of meeting?"

"No. They are away."

"You don't know where?"

"No."

"They should be a good deal nearer. You know, South Wind, that when the Indians and the whites meet, they don't speak with the same tongue. And blood will boil without fire."

"That is true," said the boy.

He frowned.

"Well," said Rory, "I'm going to swallow breakfast and go to the meeting, if I can get into it. What made you come here, South Wind?"

"To find you."

"Did you trail me down, with the other braves?"

"No, some of them are still working on your trail. But I could guess where you had gone."

"This is a very big world, South Wind," said the white man. "What made you think that I would surely come here?"

"After the war trail," answered the boy, "the braves who have taken scalps and counted victories are always the ones who are eager to get home to the people again. They wish to show their scalps and count their victories where the women can see them—and the old men and the children."

Rory Michel grinned broadly.

What was it, in fact, other than Nancy Ware that had brought him back to this spot?

And South Wind went on explaining:

"The women, the children, and the old people, they always are more ready to praise than a man's equals."

At this Rory Michel laughed aloud.

"You are right," said he. "You are going to be a great chief someday, South Wind."

"No," said the boy. "Not unless my skin changes to white or unless I die very young."

"Why do you say that?"

"The white people come and come. They are thicker than leaves in the east, and they blow west. My father has told me. They will take the country. They will crowd us into the mountains. So! But it is better to do as you will do, father. To fight hard, strike deep, and die young! That is what I wish to do!"

"I am going to the house," said Rory, much impressed by the fire and the solemnity of the boy. "After that, I shall try to get to the council where Rising Bull is to appear. You, South Wind, keep close to your

106

horse. Remember that I thank you for bringing me the warning."

"What warning?" said the boy.

"About the reward of the medicine shirt, offered to the warriors."

"Hai!" said young South Wind. "That is nothing. The next time you made medicine yourself, you would have been told all about it by your own spirits!"

Chapter 20

When Rory Michel got to the house, he went into the kitchen and found the Mexican cook crooning as she rubbed wet corn back and forth over a corrugated stone, scrubbing it into the meal from which tortillas are made.

She looked up with a frown that turned into a broad smile of welcome when she saw the face of the visitor.

"Father," said she, "may every day be full of wine and fresh meat for you."

"I hope it will be," said he, "and I hope that it will begin with this morning. What is there to eat here?"

She was up instantly and, striding between stove and table, she laid out a breakfast of coffee, bacon, and pone. He was eating this standing when Nancy Ware came into the room.

"You're the early bird," said she, leaning against the wall, her hands folded behind her.

"Does she speak English?" asked he, nodding toward the cook.

"Not a word."

"Nancy," said he, "Do you know what's in the air?"

"Trouble," said she. "That's all that I know."

"A lot of trouble," he agreed.

"How bad?"

"Knives and guns and such stuff," he answered.

She nodded.

"I had an idea it would be as black as that," she said.

She added, "We have the soldiers, though."

"You won't have them long."

"Why not? They've arranged a meeting with Rising Bull. Right down at the camp."

"I can't tell you why not. But I have the information from a source that I trust," he told her.

"You're being mysterious, Rory."

"I have to be, because it's a mystery."

"Who told you?"

"You can't ask me that. My information is to save my own hide. It isn't even supposed to be passed on."

She looked steadily at him, as though she were attempting to read his mind.

"I'll tell you what I can," he explained. "But that isn't much. One thing stands out pretty clearly."

"Tell me what it is."

"We may have to depend on our hands and our own guns."

"Who do you mean, when you say 'we'?" she asked him.

"You, your mother, and Rory Michel," he replied.

She stared again.

"Again? What?"

"I don't know. Mexicans, perhaps; Apaches.'

"Two women and one man?" she queried.

"A woman can be as good as a man," he said firmly. "You would be, Nancy. You can shoot, I take it?"

"Yes, I can shoot."

"You'll probably have to do some shooting, then. Your mother, too. You'd better screw her courage up to the sticking point."

She nodded.

"You have nerve, Nancy," he said, with a sober admiration.

She shrugged her shoulders.

"You ought to run for it, if you have a grain of sense," said she.

"Should I?"

"Yes. This is no business of yours."

"I think it may turn out to be a part of my business," he told her.

"How do you make that out?"

"Through you, Nancy."

She looked straight back at him, but the gradual color increased upon her throat and her face.

They confronted one another for a moment in this manner. And he remembered what South Wind had said to him. There was, indeed, an uncanny wisdom, he decided, in that lad.

For he knew, suddenly, that she meant more to him, by a great deal, than anything else in the world.

Then he went on eating, saying, to excuse himself, that he had business on hand.

"Where?" she asked.

"Down there in the camp where the major is going to talk to Rising Bull."

"Will you give me a single guess at what might scatter the soldiers?"

"Yes. The Apaches is my guess," said he.

"You think that the Apaches are plotting trouble?"

"I don't think that, but I think that they're ready for it."

"You think something else besides," she suggested.

"I think that there may be too much Major Talmadge in this whole business," said he.

"He doesn't know this country; he doesn't know these people," she agreed. "But he's brave."

"I'd rather have him a coward, with the right sort of knowledge, just now," said Rory.

She took a breath. Her eyes closed. He saw the white fear close over her face, over her lips, even.

Then she looked out at him again, fighting to get back her courage.

"It may pan out," he said encouragingly.

"If there's a break," she said, "father's out there, somewhere, lost in the hills!"

She made a wide gesture.

"He's better out there than he would be in here," said Rory. "You ought to see that."

"But he's heading straight back toward us. If we're surrounded, he'll be walking into a trap!"

"When is he expected?"

"This evening."

Rory tilted back his head and laughed. "This evening? Why, Nancy, the world will be made and unmade for all of us, I'm thinking, before tonight comes along. I wouldn't even dream that far ahead just now! Don't you see the look of things?"

"Some of the Mexicans want our silver bars. And some of the Apaches want our scalps."

"Perhaps they want the Mexicans' scalps, too," he suggested.

"I hadn't thought of that," said she.

"Then we may be holding the inside fort, the Mexicans the outside fort, and the Apaches will be the fire that burns us all to a crisp!"

"Why do you laugh, Rory?"

"I don't know. Because it's such a muddle, I suppose. That's the only reason that I can think of. Nancy, you get all the rifles together, will you?"

"I've done that already," said she.

"How many?"

"There really should have been twenty," she answered. "Father had arms for every one of the Mexican laborers in case there should be trouble with the Indians."

"There really should have been twenty," nodded Rory. "But did you find even two?"

"Yes, two that I had in my own room."

"The greasers stole them," suggested he.

"Yes, of course."

"And plenty of ammunition, I suppose?"

"Yes, tons of it."

"Revolvers?"

"Yes, I have two pair of 'em, thank heavens."

"Ammunition?"

"Not a lot for either rifles or revolvers. Just what I've found lying around."

He whistled softly.

"The best thing for us," he said, "is to pray that no trouble starts. If it does, pray that it won't begin till I get back from the camp and, best of all, that the soldiers aren't blown away like dead grass on the wind!"

110

They started at one another again grimly. They were beginning to see each other with a wonderful clarity and there was much on either hand worthy of observation.

Then she said: "I'm thanking heaven that I have you in the team with me. Now I've got to go and break the bad ground with mother. She's a gritty one, though. She'll groan, but she'll be a man when the pinch comes."

He nodded. He washed down the last morsel with a swallow of coffee and left the house at once. His mind was full, not of the peril that seemed to be distilling in the very air of the valley, but with the thought of Nancy Ware.

For she was all that he had hoped, and then something more. There was true steel in her!

He went down the valley at a brisk pace and came near to the tents of the camp. They were laid out in orderly rows. The horses were kept orderly, also, in a picket line. Almost at once a sentry on beat challenged him.

"Who goes there?" he asked.

"A white man," said Rory Michel, "as you can see for yourself."

"Show your face and back up," said the soldier. "That fresh lingo don't go around here."

Rory grinned suddenly at the other.

"I'm an old friend of the major's," said he. "Does that let me through the line?"

"You could be an old friend of George Washington," said the trooper, "but it wouldn't get you through unless you knew the right word."

"Here comes my word, now," said Rory.

"Where?"

"Here up the road."

"That pair of Apaches? Are they the word for you, my friend?"

"They're a pair of Apaches that the major wants to see, and I'm going with them. If you stop that pair of bucks, they'll take off your scalp and make a lining for a fan with it."

"I'll stop them," said the trooper, sticking out his

111

jaw. "Back up and give me some more room, Irish!"

Rory Michel obediently stepped back as the two Apaches brought their horses to a halt and leaped down to the ground. It was Rising Bull and a younger brave whose hideously scarred face led Rory, at once, to put him down as that younger and celebrated warrior, Black Arrow, of whom South Wind had spoken.

Rising Bull, with a gleam of pleased excitement in his eye, grunted a deep-voiced "How!" and seized upon the hand of Rory; Black Arrow, without a smile, sunk his glance like a knife into the eye of Michel.

It was not hard to guess that he was thinking of the magic shirt which makes the wearer invulnerable. Indeed, he had scars enough to make him wish for such "medicine."

What the trooper would have done with such challenges, it was hard to say but he looked as immovable as stone when suddenly Captain Burn appeared from the big central tent of the little encampment and called out instanly:

"Pass those men!"

"The Injuns?" asked the trooper in surprise.

"Yes."

"And the Irishman?"

"Of course. I wish there were twenty of him passing through at the same time."

Captain Burn came out and shook hands with Rory. He repeated the ceremony with the chiefs.

A moment later, he murmured to Rory:

"Is that war paint they have on?"

"No," said Rory. "They're wearing their pretty faces today. This is just a social call. Where's the major?"

"Writing his speech," said the captain, as he led the way forward, showing the Indians toward the central tent from which he himself had just come.

"He'd better unwrite it," said Rory. "Nobody ever knows what to say to these red men beforehand."

The captain sighed.

"You may be right, Michel," he said. "I wish myself that we were a thousand miles east from here!"

Chapter 21

When they got to the entrance of the tent, the captain went in ahead, and the guests were halted for a moment, a pause which seemed to young Rory Michel both foolish and overceremonial. In the interim, he felt the keen, bold, hostile eyes of the young chief fixed steadily upon him.

But Rising Bull was saying:

"They rode well, the young men of the Apaches, did they not? But, like fools, they tried to catch up with a medicine horse! Where is the black stallion, father?"

"He is well," said Rory. "As for the braves of the Apaches, they gave me a good chase through the hills. And now, I hope, we are better friends than ever before."

Rising Bull shook his head.

"Many things have happened," he declared. "And Big Horse has offered the value of a whole herd of horses for your scalp. Father, beware! There is only one way to make peace with the Apaches. As for me and my family, we are your family, also. Our breath is your breath, and our blood is your blood. That you know. But for the others, give them back the red eye, and they become your friends once more!"

He said it urgently, but there was little hope in his face, and he did not seem in the least surprised when Rory shook his head and replied that there was not the slightest hope that he would give back what he had fairly won.

By this time, Captain Burn had reappeared and ushered them into the big, round tent.

It was all arranged for the interview as pompously as possible. The major had made for himself a sort of desk, by turning a couple of boxes on end with boards laid across the top of these and a cloth thrown over all. Behind the table or desk, he was ensconced in a camp chair. And from this, as a sort of throne, he looked rather sternly toward the newcomers.

At the back of the tent there were half a dozen soldiers, a hard set of troopers, leaning upon their rifles, and directly in front of the entrance flap, several chairs had been placed so as to make a circle, complete with the fenced-in position of the major.

The artifice, which was to lend dignity and place to the white man, seemed to Rory so extremely transparent and futile that he almost blushed. And he felt more like blushing than ever when the Apaches, as might have been expected, after replying to the greeting of Major Talmadge and being invited to take the chairs, pushed the latter back and squatted cross-legged upon the ground.

Captain Burn sat down on one side of them instantly, and Rory did the same, keeping at the side of Rising Bull. The major, however, did not have wit enough to take this hint. He actually made a movement as though to rise and join his guests, but apparently he had already fixed his picture of himself so firmly in his mind's eye that he could not alter it. He relaxed in the chair again, gathered a frown of both dignity and perplexity upon his brow, and then directed an orderly to pass the pipes about.

Rory smiled again. If there had been only one pipe, if it had been filled and lighted with the usual ceremonial, all might have been well. But the Apaches signified that they had no desire to smoke, for the moment. They excused themselves, as it were, and, wrapping their robes more closely around them, they presented wooden faces without expression to the gaze of the troubled major.

Rory Michel suddenly remembered the pictures he had seen of life in the Apache camp, the tumult, the chattering, the gaiety, the laughing banter of even the sternest and most respected warriors. It was plain that the people knew how to assume a new face like a mask when they chose to do so.

The major, at least, spoke good Spanish, and he

began by thanking Rising Bull and his companion for coming in to answer the charge against them. The major said that, in a sense, he represented both the armed band and the judicial power of the United States. He said something more about the kindly solicitude of the White Father in Washington for his red children. And Rory noted a flash of derision pass between the two Indians.

No doubt they had heard this same nonsense many times before from the mouths of agents and the heads of punitive expeditions.

When the major ended, he wanted to know, in short, if the Apaches had found the mare and the mule foal among their animals?

Rising Bull made a speech as simple and as short as that of the other had been long.

He said: "There are a great many white men. There are not many Apaches. We don't want to fight against you unless we have to. That is why I have come here, together with a brave man, well-known among my people. Black Arrow. We have many mares with mule foals. But none of them belong to you. Most of them we took when we were making war against the Mexicans. Besides, what is all this trouble about a mare and a single foal?"

The directness and the simplicity of this speech so upset the major that he could not answer at all for a moment. Then he muttered something about the necessity of justice being done, and suddenly he broke out in English to Rory:

"You know these people young man. What should be said to them?"

"If I were you," said Rory, "I'd tell them that they are right, and that the loss of a mare and a foal is a small thing, but that you are simply using it as a means to draw closer to the Apaches. You want to have them for friends, and the whites want to be a help to the Apaches. We can't be that if stealing goes on. Tell them that the Apaches are the most wonderful thieves in the world, but that the Americans are not masters of that great art."

The major stared at Rory as though he thought the youth mad.

"Do you want me to talk," he said, "as though I admired a thief?"

The major cleared his throat. His brow was a thundercloud.

"Don't you?" asked Rory impertinently.

"I must come to the point," said he. "Bring in the man who complained of the loss!"

Instantly, a young orderly brought into the tent as ratty a specimen of frontiersman as Rory Michel had ever seen. He was one of those long and leaning fellows, with a head jutting out in front, and rather bowed shoulders, so that he had the angles and the thrusting beak of a vulture sitting on a branch and scanning the world for food, new or old!

This gawky monster was partly brown and partly crimson in color, and a special fire burned in the end of his nose. His clothes were old, soiled deerskins, with patches across both knees and in the seat of the trousers. A fur cap, most of the hair worn away, covered his head. He was as unkempt as a mangy ferret.

"Well, Terris," said the major, "here's a pair of Apache Chiefs who have come down to talk to us about the mule and the foal. They——"

"There ain't very much talkin' needed," said Terris. "If I ain't a fool, and a blind man, there sits the ornery son of a trouble that sneaked 'em both away from me!"

And he pointed straight toward Black Arrow.

The two Indians glanced at each other, but not understanding the English which had been spoken, they made no remark.

"I thought," said the major, "that you told me it was in the dusk of day, and that you could hardly see the thief?"

"Did I tell you that?" said Terris. "Well, I tell you now that a face like that one don't need to be seen in the full of the daylight. That ugly murderin' Injun carries a lantern on the prow of his ship!"

And he laughed in a high, cackling tone as he said this.

The major sighed. It was perfectly true that Black Arrow was ugly enough to be distinguished even by a half glance from among a thousand of even his ugliest fellows.

He, therefore, said to Black Arrow:

"This man says that you are the Apache who stole his mare and his mule foal. He says that he saw you in the evening of the day."

"What day was this?" said Black Arrow calmly.

"Ten days ago," said the major.

"I was in the camp ten suns ago," answered the Apache. "Rising Bull knows I was there."

Rising Bull thought for a moment and then nodded.

"That is true," he said. "Ten days ago, and fourteen days ago, he was in camp."

The frontiersman understood enough Spanish to make out this reply, and he snarled.

"Are you gonna let the Apache thieves band together and lie and weigh me down? Ain't the word of one white man worth the lyin' of ten thousand of the throat-cuttin' Apaches?"

The major sighed again. It was plain that he wished to administer justice, but he hardly knew what he should do.

Finally he said: "This is the word of one man against another."

"Two men against one man's word," said young Rory Michel.

"Who are you?" shouted the complainant, turning upon Rory.

Then he stretched out his arm and shook a very bony grimy forefinger at the boy. "You're one of them that ain't either fish, flesh, nor fowl, because you're a squaw man. You got the greasy look on your skin and the smoke in your eyes. Whatcha mean by sittin' there and sayin' that the word of two lyin' Injuns is worthy to be put alongside of the oath of an honest, upstandin', tax-payin' citizen of the United States of America?"

Rory looked earnestly upon him.

"Friend," said he, "you look like a buzzard, but you talk like a crow. There's no sense whatsoever in your cawing."

The frontiersman whirled about toward the major.

"Do I have to stand here and get myself insulted?" he shouted.

"Come out with me where there's room in the valley," said Rory, "and I'll tell you what I really think about you and your ways and your mares and your mule foals!"

"Aye, you'd murder me, with your Injuns to help you!"

"Terris," said the major, "you are sure—you speak under oath, remember—that you recognize this man, Black Arrow, as the one that stole your animals?"

"As sure as my name is Dick Terris," said the angry man, "this here is the man."

He turned on Black Arrow and yelled in Spanish: "You're the thief!"

"We have heard enough, brother," said Rising Bull, getting to his feet.

Black Arrow arose, also. To the major and Terris, he gave a sneering smile and turned toward the entrance.

And then came the tragedy.

Chapter 22

The ruffian, Terris, was standing between Major Talmadge and the entrance of the tent, and he now howled out to know if Talmadge really intended to let the red rascals go before the stolen animals had been returned or replaced.

The major, totally unable to reach a quick decision and apparently thrown quite off balance by the sudden move of the Indians to leave, parted his lips, but was incapable of speaking a word. His face swelled and crimsoned with emotion. That was all!

118

In the meantime, Black Arrow was striding past Terris.

The sight was too much for the malice in the heart of the frontiersman and, suddenly thrusting out a leg, he tripped the Indian heavily.

It would have brought most men to the ground, this tricky movement on the part of Terris. Black Arrow lunged ahead, recovered himself, and turned, with a knife in his hand.

But the knife arm was instantly seized by Rising Bull.

The flash of the steel was enough for Terris, however.

"Murder!" he yelled.

And snatching out a pistol from his belt, he fired straight into the body of Black Arrow.

The Apache swayed and lurched from the grip of Rising Bull to the ground.

"Dead Injuns are the only good ones!" whooped Terris, mad with exultation at the sight of that falling brave. He whipped out a second pistol. Dropping the first one to the floor, he tried to shoot down Rising Bull, the very man who had held back the knife of Black Arrow!

That bullet would have ended the life of the war chief, but young Rory Michel had jumped as cats jump, and he arrived just in time to jar the arm of Terris aside.

He followed the stroke with a flashing hook that sailed over the shoulder of Terris and dipped down like a swallow in mid-air, glancing over the tall man's chin as a sledge hammer glances off an anvil.

But the anvil continues to stand, and Mr. Terris did not. He sagged in three places, like a complicated hinge. He buckled at the neck, at the hips, and at the knees, and seemed to fall in three sections toward the floor.

Before he struck the floor, Rising Bull was out of the tent and on the back of his pony. The sentry, who had made such objection to the passing of Rory Michel through the lines, now was prompt enough to jerk his rifle to his shoulder and fire.

119

He thought he had knocked the red man out of the saddle, for Rising Bull had dropped to the shelter of the far side of his war horse. But a moment later he was back in the saddle once more, and jockeying a greater speed out of the pony.

Two or three other troopers sprang into saddles and waited for a word of command, but that word never came, for the major would not give it—his throat muscles being paralyzed—and Captain Burn would not give it, either, since he was kneeling at the side of the fallen Apache.

Black Arrow was dead!

"What happened?" asked the major, when his voice slowly came back to him. It was still a small sound, hardly more than a gasp.

Rory Michel gave the answer. "You've let the Apaches be kicked in the face, that's all," said he.

"Is he dead?" asked the major.

Captain Burn stood up and, as he rose, he drew the blanket of the warrior over the upturned face.

"Dead!" answered the captain, heavily, as he slowly nodded his head.

"Irregular!" breathed Major Talmadge. "Irregular and indeed most embarrassing."

He turned irresolutely from side to side.

"What's to be done about this, Burn?" he asked the captain. Burn, in distress, shook his head. Terris was sitting up with a blank look in his eyes.

"You're the judge and the jury, in this territory, just now," said young Rory Michel. "And I'll tell you what, there's only one thing to do; take this Terris out and hang him to the first tree. That'll show the Apaches that you mean justice and not murder, and it's the only thing that will show them what you mean."

Terris suddenly rose to his feet, for fear had quickly cleared his brain.

"Hey! Major Talmadge," he cried, "a body would think that the killing of an Injun was the same as the killing of a man!"

"Be quiet," said Rory Michel to the tall man.

He stepped close. His body was quivering as a bull terrier quivers before it leaps in to take a death grip.

"Be quiet," said Rory. "If I hear you speak again, I think I'll open you and see if there's anything besides sawdust stuffing inside of you!"

Tall Mr. Terris fell back a stride and stared uncertainly at the major. He opened his wide mouth to speak, but remembering the threat, he was silent.

"Very well, Mr. Michel," said the major. "I believe that I'm in charge here. I don't need to have orders given in my presence, except by a superior!"

"Give your own order, then," said Michel, "but I hope that the first one will be for the hanging of this long-legged water rat!"

"Hang him? Hang him?" said the major. "He will go back to the fort and receive whatever punishment justice awards him, but—"

Terris heaved a great sigh of relief. It was a long distance to the fort, and many would be the opportunities for escape along the way.

"Had we better bury this man?" asked Captain Burn.

"We must wait for his people to come for him," said the major.

And he looked at Rory, as though guessing that he knew far better what should be done under such circumstances.

Said Rory, seeing the glance: "If justice isn't done by you on Terris, let me make a suggestion."

"What is it?" asked the major.

"Let me take Terris out for a little trip down the valley. If he comes back, he'll come back alone. If I come back, I'll come back alone."

"He's a gunman," protested Terris, his voice shaking. "He's a regular professional man-killer. You wouldn't turn me over to him, would you, Major Talmadge?"

The lip of the major curled, for he was a brave man and loved courage in others.

"Be content, Terris," he said. "Perhaps Michel is right. But the only justice that will come to you must be through a due form of law. Michel, you must see that this man—"

"I see this," said Rory Michel. "If you don't polish

off Terris, pandemonium will break loose all over Arizona!"

"What!" exclaimed the major.

"I mean just that. The Apaches are gunpowder. This spark will be enough to set them off. Every man in your command will be in danger of his life, and so will be the lives of all the drivers of stagecoaches, all the stagecoach travelers, all the people who keep the relay posts out along the stage lines, all the men at the mines, even the small towns, unless they get word in time.

"I tell you, Major Talmadge, you're about to make a pretty red page of history unless you do justice and do it promptly. Even with Terris dead, there's something owing to the Apaches, from their way of looking at it. I tell you, Black Arrow was a big man and a brave man in their eyes. They looked up to him. And that moldy coward has murdered him here where he was helpless, in your presence.

"What would you think about Indians, if you sent an embassy under a flag of truce to 'em, and one of your men was murdered in the Indian camp? Why, you'd want to wipe out the entire Indian tribe. And that's the way that the Apaches are going to feel about this business."

He made the speech rapidly, as it came hot from his heart. And Major Talmadge shook his baffled head.

"It's a wretched business," said he. "But the forms of justice, however tardy, must be observed."

"God bless you major," whined Terris. "All that I'm askin' for is justice."

"And God help a thousand decent men and women and children who will die because of this," said Rory, gloomily. "I can see the thing, clearly enough. I can hear the yarns that will come in of the atrocities. Believe me, major, the Indians don't need teachers when it comes to matters of murder. You've given them a start, and they'll run downhill all the rest of the way. Have I heard your final word in the matter?"

The major was irritated by a sense of helplessness. He could not help feeling the profound justice in the words of Rory Michel, and yet he could not change his own stiffly disciplined mind. Before him now loomed the thought of a court-martial, more vivid than the picture of the burning homes and the slaughtered settlers in Arizona.

"I can only do what conscience allows me to do," he reiterated.

"Then," said Rory, "I wash my hands of the lot of you."

He stepped to the entrance to the tent. There he paused and turned.

"I'll give you one piece of good advice," said he.

The major glared at him. He really wanted to hear the advice, but he could not ask for it.

"Get all of these tin soldiers together," said Rory, "and start them burning up some ammunition. Teach 'em to shoot. Get in some real mountain men to show 'em how to use cover. Try to turn these soldiers of yours into frontiersmen and Indian fighters inside of twenty-four hours, because that's more than the leeway that you'll have. After that, if you can't defend yourselves, the Apaches will lift your hair. Good-by!"

He turned on his heel and walked from the tent, from the encampment, and slowly up the road toward the Ware mine and the house where Nancy and her mother were.

He was dark in mind and soul.

It seemed to him, suddenly, that waters of danger had flowed up the valley and that they were truly alone, the three of them—he and the girl and her mother.

One thing must be done at once—to persuade the two of them to leave the house and take shelter with the soldiers.

Chapter 23

He found the girl busy in the front of the house; he was astonished to hear her singing softly as he came up, and she called out cheerfully when he spoke:

"What is it, Rory?"

"Talmadge is a fool," he answered in grief, "the soldiers are protecting a murderer; the Apache Black Arrow is dead; the whole tribe is going to turn loose, and there will be the deuce to pay all over Arizona."

She came out of the front door and met him as he ended this wretched catalogue.

He said it over again. He told how he had seen Black Arrow slaughtered, and nothing done about it, except for the welt that he had himself raised along the jaw of Dick Terris. She mantled with anger, as she heard the thing.

"Now," said he, "there's only one thing to be done."

"What's that?"

"You and your mother and I, we three have got to get out there with the troops, no matter what you think of the commander. Poor Talmadge is not a bad fellow. He simply doesn't know what to do with himself and his men in this part of the world."

"We're to pick up and move?" said she.

She shook her head.

"Why do you shake your head?" he asked, thoroughly provoked.

"Well, we'll talk to mother. We'll see what she has to say."

They found Mrs. Ware looking as still and as gray as a stone. She had grown old overnight, and her wistful, pathetic eyes were fixed vaguely before her, as though inquiring of the future what blow was about to be leveled at her.

"Mother," said Nancy Ware, in her brisk and yet kindly manner, "Rory Michel has come to tell us that there's trouble in the air. One of the great Apache chiefs has been killed in the presence of the troops, and there'll be an Indian war buzzing around our ears in no time. Rory says that we must pack at once and join the troops."

"Pack?" said Mrs. Ware. "What of the silver, Nancy?"

"That could be packed on the horses and the mules you have here at the mine," said Rory, instantly.

Mrs. Ware stared helplessly at him.

124

"There's Dean, too," said she, almost as though her husband were a secondary consideration.

"He's out there in the hills with plenty of good horses and mules. He can take care of himself. He's no baby," said Rory, with confident vigor.

"You know, Rory," said Mrs. Ware, "that you're young and quick and as active as a cat. But Dean is not a youngster any longer. He's not even as young as he sometimes seems to feel, I'm afraid!"

She shook her head, watching Rory all the while as though she chiefly feared that he would disapprove of what she had said.

He answered her: "Well, Mrs. Ware, tell me what good it would be for Dean Ware to come here and find you and Nancy dead?"

"No, that would be no good," she answered, with a childish simplicity.

"And would you be any help to him after he came or just a burden on his hands?" went on Rory, aggressively logical.

"Perhaps we'd be a burden," she said, "but—"

"But what?" insisted Rlry.

"But if we went away, that would be deserting our post, in a way," said Mrs. Ware.

"Deserting your post?" cried Rory.

"For me, I mean," said the mother, looking anxiously toward her girl, "but not for Nancy. Nancy ought to go. I'll keep the place running along until—"

"Hush, mother!" said Nancy Ware, and she slipped her arm inside that of Mrs. Ware.

"You wouldn't have to stay, Nancy," said the mother, much moved.

"I wouldn't dream of going," said Nancy. "I just brought Rory to you so that you could say the thing first."

"Nancy," argued Rory Michel, "there's no sense in what you suggest!"

"I know there isn't," said Nancy, strangely. "But that's what we're going to do, I'm afraid."

"God bless you, Nancy, you strange child!" said Mrs. Ware.

"Nancy, you're talking like an idiot," said Rory, more heated than ever.

"You run along and take your place with the troops," said the girl. "The Apaches may come swooping any moment. Go along with yourself, Rory. You've saved our horses for us once and our necks another time. Now save your own!"

"I'm to run away and leave you, am I?" demanded Rory.

"Of course, you are."

"You know I won't do that," said he.

"Don't sulk, Rory," said the girl. "We don't want you to risk yourself here!"

"I'll stay, confound it!" said Rory, with a very poor grace. "But there's prickles up and down my spine. I smell blood, in fact!" He spoke savagely, and Mrs. Ware murmured under her breath and began to tremble.

"You tremble now," said Rory, pressing even this brutal advantage, "but you'll tremble a lot more when you find the time come on you, and you hear the red men shooting. They won't be men, then. They'll be red demons. Besides, it's not only death that I'm talking about."

Mrs. Ware sank down into the chair, still clutching with one hand at the arm of her girl.

"Nancy," she softly whispered, "you must go! He's right! You must go at once!"

"And you?" asked Nancy.

"I'll stay. I have to stay. I know it isn't sense. I know that Dean would order me to go, if he were here. But to leave the place where he expects to find me, I can't do that! There's something in me that won't let me!"

It seemed to Rory that he was seeing not this gray-faced woman but another figure, half-hidden behind the centuries, a Roman soldier at his post, inescapable danger rolling upon him and nothing to keep him at the place of peril except that his captain had not yet given the order to retire. There were centuries in between, but the spirit was the same.

His anger fled from him and left him clothed only with pity and a sad understanding. They were better

126

people than he, he felt. He had felt so before this, but now he thought that he understood almost the entire depth of the gulf between.

"You see how it is, Rory," said the girl. "She won't go. If she did, I wouldn't. Dad expects to find us here. He'll fight through fire to get to us, when trouble begins. And I won't have him come to an empty house."

"You see," explained the mother, attempting to be cheerful, "the soldiers may be the main focus for the anger of the Indians. We haven't harmed the Indians at all!"

"You don't understand the way the Indian figures things," said Rory. "If a red man is killed by a white, all the whites are responsible. If a Comanche kills an Apache, all the Comanches are guilty. They feel the same way about the whites. We're just another tribe, in their eyes. They'll not overlook this place. A woman's scalp is as good as a man's to them. All the better because it's more easily taken!"

Mrs. Ware shuddered, but she shook her head, clinging to her line of resistance.

"It's a bitter thing, Rory," she said, "but I must do the only thing that I see before me that I'm capable of doing!"

"Well," he answered, "I'll argue no more. Only, you understand that if the Indians don't come for you, the Mexicans here at the mine are probably going to rise and try to murder you for the sake of the silver?"

"Great Heavens!" cried Mrs. Ware.

"It's true. I think Nancy has guessed it, too."

"Nancy!" exclaimed the mother. "It can't be! Not these men who have lived here with us so long?"

"They're a lot of renegades, you know," said Nancy, with the same cool calm. "Refugees even from Mexican law. They're capable of doing anything."

"Then, may God protect us!" cried Mrs. Ware.

A knock came at the front door and, without waiting for a response or an invitation to enter, Captain Burn came striding into the room. His service saber was hanging at his spurred heels. His epaulets shone upon his shoulders, and the metal braid upon his coat and

127

trousers. His boots glistened like silver. Altogether, he made almost a medieval picture of chivalry and valor, Slender young Rory Michel, in comparison, was hardly worth noting.

"Mrs. Ware," said Captain Burn, "the major sends his compliments, and wishes me to state that he will be very happy to offer you shelter among the troops, because it appears that trouble is in the air, so to speak. I don't want to alarm you, but the Apaches—"

"She knows the whole story, and you're wasting your breath," said Rory. "She won't budge. And neither will Nancy. They've gone mad. They're going to wait here to see if Dean Ware won't come blowing back to them through the hurricane!"

"Wait? Wait here?" exclaimed the captain. "Do you really mean it?"

"Ask them! Ask them!" said Rory, furiously. "I've talked myself dry in the throat, but it's no good!"

The captain, however, did not ask them. Mrs. Ware had begun to cry, not covering her face, and the tears rolled down unheeded. Once more her misty eyes were looking straight before her at unheard-of trouble.

"Bless my soul!" murmured the amazed captain.

Then he added: "It's a thing that I cannot believe. I mean to say that the danger is really—"

"They know everything, I tell you," said Rory. "And they won't stir. I almost hope—" He left a savage comment unspoken.

Then he added: "You can't do anything here, captain. Go back to your command."

"And you?" asked the captain.

"Oh, there'd better be three fools than two. I'm staying on here for a while."

"Hush!" cried Nancy. "Listen! what is it?"

It sounded like thunder, but a strange thunder that rolled up from the middle of the earth.

Chapter 24

They ran at once to the front of the house and they were in time to see disaster over which they had no more control and in which they could take no more part than if it was an earthquake.

The focus and center was the camp of the soldiers.

The background was the flattopped mesa of the lower valley, seamed and engraved with blue on one side and golden sunshine on the other. The cause of the disturbance was a swarm of Indians which streamed out of the gullies and rushed upon the encampment of the soldiers.

As for Major Talmadge's command, it was rapidly forming on horseback. Tents were being struck, baggage wagons were being equipped with teams and the loads were still being flung upon them.

Despite the warning given by Rory Michel, it seemed that the troops were totally unprepared, and the Apaches had completely surprised them. The battle front of the soldiers they avoided. In wave upon wave they charged upon the cavalry but, when they were close, the charging Indians broke to one side and to the other, as though upon a rock, and sweeping around the flanks of the mounted men, they closed on the baggage train to the rear.

Captain Burn grabbed his trailing saber with one hand, wrenched out a revolver, and started running down the road.

"That won't do," said Nancy Ware calmly to Rory.

But he had already started.

He overtook the captain in a moment and took hold of his arm.

"Let me go!" exclaimed Burn.

"It's no good," said Rory Michel. "You can't help. You're only one. And that flood would pick you up and dissolve you like sand."

He nodded toward the sweep of the charging Indians. Their yells now filled the air, like the screaming of demons. And Captain Burn shuddered as he listened.

"You're right, Michel," he said. "You're absolutely right. There's nothing that I can do. I'm helpless. The ship's at sea," he added, "and I'm left on dry land like a fool and a deserter! I only thought—"

"You only thought that you were doing the right and decent thing when you brought up the message from the major. And you put that message into the major's mind," said Rory. "Well, you're right. You've done the decent and the right thing. You'll die for it. Most of those soldiers will get away. But you'll stay here and die with us. That's simple and plain as the nose on your face!"

The captain turned and stared at him.

"I suppose that you're right, Michel," said he. "And it doesn't much matter where I die, since I'm missing from my command on a day like this."

"Stuff!" said Rory Michel. "Just watch those beggars ride, those Indians. They seem to be born on horseback!"

In fact, the Apaches scurried about the lethargic host of the cavalry like sea gulls flying against a heavy wind.

And the cavalry, outnumbered four or five to one, began to retreat. They moved backward in good order for a time, but presently the pace increased.

The major, easily distinguishable through the brilliance of his uniform, was seen ranging up and down the ranks. Now and then, he issued at the head of a few squads to meet one of the threatened Indian attacks with a countercharge. Always the Apaches whirled about and let the cavalry go thundering through a gap; then, turning as agile as birds, they harassed the military with flights of arrows and with bullets.

"They enjoy it," said Rory Michel. "They love that sort of thing. And the cavalry doesn't know what it's all about. It's a new thing to them. Why, they're children. And the Apaches are experienced men at this game!"

So it seemed.

The calvary, swept back by the Indians, although not

a single saddle had been emptied, now broke into a sudden gallop to the rear.

The baggage, by this maneuver, was instantly lost. The drivers of the wagons, each man cutting the traces of one of his animals, sprang on the backs of the horses or mules and raced along with the main body of the troops. The wagons themselves were left standing.

These wagons were like separate rocks, holding up or partially damming a flood. When the Indians reached them, their love of plunder overcame their desire to count victories and take scalps. They did not follow the retreating whites but, dismounting, they flung themselves upon the loot.

As Captain Burn in an agony pointed out, a slight rally and a charge of the cavalry, no matter how disorderly, would have swept the Apaches before them in a rout. But there was no rallying!

The major in his shining uniform could be seen ranging here and there. His sword flashed as he struck man after man with the flat of it. But the soldiers had had enough of this maelstrom of red men. They poured back and then, gathering speed, the whole mass of them rushed away headlong for safety.

Captain Burn groaned as he watched the flight.

He saw some few handfuls of the reds galloping madly in pursuit, while the remainder were huddled around the wagons, plundering. He saw the major rally, at last, a few scattering troops, and before their countercharge the madly onrushing Apaches turned tail and fled without shame, though still they outnumbered the men who were brought against them.

But the Indian warfare is to strike with safety, not simply to win a victory. As for victory, it was already, in a sense, secured, since the entire baggage train had fallen into their hands. As for the soldiers, no doubt they could be followed at their further leisure.

Still, in spite of the valiant effort of the major, the main body of his troops continued their flight, unpursued except by their own panic.

Rory began to look carefully over the ground but, so far as he could see, there was not a single corpse, either of Indian or white man, lying anywhere.

"The most shameful day in the history of the American army!" groaned the desperate captain.

"No," said Rory, "but their imaginations beat those fellows. You take 'em, man for man, they probably could lick ten times their weight in red men. But they didn't know the game. Twenty old mountain men would have banded together and split those Indian charges; aye, and left a good many empty saddles while they were doing the trick. But that cavalry lot saw that it was being badly outnumbered and, therefore, they ran for it.

"Against odds of five to one, no sensible man thinks of standing very long. So they ran for it. Well, they simply don't know the Indians, but by thunder, they'll know the red men better before ever they see home again."

He said the last through his clenched teeth.

"They're gone!" was all that Captain Burn could say, out of a hollow throat.

"They're gone," repeated Rory Michel after him. "And the thing for us to do is to get back to the house, there, and turn it into the best sort of a fort that we can!"

Captain Burn seemed to be withdrawing himself from a mist. He sighed as he looked around him and at last he said: "You're right, Michel, you're entirely right, and I've been acting like a child about spilled milk."

Yet he lingered a step or two behind, as they retraced their steps toward the house. Now and again, he turned his head to follow the flight of the cavalry far down the valley. It seemed as though he could not believe in the shameful fact, even after he had seen it.

Rory went up to the two women with the most cheerful of smiles.

"You see how it is?" said he.

Mrs. Ware said nothing. Her face was stone.

But Nancy answered:

"I know, Rory. I heard you prophesy the whole affair. I couldn't believe what I heard, but you were right. They've been scattered like dry grass blown down a wind, and now we're left alone!"

"There's no reason why we can't stand a siege," said Rory. "We have food enough and courage enough, and those are the two things that stock the biggest town against the longest siege. Nancy, you can get back to the house and start forming the habit of wearing a Colt belted around you. Teach your mother to do the same thing. Carry a rifle for a walking stick. And think that you're walking in a forest full of Indians every step that you take in the house. Keep an eye to the pantry; keep an eye to the silver in the cellar. I have something else to do just now."

Chapter 25

He went straight out to the barn. Captain Burn had called after him, as he started: "Michel, you're the captain, here. Tell me what to do, will you?"

"Put some heart in the ladies, Burn," answered Rory over his shoulder, "and that won't be hard to do, either."

The captain had nodded and gone into the house with the women. It was plain that he would be better, in a pinch, than his good nature and his stiff manner promised. He would fight until he dropped.

Moreover, he had already accepted the fact that he was not the one who knew how to deal with this situation, and Rory Michel felt a sudden warmth of affection for the big, simple, true heart of the captain.

With such a man as this in his hands, he ought to be able to do very much, indeed.

But the Doctor was the next thing in the mind of Rory.

He had forgotten the long months of agony which he had spent along the trail of the geat horse and now he was ready to fight again, to the last drop of his blood, for the black stallion.

Whatever happened, he would lose the horse only one moment before he lost his own life! So he went on toward the barn.

The instant that he entered a voice hailed him. "Father, I have been waiting here!"

He turned sharply to the side, revolver in hand, but when he saw the speaker, the muzzle of the gun declined. It was South Wind.

He was not as Rory had seen him before. Over his shoulders was draped an army blanket and an army rifle was in his hands. Plainly he had been at the looting of the wagons early in the fight.

"You have filled your hands since I saw you last, South Wind," said he.

The boy looked down at the spoils and then shrugged his shoulders.

"There was much more," said he, "but I hurried away. I needed to see you, father."

"For what, South Wind?"

"Because the Apaches are very angry, father. They have made their knives sharp and loaded their rifles. They will take scalps and count many victories. Black Arrow was murdered by the whites!"

The face of the boy contracted and grew ugly as he spoke.

"What does Rising Bull say?" asked Rory.

"What he says is not a great thing to the Apaches just now," answered the lad. "The braves turn their heads away when the chief comes near them. They say that he persuaded Black Arrow to go down with him and talk as a friend to the soldiers. Now Black Arrow is dead! And the only voice among the warriors is Big Horse."

"And Big Horse wants to see me very badly, I suppose?" said Rory Michel.

"Every day he makes strong medicine. He wants to see you dead. So do many of the other warriors," said South Wind. "They saw Big Horse wearing the medicine shirt at the fight. And the bullets turned away and would not harm him. He rode straight up to the soldiers and laughed. He was not at all afraid, so that we could all see that what he says about the shirt is true.

134

"Father," went on the boy, with a change of voice, "all of these people are dead. They cannot escape. The Apaches will follow the soldiers for a little, but some of them remain behind to watch after the whites who are here. They watch after you, also, because Big Horse is with them. Do not stay here. If you stay, you are dead, too, as surely as though the bullets already had struck through your body, and your scalp had been taken, and the victories counted upon you. But still you have the black horse. Now saddle him and gallop away. Then even Big Horse, I think, cannot stop you, no matter how strong his medicine may be!"

Rory looked calmly at the boy. There was such a mixture of truth and foolish superstitition in what South Wind was saying that he found it hard to reply for a moment. Then he said: "Listen to me!"

"Who am I," said the boy, "that I should close up my ears against you?"

"Big Horse makes a strong medicine, does he not?"

"Yes. All the tribe knows that."

"But his medicine could not cure you?"

"That is true."

"And my medicine healed you?"

"Here I stand!" said the boy.

"Very well," said Rory. "No matter what Big Horse may do, my medicine is still stronger than his. In the battle, or in the tepee, he is only a child. Take him that message from me, South Wind. Tell him that one of these days I'm going to come for him, hunting as if for a deer. Then he is dead. If he runs away, the black horse will overtake him. If he stands to fight, I'll show him how I break the spell of medicine shirts. Will you tell Big Horse these things from me?"

The boy stared with open eyes.

"Do you mean it, father?" said he.

"Yes. I mean it. Just now, I am going to stay here with the people of this place, so that they won't have to be afraid. They are my people. I am sorry about the death of Black Arrow. But those who are in this house had nothing to do with that death."

"They are all whites," scowled South Wind.

"The Comanches are red, like the Apaches," pointed

135

out Rory. "Do the Apaches have to answer every time the Comanches take the scalp of a white man? You know that they don't, and the people in this house have never harmed the Apaches."

South Wind shook his head. "When I hear you, I believe you," he said. "But I am only young. How should I speak to the warriors who have counted victories? They will not even listen to my father, now. Yet I shall tell them all the things that you have said. Father, you will not go?"

"No," said Rory. "Neither would you go, South Wind, if you thought that you could help friends."

"I am sorry," said the boy. "It may be that a time may come when I shall be able to help you, father. Then you will see that my hands do not halt and stumble! Yet I wish that you were not to die!"

There was a chill in the very heart of Rory, but he managed to shake his head and smile.

"There is no fear in me, South Wind," he said. "I am sorry to make medicine against the Apaches. I have done something for them. I hoped that my lodge could open to them, and that their lodges would be open to me. But now they come to kill me. You will see that they have no power. Their bullets will turn in the air. Their knives will have thick edges. All of this shall be as I say. South Wind, farewell!"

The boy took a deep breath, hesitated, and then gripped the hand of his benefactor. Then Rory went on toward the stallion. He saddled and bridled the big horse, then loaded him down heavily with clean oats and with a mass of hay. So loaded, he turned to see South Wind still waiting near the door of the barn, but a moment later the young Apache disappeared; and as Rory went on from the barn toward the house, he could hear the rapid beat of a pony's hoofs rattling off into the distance.

There was sufficient dismay in the heart of Rory by this time. If he had felt closed in and hopeless before, he was now tenfold assured that he was lost in this cause. Still, he could not force himself to turn back.

Nancy Ware, leaning on a rifle, was waiting for him when he came up to the veranda.

"Are you bringing the Doctor?" he asked.

"Yes. There's a place for him in one of the empty rooms, if you don't mind."

"You know, Rory," said she, "that when they start shooting, it's fairly easy for bullets to strike a target as big as a horse."

"Their bullets won't strike," he assured her. "I've made medicine, and all of their bullets are going to be turned away from flesh."

He snapped his fingers in the air and she smiled back at him.

"Hurry up, Rory," she said. "Get him inside. There come some of the red rascals and the Mexicans are getting ready to make trouble at the back of the house. Three of them have asked to get into the cellar. They say that they want to get at the old drills there. But we know better than that. They won't be bothering with iron junk when there's silver beside it in the same cellar. Captain Burn is back there now. But he may need help."

Rory took the stallion in. Daintily the great horse trod the steps, stretched out his neck and sniffed inside the front door, then like a ballet dancer tip-toed across the big room and went through the doorway beyond, lowering his head to do so. It was a small chamber upon which one window opened. And there Rory bedded the stallion down.

As he pointed out to the girl who stood by, watching, the Doctor would act almost as another member of the defending force. No one could possibly force that window without bringing a loud alarm from the black horse.

Then he went back to attend to other details of the defense and left the Doctor whinnying softly behind him.

From the front of the house, Rory scanned the valley, and there he saw two or three small knots of Indians scattering out into a widely spaced line as they came up toward the mine. The great bulk of the riders had disappeared after the troopers.

There was not even a dust cloud, by this time, to mark where they had swept down the valley.

Plainly they meant business. He did not need even the warnings of South Wind to tell him that.

But there was grace for a few moments.

He went to the back of the house, and there he could hear the captain arguing loudly and in bad Mexican with a group of the laborers.

Suddenly one of the men outside cried out: "Listen to me! We have finished talking. We give you a last chance! Will you open the door and let us in?"

Rory came up and looked out through a crack in the flimsy wall near the door. He could see that Miguel, the half-breed son of Alicia, was the spokesman, young as he was, for the entire party. And the whole body of men from the mine had gathered.

"You scoundrel!" exclaimed the excited captain, "don't you think that we understand?"

"What do you understand?" demanded Miguel, insolently.

"We know very well that you want the silver, and we'll see you hanged before we let you at it!"

"We may be hanged, when our time comes," said Miguel, as complacently as ever. "But now we want the door opened or we'll open it ourselves with powder! Are you ready for that?"

He laughed loudly, as he asked the question.

"And if a bullet is fired." he went on, his voice changing to a higher and more threatening tone, "if a bullet is fired, then we blast the door open, and you are dead; all of you inside that house are dead!"

A deep-throated, brief shout from the other agreed heartily with the words of the spokesman.

Mrs. Ware, with a faint moan, sank into a chair.

"There's no use, Captain Burn," she said. "If only Dean could know what danger we've been in before we submitted to the stealing of the silver, but what can so few of us do against so many?"

"I'm hanged if I know. They have a ton of powder, if they want to use it," said the perplexed captain. "And they're all expert miners. They could blow this house and all of us to the sky, if they wanted to. I suppose that I'll have to open the door?"

138

"Let the door be," said Rory, through his teeth. "I'll give the brown demons something to think about."

He stepped suddenly to a window.

"Hai, Miguel!" he called.

The whole body of the Mexicans turned toward him. Several jerked up guns and leveled them, but others knocked the weapons aside.

"Father," said Miguel, shamefacedly, "come out to us. We are your children. In that house there is only danger for you and you have done us much kindness and good."

"I'm going to do you more kindness, Miguel," said Rory, pleasantly. "Go to the front of the house and see the Apaches riding up the valley. They've started under the Mexican moon, and they're hungry for scalps, Miguel!"

Chapter 26

There was a murmuring outcry of dread which, for the moment, was music to the angry ears of Rory Michel. The entire body of the Mexicans bolted around the sides of the house, all except one older man who stood still and cursed the Americano for a liar, and swore that the Apaches were all gone to hunt down the cowardly soldiers. They, the Mexicans, would remain long enough to take what they wished from the mine, and then they would go happily homeward, and all of them could live as gentlemen the rest of their lives!

He had almost finished his impassioned little speech, when loud outcries from the Mexicans proved the truth of Rory's warning. Back they came, pouring.

It seemed that young Miguel was, to a degree, the leading spirit of the crowd. Now he stood in the center of the yard behind the house and bawled out frantic orders to every man to get to his house and carry the household goods to the inner row of dwellings.

The arrangement of the huts was perfectly simple. They huddled in a semicircle behind the house of the master of the mine. There were some twenty Mexicans employed in the mine, at one thing or another, and these, with their families when they had any, lived in six small shacks which had been built in a semicircle, in a double line.

The shouting orders of Miguel soon had their effect. His companions, galvanized with terror, rushed to do his bidding. For in time of need nothing is so welcome as the voice of authority.

The furnishings, which were on the whole few and simple, were being thrown from the outer line of the huts.

Between these orders, he had been arguing the case with Rory.

"Senor, our father," said he, "consider that the Apaches are ten times more hungry for the scalps of white men than for the scalps of poor peons. Consider that they will storm the house and there are only two men to shield it. But once you have us inside, we are all safe."

"What would you do, Miguel?" said Rory. "Would you have us all crowded one upon another? No, no, we need elbow room and so does the silver in the cellar!"

"As for the silver," began Miguel, "I swear—"

"You burn ten thousand extra years for one false oath, Miguel," said Rory. "Don't swear it. But tell me like an honest man, do you think that I can be fool enough to let you and all the other Mexican knives into this house?"

Miguel did not have an answer for this last remark. In the meantime, however, he had successfully cleaned out the outer line of the houses and big charges of blasting powder had been placed in them.

The Mexicans, however, now streamed back into the inner yard which lay between the inner houses and the dwelling of the owner. They were frantic with excitement. They threw up their hands with wild supplica-

140

tions to the figure of Rory Michel, who was to be seen calmly seated in a window, smoking a Mexican cigarette.

He shook his head and made them reassuring signs. As for the main house itself, it seemed that there was little fear for it at the present moment. The Indians had worked around to the rear and seemed intent upon rushing the homes of the laborers. Once they gained these shelters, of course, it would not be long before they poured all over the larger building.

Miguel was gone from his central post now to supervise the blowing up of the outer row. A great whooping burst out from the Apaches. Like fiends blown on an infernal wind, those screeches came toward the house, borne on a rolling thunder of hoofbeats. The Mexicans within the yard responded with a tingling cry of despair.

Captain Burn rushed to Rory.

"Rory," said he, "you know more about this sort of business than I do, but it seems to me that we ought to be out there helping the Mexicans turn back the Apaches. A couple of cool men, a couple of rifles added—"

"While a few of the Apaches take a crack at our front door and come in and murder the women?" answered Rory. "No, we'll sit the way we are. If some of the Mexicans die, they've brought it on themselves. But I don't think they'll die. That Miguel ought to be a general. He has a brain in his head. Hai! There it goes!"

The screaming of the Apaches as they poured up in the charge sounded nearer and louder every moment. Now, as though to answer and overwhelm that hideous noise, in rapid succession six great explosions shook the ground, filled the air with flying fragments that rained down on the roofs, crashing, and hurtled into the yard, endangering every head there.

There was a deep groan of terror and wonder from the Mexicans. Far beyond, the Apache voice, howling like disappointed wolves, drew rapidly away.

Miguel came striding back into the yard powder-blackened, but bearing himself with the dignity of a hero. He had saved the day, and he was willing to let his pride appear.

"They are gone, father!" he shouted joyously to Rory.

"I told you that they would not win," answered Rory, with much composure.

The Mexicans broke into a frantic jubilee at the same moment, but Rory beckoned the son of Alicia to the window. He leaned out and called in his ear:

"They haven't time to celebrate like this, Miguel. You've blown some holes in the ground and piled broken rock everywhere. But the Apaches will come back. You'd better start every man, woman and child of the lot to piling up the fragments of masonry into walls to join hut to hut, and the ends of the wall ought to fit against this building. You understand?"

"Hai, father!" said Miguel. "Of course, you are right. I'll drive them as a sheep dog drives sheep. They have no wits whatsoever of their own, poor fools that they are!"

He was as good as his words. He ran here and there, shouting, ordering, breaking up the foolish celebration. And though, here and there, teeth flashed and even a knife or two was bared, yet the peons seemed to realize that their leader had struck upon a wise idea again.

Off went the whole busy swarm of them to do the work. There was merely a crude piling up of the building materials, of course, and therefore the wall arose like magic, higher and higher. It was breast-high, then as tall as the head of a tall man, before Miguel yelled permission to give over the labor.

Now that it was completed, Miguel walked up and down on the top of the wall where it fitted against the house near Rory Michel's window.

"The thing is done, father, as you see!" said he.

"Aye," said Rory. "You have the right way with those people. You know how to make them work for you, amigo! You have turned this all into a fort—a good, strong fort. You should be a general, Miguel. That's the truth of it."

"I have always wanted to be a soldier," said Miguel,

immensely pleased. "There come the sneaking Apaches again. I tell you, father, that they could have taken this place at the first rush, if they only had known. But now the heart is up in my people. They are steady to shoot straight. You will see! They will break the teeth of the next charge. Hai! They will knock the teeth of that charge down the cursed Apache throats!"

"They will," said Rory, "with you to lead 'em, Miguel."

"And you in the house," said Miguel. "How is it with you? Will you have some picked men to help you defend the place, father?"

"This house?" said Rory, as though surprised. "Why, the Apaches are nothing to us, Miguel. They will never take this house. Only look after yourself and your people, and we'll take care of the big house."

"You are there, father," said the young Mexican, "and you are an army."

He turned on the wall, calling to the miners to take their places at windows, with rifles ready.

"Hold their fire!" said Rory. "Make them wait till you give the word. They've heard bullets whistling in the air before today, but they hate the feel of 'em jolting home through flesh and bone. Hold the fire, Miguel!"

The idea made Miguel show his teeth with pleasure. And quickly he rattled out the necessary orders.

A pause followed. Miguel had jumped from the wall and had taken up his post where he could look out through one of the back windows of the huts. A crying child was hushed frantically by its mother. Dead silence fell over the place.

From the distance, unseen by those who waited with Rory, the Apaches were approaching. There was no doubt of that. The very depth of the silence proved that they were working nearer and nearer, no doubt taking advantage of every post of shelter among the rocks and in the brush.

Their plan would be to try to work up very close, and then rush the defenders. Rory began to hum softly himself, and heard the quiet voice of Nancy near him.

"I think that you like it, Rory," said she.

He looked sharply up at her.

"Ask yourself, Nancy," he answered. "You feel about as I do. What does it mean to you?"

"A lightness in the head. A giddy feeling," she returned.

"You're between smiling and laughing," said he. "You might have been a man, Nancy."

"The captain's watching things from the front of the house," she answered. "Is that enough?"

"Of course, it's enough," said he. "They won't try to blanket the whole place. They haven't enough men and— There they go!"

The voice of Miguel, raised hoarse and sharp, barked out the order, and instantly there was a deep-throat roar of many rifles, exploding in a single moment.

For answer came screeching cries of defiance, of rage. The babel continued.

"They're hurt. Something worse than wasps has stung 'em," said Rory cheerfully. "That's music, Nancy. Listen to 'em howl and yip!"

"I'd like to see what's happening. I wish the huts didn't shut off the view!" exclaimed the girl. "That Miguel, he's a man, Rory."

"Wait a moment," said Rory, gravely. "Maybe we'll need more men than Miguel, at that!"

As he spoke, something ripped through the roof of the kitchen in which they were talking and thudded heavily against the opposite wall.

"I'm a fool," said Rory. "I forgot the barn. From the top of that, they can knock holes through us to their hearts' content!"

Chapter 27

The jubilation of the Mexicans over the second repulse of the Indians, was checked at the same instant. Even into the taller house of the mine owner, the rifle bullets could angle down from the roof-ridge of the barn; the lowbuilt huts of the Mexicans offered a far more vulnerable target, however, and soon the leaden slugs were sweeping through.

Miguel, yelping like the sheep dog with which he already had compared himself, ordered his men, with their women and children, to take shelter close under the walls, and the order was strictly obeyed.

Not a soul had so far been wounded. By the exercise of precaution, the people in the house, also, could avoid the angle of the downward driving shots.

"It won't be so bad," said Nancy, when they had a chance to observe the effects of the new fire.

He looked absently at her, for a moment, before he answered. His mind was dwelling, at that particular moment, upon Dean Ware and his thoughts were not altogether gentle.

It was bad enough, he thought, for Ware to go off from the mine at such a time, when he might have guessed that trouble was in the air. Had he not had Apaches rifles leveled at him through the windows of his own dining room? And, though it was true that Ware had not taken a job either easy or safe in traveling about the country to collect the debts which were owing to him, still it seemed to young Rory Michel that the owner might have left the cook, Blucher, and the bookkeeper, Tod Merritt, at the mine.

He had not, however. Both were gone with him, and the women were left in charge of the chance care of Rory and Captain Burn.

145

It angered Rory more than he could say to look back over this affair and perceive what he felt to be rather the stupidity than the real selfishness of Ware. The man seemed incapable of understanding people and conditions.

So it was that Nancy had to repeat her remark before he exactly understood it.

"You don't know how badly off we are, Nancy," said he. "That dropping fire will keep the Mexicans huddling for security against the base of the walls of their huts. And while they're lying there, suppose that the Apaches give them another rush, and then what will happen?"

She shuddered.

"I hadn't thought of that," she admitted.

"I don't want to think of it, either," said he. "Mind yourself, now, and keep close to this wall of the house. Otherwise, you'll be tagged by a perfectly good army bullet."

"Where are you going, Rory?" she asked, as he rose from the window sill.

"I'm touring around the place. That's all."

His tour took him slipping through the rear door of the house, in the first place. In the central hut he found Miguel, with half a dozen Mexicans huddled against the wall which was nearest to the barn.

"Down, down, father!" cried several voices, as he entered.

And, at the same time, a bullet smashed through the window on the danger side of the hut, and several more ripped through the fragile roofing. A whoop came from the Apaches on the barn top, as they poured in their volley.

The very knees of Rory sagged with desire to take shelter, but he forced himself to remain erect.

"Take cover, father!" shouted the shrill voice of old Alicia.

"There's no reason for so much fear," he answered. "You see these Apache bullets don't understand very well how to find the mark. Miguel, come here for a moment."

Miguel, after rolling his eyes about him, once or

146

twice, was spurred to his feet by pride. He stood before the white man, but still his glance was uneasy, and his whole attitude that of one ready to jump in any direction for safety.

"Miguel," said Rory, "who's keeping the lookout between this place and the barn?"

"The lookout?" said Miguel, gaping. "Who wants to be a dead man? Is anybody going to stand in front of the windows that face on that side? Look!"

He himself went near the window and held out a rifle, so that the barrel extended across the aperture. Two or three reports instantly rang out from the barn top and the rifle was actually knocked out of the hand of Miguel.

He sprang back with a shout of alarm.

"Look, the demons!" he groaned. "They can even hit a streak of light! Hai! You ask me who will keep the lookout on this side of the houses? Only dead men, father!"

Rory was gritting his teeth. He knew very well that not accuracy so much as chance had knocked the gun from the grasp of Miguel, but it was just as impressive to the Mexicans. They paid no heed to the noise which the other bullets had made as they had thumped into the side of the house. All that mattered was the lucky one which had clanged against the barrel of the rifle.

They scattered back from the region of the window as though death were literally breathing from it! At one stroke, Rory saw that the morale of the men was ruined.

The story of this would sweep the rounds. The Mexicans would convince themselves, after such marksmanship, that they were matched against uncanny redskins who could, as Miguel so forcibly put it, hit the wavering gleam of a ray of sunshine. That very night they were apt to desert, slipping away, one after another.

Worse than that, at the first war whoop near the walls, every man of them was likely to take to his heels, even though he were running from sudden to lingering death. For these reasons, Rory Michel ground his teeth.

He saw that he would have to do something quickly

to restore the balance; and at that very window, he must do it.

So he stepped boldly up to the aperture, saying: "You see, Miguel, that was only luck. It was a chance bullet. Just a mere chance!"

"Hai!" Groaned Miguel. "You may say that, father, but you are standing at the side of the window, not fairly in front of it."

"Look!" said Rory.

He waved his revolver in front of the window. There was the same spurt of rifle fire, but this time three bullets were distinctly heard to pound against the side of the house, and not one entered the gap.

Rory turned toward the shrinking Mexicans.

"You see, Miguel?" said he. "That other time, it was only luck."

"Well, said Miguel, "if I had been where the rifle was, I would not have lived to find out that it was only luck!"

There was inescapable point to this remark. Rory sighed. A demonstration as cheap as his would not do. He had to find something more striking, and now he wondered why this window was being surveyed so closely from the barn that the first movement inside it called forth such a burst of fire?

He stepped closer and, keeping his head sheltered, peered out as far as he could with safety. He commanded, in this manner, about half of the view from the window, and he could look out on the right half of the corral, the brush that grew between the fences and the shacks, and the rocks and trees on the higher ground beyond. Nowhere, did he mark anything suspicious, though he strained his eyes for a long moment.

He circled back through the room and came up to the window on the opposite side, saying to Miguel: "You see how easy it is, Miguel? You look from one side, and then from another. I don't suppose you think that they can shoot around corners?"

One of the more elderly Mexicans now answered: "That may be very true, father, but we find in this life a great deal more than the eye can always see!"

"Aye," said Rory, promptly, "such things as

148

Apaches' knives that strike in the dark and stick as deep as the heart."

He could see the Mexicans literally turn green.

In the meantime, he was staring out from the farther side of the window, and now he could see the entire sweep of the barn and the remainder of the corral. There were some very low hummocks, some brush also near the house, but nothing that could possibly shelter a man. His first fear that the redskins might have been stalking the house at that very moment grew easier.

They held the barn in strength, however. Beyond it arose a broadtopped column of smoke, a sure sign that the Indians were at their cookery at that spot. No doubt, the cattle or the horses of Ware would supply their larder.

But the chief post of the Apaches was behind the very ridge of the roof of the barn, which acted as their breastworks when they wished to open fire. As Rory scanned that roof, he saw a head and shoulders suddenly appear above the line of it with a leveled rifle, and the next instant a bullet hummed through the window and clipped a bit of cloth from the shoulder of Rory's coat.

"Hai! father! You are hit?" cried two or three of the Mexicans, in one voice.

"I? Not at all," said Rory. "Their medicine is not strong. They have not hurt a soul in the place, up to this time, and think of all the bullets they have fired."

"They will eat us with knives, not with fire," muttered old Alicia.

It seemed to Rory pretty thoroughly demonstrated that nothing could be more dangerous than to attempt to maintain a lookout on this side of the house. But, without such watchfulness, steadily maintained, how were they to keep the Apaches at any distance, by day, to say nothing of the night!

All the lives inside those buildings would be put out in a red flow of blood as soon as darkness fell, he saw at once.

Unless something were done—and, as he thought of this, he saw one of the bushes near the house move slightly forward! He was not mistaken. It stirred again,

149

only inches at a time, and now, snatching a rifle from the hands of the nearest of the Mexicans, Rory took careful aim at the bottom of the suspicious shrub and fired.

A loud yell answered him. The bush disappeared and out of the very ground sprang an Apache who leaped into the air like a rabbit making its spry hop, then raced away for the barn. But, as he reached the corral fence, the rifle spoke again in the hands of Rory, and he saw the brave slump down and hang limp over the lowest bar of the fence, dying or dead!

Chapter 28

Only after this happened, and the Apache was definitely down, did Rory become aware that a score of bullets had hurtled through the window from which he was firing. The floor of the house was liberally plowed up, and the Mexicans along the walls were yelling and shrieking, as the dirt spattered upon them.

Then Rory stepped back.

"You see, Miguel," said he. "There's no good medicine in their bullets. And unless you keep a close lookout, those Apaches will surely steal up close enough to the houses to jump into 'em. You saw how near that brave was?"

Miguel who had been standing almost immediately behind Rory, had seen everything that had met the eye of his chief.

"Father," he said now, "you have no fear!"

"Of course, I have," said Rory, "but not when I'm standing up to people who shoot as badly as those Apaches. You saw how they missed me!"

Further talk became almost impossible for a moment.

The fall of the warrior was instantly known to all the

beleaguering forces, it appeared, and it seemed that he was a well-known man, for a chorus of loud yells went up from the encircling throng, hideous canterwauling lamentations, howls for revenge and promises of death.

At the same time, every weapon the Indians were master of was turned upon the houses.

Rory sat down by the wall and made himself a cigarette, Mexican style, sitting cross-legged while he smoked it.

"They're using up a lot of powder and lead," said Rory. "They're knocking up some dust and chipping off some rock splinters. But that's all. Do you feel better, Miguel?"

Miguel was actually laughing and, as the outburst of firing died down and only one woman's voice sounded in a high-pitched, tingling lament for the dead, all the Mexicans in the room joined in the laughter and began a great chattering.

Rory sighed with relief, for he knew that the tension had been broken. The bravest of men may be afraid when the fight commences, but now that a blow had been struck and an enemy had fallen, every rifleman in the place would feel encouraged to imitate that excellent example.

He remained until his cigarette was finished. They were actually exchanging jokes before he left, and he had the satisfaction of seeing a keen-eyed fellow posted beside the window and keeping the lookout.

"Although, father," said Miguel, "we have not eyes like yours, that look right through the solid ground."

"Go into the other huts, Miguel," directed Rory. "Show them how to keep the lookout. We are going to keep them off, but we must have our eyes open, Miguel."

Miguel thrust out his jaw.

"We will kill them like sheep, before the end," he boasted. "Don't worry about us. We are all awake, now!"

Rory went back to the house, and there he found the captain and Nancy in a state of much excitement.

"Who did it?" said the captain. "I was looking out through a chink at the very spot, I think, but I didn't

151

see that Apache. He'd turned himself into grass and ground, it seemed to me! Some of those Mexicans must have eyes, Rory."

"They have eyes, all right," agreed Rory. "And we're going to keep the red rascals off, I've no doubt. I've brought in an extra pair of rifles. We made need 'em in here. They have plenty to go around out there."

He asked after Mrs. Ware and learned that she was lying down. The report of the Indian's death and the outbreak of yelling and gunfire that followed it had unnerved her. Now Nancy went off to look to her, and the captain fell into quiet, serious conversation with Rory.

"Michel," said he, "I know that what you've said was to raise the spirits of the three of us in here. But you're aware, as well as I am, that we've got a lost cause here?"

"A lost cause?" said Rory. "And why?"

"Because of the barn, of course," answered the captain. "Even if that were out of the way, we'd be in trouble enough, no doubt—there are such a lot of those Apaches. And they shoot straight enough, too. See what they've done to the roof, for one thing! But with the barn there, we've got the enemy in the very house, so to speak. As soon as it grows dark, they can rush us whenever they see fit. Do you think that the Mexicans will really stand up to the shock, in case that happens?"

"They'll fight well enough in the daylight—now," said Rory. "Their hearts are up. After dark—well, I'm not so sure. The whole gang of the Indians can bunch behind the barn and rush us from there. They'd come through the night and be swarming around us before we knew what was up!"

"The very thing that I've been thinking about," said the captain. "That place is too close, too infernally close. There'll be a moon, tonight, of course, but it rises fairly late. Before moonrise, I've an idea that we may all see our finish, Rory!"

The latter looked the soldier squarely in the face and saw that there was apprehension, but no shrinking in his eye.

"We will see our finish, probably," admitted Rory.

152

"We've got about one chance in ten, I suppose, of living through the night."

The captain nodded. He went on:

"I've been thinking the thing over. The worst time for visibility is between day and dark, you know. Twilight time is the worst of all. Even starlight is almost better than that, I suppose. Because the eyes don't get accustomed to the changing light. Now, then, we might use that time."

"For what?" said Rory.

"For slipping away. The Indians won't be expecting that."

"Slip away, with the whole tribe of Mexicans and these women? That would simply mean a massacre. Even if the Indians were blind, their ears would tell 'em what was happening. In a wind and rain storm—well, there might be one chance in a hundred, but not on a still evening like the ones we've been having lately."

The captain nodded.

"I know you're right," he said. "But it's the only thing I can think of. And to sit quietly here and wait for death—that's a hard thing to do, Rory. You know how hard that is!"

"Yes, it's hard, all right."

"If I had even no more than a little three-pounder in here, we could mount it and knock the Indians out of that barn and off it! But that's a daydream of course. Only, I've been imagining the howl those demons would put up if a shell were to drop through the roof and burst in the mow of that barn. I can't help thinking about that!"

"Well, we have no cannon," said Rory, a little sharply.

"And no shells," replied the soldier, with a sigh. "One incendiary shell—well, I might as well wish for a legion of angels to fly down from heaven and rescue us. I know that we can't have it."

"Incendiary, incendiary!" murmured Rory.

Suddenly he began to stare at the other with an empty eye, as a man will do when his mind is crowded with many thoughts.

"What's in the air?" asked Burn.

"You know munitions and their manufacture pretty well, I suppose," said Rory.

"I know them pretty well. Yes. That was my special branch."

"Could you make a bomb, Burn? I mean, a bomb that would stave in the side of the barn and shoot it full of burning powder, or some such business?"

The captain scowled. "What have we got to shoot the bomb or throw it at its target?" he asked.

"You make the bomb," said Rory. "Then one of us might be the howitzer."

"The what?" asked the captain.

"One of us could carry the bomb and drop it beside the barn, in that same half light that you've been talking about at the end of the sunset, Burn!"

The captain stared, more wide-eyed than ever.

"What do you mean, Rory?" he asked. "One of us could carry a bomb across the open all the way to the barn; climb through a fence; run on again; plant the charge; fire the fuse; why, he'd be dead a hundred times. The Apaches would blow him into such small pieces that they wouldn't even be able to salvage a scalp from the remains!"

But Rory had begun to walk up and down, humming softly to himself.

At length he said:

"Look here, Burn, you have a lot of materials here —powder, scrap iron, lead, fuses galore. You make a bomb. Make one with a twenty-second fuse hitched onto it, say. And when the end of the day comes, then we can decide whether the bomb is worthless or not. You've nothing better to do with your time, have you?"

"No," argued the captain, "but what's the good of—"

"I don't know what the good of it may be," snapped Rory. "But something is always better than nothing. Make the bomb, I say, and then we'll see!"

The captain did not argue any longer.

As a matter of fact, he was pleased to have something that would fill his hands and part of his mind during the rest of that weary day.

The fighting had ended, shortly after noon. That is

154

to say, there was no longer even the most desultory fire maintained from the barn, and men could show themselves at the windows of the house or of the huts without being shot at.

A brilliant, powerful sun, such as shines in Arizona alone, took charge of the landscape and buried everything in a watery sheen of heat waves that rose and swayed and danced under the eye. The heat grew oppressive in the house. They were gasping for breath in the smaller house. Some of the Mexican children began to wail, fretfully, though they had remained as still as fawns during the danger of the first attack.

Such a heat might bring wind, and the wind might raise clouds—but vainly the watchers stared toward the encircling horizon. Not a hint of a shadow arose. And so the day sloped toward the end, and the sun reddened and puffed his cheeks in the west. There would be no heavy-mantling storm to cover an escape.

If any hope remained now for the garrison, it was in the hands of the captain, who was carefully, delicately, giving the last touches in the making of his bomb.

Chapter 29

The bomb constructed by Captain Burn was not exactly a thing of beauty or a joy forever. It consisted chiefly of sheet lead, quite thin, and held into a firmer structure by bands of rough iron which the captain had worked around the mass of the central core.

There was a short length of fuse attached to the bomb, and Nancy Ware, who had been helping somewhat, declared that this pigtail, as she called it, made the thing like the letter "Q" in three ample dimensions.

She had helped patiently, running errands, holding, twisting, turning, fetching tools at the bidding of the captain. All she knew was that the mysterious object was a bomb. How it was to be used, she could not guess. She merely suggested that it must be for the purpose of breaking up some mass attack.

"That's not a bad idea," said young Rory Michel. "I wish that we had a dozen of these things lying about."

"I don't," answered the captain. "If we had that many, a stray bullet would be too likely to graze one of 'em and blow us all to kingdom come."

"That's a pleasanter way of going than the way that we're likely to find," said Nancy, shrugging her shoulders. "But let that go. If we—"

"Oh, great heavens!" cried Mrs. Ware. "They're surrendering."

"Surrendering, my foot!" said Nancy, turning to her mother as the latter ran in from a front room.

"I see them waving a white flag!" cried Mrs. Ware. "What else could that mean? Right from the corner, of the barn, they're waving the flag!"

"They surely want to parley," said the captain. "Shall we show a white flag in turn, as an invitation, Rory?"

"Why not? There's nothing but Indian deviltry behind it, no doubt, but then we may as well learn what they want."

So they prepared a towel on a broomstick and waved it out a window. They had hardly begun to wave, when there was a withdrawal of the white flag that showed beyond the corner of the barn. Rory, from the rear of the house, called to Miguel to make sure that no one should open fire, in case a single Indian, or even two of them, appeared coming toward the place.

He had hardly given that warning, when a single rider came on a dancing pony from behind the barn and started toward the house. He was brilliant with war paint and stripped to the waist. In the gold of the sunset light, he looked like something created of burning copper, so did he glow and shine.

"Look! Look!" cried Nancy. "I've never seen anything half so beautiful. See him come, like a hawk on the wing! There, he's going to crash into the corral fence, no, he's over it! That's riding, Rory!"

"He can ride better than that," said Rory. "That's

156

the lad that I told you about. That's young South Wind. He's the one who's bringing us a message of some sort. A good one, I hope."

"Bless him," said the girl, generous in her enthusiasm. "I never saw such a picture of a lad! And see that spear! He comes charging as though he meant to drive that spear clear through the wall of the house!"

Young South Wind galloped in this most frantic manner straight up to the Ware house, and there he pulled his pony to a halt and lifted one hand while the little horse still danced with eagerness.

"Hai, South Wind!" called out Rory, without dignity in his manner of speaking. And he leaned deliberately out of the window!

"Don't do that!" cried Nancy. "They may shoot! They know that you're our strength—half our strength, I mean!" she added, glancing rather guiltily at the captain.

But he shook his head in the greatest humility and good nature as Rory answered her:

"They won't shoot. They're not risking the death of such a fellow as South Wind. How is it, South Wind?" he added directly to the youth.

"Father," said the boy, "draw back a little under cover. There are some hard eyes and hard hearts among those men who are waiting yonder. One of them may shoot before he thinks."

"I take a chance," said Rory. "One has to do that."

"Then I come closer," said South Wind, generously, "so that if they fire, they are more likely to strike me. That may hold them back, a little."

He rode closer, accordingly, and sat on the back of the pony immediately under the window from which Rory leaned.

"Here you are, South Wind," said the white man. "And I'm glad to see you again. That was well ridden, just now. We've been admiring you. How is your father, South Wind, and the rest of the chiefs and the braves?"

"They are all sad for the death of Black Arrow," said the boy. "We have driven the white soldiers, but we have killed none of them. We have hurt a great many of them, but we have not emptied a single saddle. And now comes worse fortune, and Spotted Antelope lies dead, yonder, fallen over the bar of the fence like an empty pelt, rather than a strong young warrior. This cannot be very happy day for the Apaches, father."

"You see how the thing runs, South Wind," said Rory. "I told you before about the medicine of Big Horse and the rest was not very strong. You can see it now for yourself."

"I have seen that and so have the chiefs," said the boy. "They are not very pleased with Big Horse. He is making medicine still, and this time he promises to make such a kind of medicine that every scalp within these walls shall fall into our hands. Do you hear, father? Every scalp!"

He solemnly raised a warning forefinger.

"I hear, of course," said Rory Michel.

"Now, then," said the boy, "it would not have to be a very strong medicine, either. It is not long, father, before the darkness comes."

He lowered his voice as he said this.

"And then the Apaches attack, of course," said Rory.

"I have not said that. I cannot say such a thing. But we are many, and you are few in here!"

"A few men, and a strong medicine," insisted Rory.

The boy sighed and shook his head. "The bravest man," he declared in answer, "always talks even more bravely than he feels. That is like you, father. I know that you will never talk like a woman. I am proud when I hear you speak. So I shall like to speak, one day, before I am to die. But now, hear me, because I am about to say the thing that will be good for you."

"Tell me, South Wind."

"I have talked to the chiefs, Rather, my father has talked for me, and he has made them promise, in spite of Big Horse, to let you live."

"Am I to live, really?"

"Yes, you are to live. You have done a great and famous thing for the Apaches. They have not forgotten.

158

My father has talked to every one of the chiefs and to the oldest warriors. They are willing to let you live, and all that they ask in return for your life is the return of the red eye. '

"Go on, Rory," urged the captain, as Rory was silent for a moment, astonished by this offer.

"Yes, yes," said Nancy Ware, hurriedly. "There's no hope in here. Not for any of us."

Rory turned to her and favored her with a very faint and very odd smile.

"I'm to run away, Nan, am I?" said he.

Then Mrs. Ware said, gravely: "We are all to die, Rory. I feel it. We all feel and know it. If your life can be spared, go, and God bless you for what you've done already, and what you've tried to do!"

"More than enough already," said Nancy.

Rory turned his back on them and their words. He faced the Indian again.

"Go back to the chiefs, South Wind," he said, "and tell them that there is a young girl here who has done no harm to any of the Apaches. If they will agree to let her go free—if I can see her ride freely out of sight down the valley, then I'll give up the ruby. And, with her out of the way, they can take my scalp if they're able. Is that clear to you?"

"Hai!" cried the boy, indignant, "I come to you, father, and talk to you of your own life, which is worth more than herds of horses and robes, tepees and pack loads of beads, knives and rifles. I offer you your own life and, instead of taking that, you offer to give in exchange the life of a young squaw. I have seen her, too. There is no more strength in her arms than in the arms of a child. She would never be able to keep your tepee and make your clothes, sharpen your weapons and cook for you, do beadwork and everything else that it is fitting a woman should be able to do! What sort of talk is this, father? I offer you life; and you laugh in my face!'

"I'm not laughing in your face. Look!"

He drew the ruby from his pocket, shook it out of its

159

wrapping of chamois, and let it flash its brilliance in the eyes of the lad.

"You see it, South Wind. That I shall give for the life of the girl, if they will let her go free. Otherwise, I give them nothing, and trust all to the strength of the medicine which I am making now against the Apaches."

The boy was silent for a moment, breathing hard.

"My father has spoken?" he said at last.

"I've said the thing that I mean," said Rory. "If there is an acceptance, you'll come back to get the stone. If not, wave the white flag once more from the end of the barn, and we'll know that it is war to the finish."

"You have spoken," said South Wind. "Father, farewell!"

He raised his right hand in a stiff and solemn salute, then jerking his pony about, he returned to the barn in the same bullet-like course which he had pursued before, leaping the bars of the fence.

"Rory," said the girl, "you know that you've thrown yourself away."

"I know nothing, till the thing's proved," said Rory.

"Will they—" began Mrs. Ware.

"What is that red stone?" asked the captain, curiously.

"A ruby worth a crown," said Rory, quietly.

Just then there was an angry uproar of voices from the Apaches, and the next instant the white flag was brandished in a single flourish from the corner of the barn.

160

Chapter 30

"You've chucked hope behind you, Rory," said Captain Burn, looking at the boy. "It's a thing I would have wanted to do in your place but I don't know that I would have had the nerve!"

Mrs. Ware drew herself up with a good deal of dignity.

"Children," she said, her gesture including the two men as well as her daughter, "It seems that the time has come when we are about to die, and I imagine that our chief interest should be to die well. There are four of us here. But we're not the only ones. Before moonrise, I know that my poor husband will be drawing near this place, and I only hope that we may be able to defend ourselves long enough to warn him with the noise of the shooting, while he's still at a distance. Otherwise, he will be walking straight into the same death trap that holds us all!

"I know that you, captain, and you, Rory, are brave men. I know that Nancy will never fail in a crisis. There's only one weak link in the chain and that is I. I've never lifted a hand against another human being. But tonight I must try to do my best for Dean's sake. I am going to use this rifle when the time comes and I pray that when I shoot, the bullet will find a mark."

As she spoke, she picked up a heavy rifle and gripped it in her trembling hands. The men were impressed. Perhaps the girl was, also, but she replied:

"You know, mother, that you'll be dying ten times an hour from now on to the finish—and then there won't be the sort of a finish that you expect. After all, there's a chance!"

Mrs. Ware managed a smile.

"But what chance is there?" she asked.

"There's Rory's chance," said Nancy. "His luck is what I'm betting on. Rory's luck, that never fails."

And she laughed as she spoke.

Rory Michel left them and went into the adjoining room where the black stallion was stabled. The sun was down now and, since this room's window looked to the east, very little of the sunset light entered the chamber; yet the glossy skin of the Doctor was glimmering in the half light. He thrust out his head toward his master and whinnied as softly as a human whisper.

Rory Michel stood for a moment in the dimness with one arm around the beautiful head of the horse and as he lingered, he saw the long months of the trail flow once more before his eyes and through his heart, the agony, the hope, the despair, the grimness of that effort.

Now the prize was his. If he cast open the front door of the house and bolted it at the full speed of the great horse, who could say that the bullets of the Indians would find him in the treacherous half light of the day's end?

But that was not the goal in the eye of Rory. He had first another task before him.

He saddled and bridled the horse and led him in to the next room, and the Doctor moved gingerly, sometimes raising his head a little and sniffing, for there was a distinct odor of burned powder in the air.

The other three turned questioningly to Rory. What was in his mind they could not guess, but they knew, all of them, that he was their chief hope. He had done much already, so much that they hesitated to place a definite limit upon his possibilities.

"Why the saddle and the bridle, Rory?" asked the captain.

"This is the gun to shoot the bomb, Burn," said Rory. "How many seconds will that fuse take to burn?"

"About a minute," said the captain.

"Cut off two thirds of it," said Rory.

"But—"

162

"Do it man," urged Rory. "That will be long enough."

The captain stared at him, then, without a word, drew a knife and cut the fuse.

"Nancy," ordered Rory, "stand by the front door there, and jerk it open when I give the word."

The girl, likewise in silence, nodded and immediately stepped to the door.

Rory Michel leaped into the saddle, his head almost touching the ceiling. After that, he swung over, Indian fashion, and hung along the side of the stallion.

"Give me the bomb, now," he called.

Burn brought it to him. "Rory," he said, "I know, now, what you have in mind. God bless you for the idea. It makes me see that you're the bravest fellow in the world, but you'll never get there!"

"Maybe not," said Michel. "But I'm trying."

He took the bomb in the hollow of his left arm. It was on the left side of the stallion that he lay stretched out, for this would be the side turned most from the barn when he issued from the house.

"Light the fuse, now," he commanded.

Captain Burn obediently touched light to the end of the fuse, which instantly began to sputter like a living thing.

"The door, Nancy!" called Rory.

"The door!" she repeated, and jerked it open, as he had ordered.

"Now, Doctor!" muttered Rory to the horse.

But he hardly needed to urge the good animal to its work. The brightness of the outdoors impelled the stallion, and perhaps a sense of something impending, which horses will sometimes feel as keenly as their masters. At any rate, he made one or two quick, catlike steps forward, and then shot through the door like a projectile through the throat of a gun.

The first leap landed him on the veranda, crashing upon the boards, and skidding violently. It looked to those who remained in the room, holding their breath, as though horse and rider must have a ruinous fall, but a fraction of a second later the Doctor had struck the firm ground and was rushing away in a streak, not down the valley toward safety for itself and its rider, but straight on toward the barn where the Indians were posted.

Leaving the doorway, which no longer afforded them a view of that wild ride, all three rushed to the window on the western side of the building, and there they crowded to watch the progress of Rory. By the time they got to their observation post, the Doctor was taking the corral fence with a bound like the spring of a bird from the ground into the air, supported by the strong beat of wings.

And still, though half the distance between the house and the barn had been covered, there was not a whisper, not a single sign from the Apaches.

"They're waiting, with their guns trained on him," moaned Mrs. Ware. "They're laughing at him, and, then, they'll blow him to bits with a volley. O God, save and protect him, the gallant lad! Poor Rory, poor Rory! There are plenty more humans like us, but there never will be another like him!"

"Hush!" said Nancy Ware. "Don't speak! Don't whisper, even; Satan himself would never have thought of such a plan as this one of Rory's!"

The Indians, however, were not waiting with leveled guns as Mrs. Ware suspected, and now they gave proof by setting up a sudden yell of alarm and bewilderment at the sight of the single horseman who came charging straight down upon their stronghold.

They could not understand the thing. It was madness, and madness is sent by the Sky People upon unfotunate humans.

With his own eyes, Captain Burn saw a brave spring out from the corner of the barn with a rifle at the ready in his hands, but he failed to make any effort to level the gun or to fire. Apparently bewilderment had frozen his limbs and his brain. Several others appeared upon the ridge of the barn, one of them standing bolt upright to stare at this wildest of wild charges. For who could imagine any sensible creature actually charging into the mouth of death in this fashion?

There was little time for thought, for that matter. The black stallion had struck his pace, and such a speed as his never had burned up the prairies or swept over the mountains upon four legs. He was over the corral fence, across the inclosure, and then veering at the very side of the barn itself, at the moment when it seemed the purpose of Rory to drive straight on through the wall of the barn!

But at the last moment, the horse swerved violently, and not a bullet had been fired as the rider, straightening in the saddle suddenly, hurled his missile straight through the nearest open window and dashed on toward the fence at the corner, that same corner behind which stood the Apache with laggard rifle.

Captain Burn, calmly, had taken aim to cover that warrior, and as the man finally jerked up his gun, as an uproar of alarm burst out from the Indians inside the barn, Burn pulled the trigger.

The Apache fired, but he fired blindly into the air, leaped up, toppled backward to the ground, and then went wriggling off through the grass to get to cover.

In the meantime, the stallion had leaped the fence the second time. And while it was in the air, the bomb exploded.

All of these things had been crowded compactly into twenty short seconds!

It was not a great roar that the bomb of the captain made. The materials which confined the powder were too loosely and hastily put together for that, no doubt, but the report was a dull, bursting sound, as though a vast paper bag had been inflated and then struck hard with the flat of the palm.

There was sufficient force in the explosion to make the barn shudder visibly, and then jets of black smoke burst out at the windows and at the door, followed immediately by flashes of crimson plainly visible in the dark interior of the building.

The noise of the bomb had not been great, but the

outcry of the amazed and infuriated Apaches was indeed, sufficient to split the sky fairly open.

Loud and wildly shrilling, they whooped and roared. And suddenly a score of rifles were turned upon the fugitive.

But he was already a few seconds away, and every second meant much, in that light, with the stallion straining to his utmost greyhound speed. Rods flashed behind him before the shooting began, and he plunged on to what he felt was a very safe distance indeed. At the same time, when the yelling of the Indians rose to a higher pitch of rage and despair and vexation, he stood up straight in his stirrups and waved back to his friends in the house of Ware.

Chapter 31

Return to the Ware house was obviously cut off. Not only were too many rifles gathered behind him, but now a farflung volley of Apache horsemen swept out from the vicinity of the barn and raced after him.

So he settled down to riding and, after a few hundred yards, he had the satisfaction of seeing the pursuers give up the chase. Perhaps it was because they recognized the manifest superiority of the stallion. Perhaps it was because they wished to return to see the full effect of the disaster which he had caused.

They Rory Michel himself drew rein and from the top of a considerable hummock he looked back up the valley toward the Ware place.

The barn was now throwing out flames from every window and, even as Rory paused, he saw a red arm break through the roof and stand up against the sky. The incendiary bomb had done its work perfectly.

That was not all. The glare from the burning building promised to last a big part of the night and that illumination would make light for the besieged. The most daring of the Apaches would not dare to rush the defenders through such a glow as bathed the entire vicinity. And, by the time the firelight died out, there would be a bright moon shining.

Rory Michel began to whistle softly, contented with himself. On the hummock he waited until he saw the nearer end of the barn fall in.

Like the opening of a furnace door, it revealed a vast pool of fire, and now a crimson maelstrom rushed up into the sky. But it revealed no Apaches lurking nearby. They had taken refuge at a distance, and down the wind came the noise of their yelling, like disappointed fiends.

If they had wanted the scalp of Rory Michel before, what must be their passion for it now?

Even if he could not get back to the house and rejoin the defenders, he had sufficient work planned. Ware and his two companions were by this time coming up the valley, in all probability, and it was necessary to warn them as quickly as possible. Perhaps the Apaches knew of the impending arrival of the treasure wagon, and they might well have planted an ambush to intercept it.

At any rate, Rory went forward carefully, keeping the stallion to an easy canter and leaning to peer into the shadows.

A wind was rising now. It seemed as though the burning of the barn had started it, and when he looked back he could see the flames fanning far out to the side. He hardly knew whether to curse or bless the rise of the storm. Though it would cover the sounds that otherwise might have reached him, yet it was likely to muffle the noise of his own approach if hostile ears were listening.

He was now drawing into the mouth of the valley where it widened, and the ground was a succession of easily sloping waves. Small patches of oaks and of skeleton cactus forms were lifting here and there against the stars, from the higher places, and every one

167

of these might be covert for a band of wild Apaches. They could hide themselves where there seemed hardly room for a coyote to curl itself up.

It was like moving past door after door of yawning danger, and his nerves grew as tense as violin strings, screwed to the snapping point.

Twice he dismounted to lie flat upon the ground and, his ear pressed close, attempted to hear whatever noises of wheels or hoofs might be stirring abroad, but he could detect no distinct sound, until the second time, when it seemed to Rory that he heard, far off down the road, that dull, repeated chucking sound such as the wheels of a heavy wagon make.

He could not be sure but, mounting, he rode up to the top of the next rise of ground. And there he saw what he wanted.

The road here pointed almost directly toward the east, where the sky was flushing with dull crimson above the rising moon. Half of the head of the moon had already appeared, and across that disk moved a little black etching of a covered wagon, drawn by patiently nodding mules.

Rory Michel sighed with relief.

There were several intervening ridges, but he did not hurry to cross them. Instead, he looked for a moment to the stallion. The cinches of the saddle were a shade loose. He tightened them, and patted the sleek, hot neck of his horse before he remounted and went on at a contented dogtrot. There was surely no need of haste now. And what held back Rory was the knowledge that he had such bad news for Ware.

There would be four of them together, and four determined men could manage a great deal, even against such a throng of wolfish Apaches. In the dark of the next night, for instance, they could rush through the Apache watchers and get to the house. Perhaps one or two of them might fall, but those who lived would be an excellent addition to the garrison of the fort.

Even such a small stroke as this might, in addition, be enough to discourage the impatient Indians. They

168

were notoriously ill at ease in siege tactics, and already they had probably found the Ware place unexpectedly stubborn.

Still another hope appeared in his mind. The mere desire to murder the whites and the Mexicans in the Ware place could not have been so overwhelming in the minds of the Apaches. They already had the plunder which they most desired, the guns and ammunition from the cavalry, and the livestock from the Ware outfit. They would gain but little more by the sack of the houses. And they were apt to pay for it with blood; they had already paid some installments in advance!

In fact, the cause of their bulldog grip upon the place must have been their desire to get at Rory Michel and, now that Rory was gone from the house, what would they do? If Big Horse had his way, he would urge that the whole tribe take up the trail behind the fugitive rider. Others might object that the black stallion already had outdistanced them on more than one occasion. And perhaps the council would determine upon some other target at which to strike.

In case the Apaches clung to their prey, other things might be attempted. For instance, he might ride to find the driven and humiliated command of the major. By this time, the troopers were probably boiling with eagerness to avenge their rout. They might follow willingly, if they were to be taken back to the fight against the same Apache band.

If that were done he, Rory, could fairly well guarantee them against surprise along the way!

These were the matters which Rory turned busily in his mind. But he was beginning to wonder why he did not have sight of the wagon. He had crossed two of the intervening ridges already; the third one should have been topped by the wagon before this.

However, when he came to the top of the third ridge, the matter was explained. The wagon had halted there. He saw the mules spanned out, two and two, before the

169

big, clumsy vehicle. And he saw even the dull silhouette of the driver of the seat.

So Rory shouted cheerfully and waved his hand. All was for the best, and he never had felt so rich in good fortune as he did at that instant of beginning the canter down the slope.

The moon was up a bit in a clear sky by this time. There were just a few wisps of clouds flung in its face by the wind, so that the broad, yellow shield seemed to be rushing through the sky like a cannonball. The light was fairly bright withal, and Rory told himself that they could not dare to attempt to penetrate the Apache lines under such a moon as this. Not until the dawn commenced, and the twilight of the early day was there, then they might rush, at that sleepiest of all hours for men and beast!

The plan was matured in his quick brain as he came down to the bottom of the hollow and called, as he rode: "Hello, Ware! Hello!"

Suddenly he thought he saw, dimly, a struggle in the brush beside the road, where it grew thick, and the next moment a form rushed wildly out, waving both hands above its head, and the voice of the bookkeeper, raised to a hoarse scream, like the screech of a hawk, rang in his ears.

"Rory! Rory! Apaches! Run for it—run!"

It was the jolly little bookkeeper.

And now, from the brush behind the man, leaped a half-naked man, his body gleaming in the coppery moonshine. From his head streamed long hair and a feathery headdress. In his hand he wielded a short-handled ax and this weapon arose and circled fiercely as the Indian sprang in. The blow fell upon the devoted head of the bookkeeper, and down he dropped, falling heavily, arms outspread, upon the road.

At the same time, the entire hollow was alive with men, springing up under the very nose of the rider. Horses, too, were conjured from the shrubs, from the brush, from the rocks, and warriors were leaping upon their backs as Rory made the stallion spin to the right.

He could thank his fortune that the stallion was as

badly frightened as he, and needed no word of command, no touch of heel to make it flow in one gleaming streak down the hollow.

All the wild noises of an inferno awoke and lived around him, demons wailing and yelling with desire, and with hatred. Bows twanged and rifles rang loudly on the night air.

The hat was knocked from his head—not the first time in his life that this had happened—and then he felt two or three unimportant little tugs at his coat; hardly perceptible twitches which, nevertheless, he knew were the fingers of death plucking at him.

He pulled the stallion right and left as he fled, and the big horse seemed to understand the business of dodging flight as though from long practice. Then, in an instant, they were among rocks that jutted up like teeth and closed in a wall behind them. The uproar, the clamor of the rifles, were shut away from them for a moment, and only came again as Rory and the stallion reached the summit of the next hillock.

He glanced back to see that a score of warriors were flowing after him. The moon gleamed on their bare shoulders and on the tossing, decorated heads of their ponies.

It was like a level flight of evil spirits.

Then Rory pointed the head of the Doctor down the farther slope and gave him a free rein to fly like a hawk to safety.

Chapter 32

As a hawk strikes at its quarry and then swings far away through the sky, baffled, but ready to pounce again, so Rory Michel fled through the hills and, when he heard the roar of hoofs die down behind him he circled back to come to the point where he had seen the abandoned wagon.

He did not know exactly what he could do. If the Indians were busy, when he arrived, in the plundering of the wagon, it might be that he could accomplish something—unless all the men of the white party had perished as the bookkeeper had.

At any rate, he would go rounding back to accomplish what he could.

What filled him with wonder was the manner of the end of the little bookkeeper. That insignificant round-faced fellow had been a hero in the end, not for the sake of any great friend either. For he had always held somewhat aloof from Rory Michel, suspiciously, as though he did not know what to make of that wanderer. But when the pinch came, he had been willing to bring sudden death on himself in order to warn Rory away from that trap.

It amazed Rory Michel. He had seen brave acts before, but never had he seen a thing that stirred him more than this!

What was to be said of the Apaches then?

Strangely enough, Rory felt no bitterness toward them. He had lived among them. He had seen them like gay children romping and playing together. He had experienced their generosity, their impulsiveness, their kindness. If they were savages, now, it was because they knew of no other way to act in time of war. As well as panthers from the jungle to act like house cats as to expect from Apache blood, once roused, the ways of civilized creatures!

And Rory, knowing what they were, looked upon them with a sort of impersonal interest, not as villains. He considered them as he would have considered gunpowder, something to be treated with infinite caution, but something which in itself might be more useful than dangerous.

So he came rounding back through the night until he swung up near the hollow from the side opposite to that where he had fled.

He could see clearly what was happening, for the

172

Indians were holding up a lantern, as it were, to their own doings. They had kindled a fire of brush, and by this illumination they were proceeding the looting of the wagon.

It was not in bar silver alone, it appeared, that Ware had collected the debts owing to him. He had picked up a great many articles of trade, as well as cash. A barrel of sugar had been staved in, and the red men were scooping it out by the handful and pouring it down their throats.

As children sit on a board fence and kick their heels while they eat pie, so the Apaches could not be still while the sweet stuff was flooding their throats, but every now and then they bounded into the air, awkwardly, and flung their arms about, usually with weapons in them that often grazed against some other person.

They had liquid to wash down the feast of sugar also. That liquid they drew from three casks which they had rolled out from the wagon bed. And by the squat, iron-bound look of the barrels, Rory could guess that the contents were whisky.

He breathed a little sigh of relief when he saw this.

For he knew that an Indian is soon drunk, soon furious, soon helpless. Helpless he wished them all, if only the contents of the whisky barrels were not spilled.

But what had become of the entire white party?

Dead, he made up his mind, at first.

He tethered the stallion at a good distance, in a coppice. Then he worked his way from cactus to cactus, from rock to rock, from shrub to shrub, coming momently nearer to the uproar about the wagon. If they had taken three scalps, counted their victories upon the dead, and managed to loot the wagon, it was no wonder that they were celebrating, for this was a glorious victory.

He came so close that at last he was sheltered behind a thick, spreading cactus not ten yards from the nearest of the prancing redskins. Here he reared up his head with caution and, looking through the glinting spines that sprang from the cactus leaves, he saw the entire picture, somewhat as one might look out through the scanty lashes of half-closed eyes.

The first thing that met his glance was a joy to him, for it was the broad-shouldered silhouette of Dean Ware squatting between him and the fire. He was tied hand and foot and, the better to secure him, the thong that bound his hands together behind his back passed on to the bridle of an Indian pony. If he attempted to move, he would soon have the animal plunging, and draw the attention of all toward him.

As for the cook, Blucher was dead and done for. He lay beside the wagon. Enough light struck his face to enable the watcher to recognize him and then he turned his eyes hastily away from the horror that he had seen.

Now he lay flat again, feeling weak and unnerved, amazed at this revolt of his nerves, he who felt that he could look on any horror in the world. But now the stillness of the dead and the madness of the living had made too sharp a contrast.

At first, no one paid any attention to Dean Ware, but presently one of the savages began to prance about in front of the captive with a tomahawk that cut circles about the ears of the white man. By the confused face of the Apache, young Rory judged that one of those blows might turn from play to earnest, and Ware's life would end that moment, but here a squat, waddling, powerfully made warrior approached the other and waved him away from Ware.

He who was warned off was in the prime of middle age: the other was comparatively a youngster, and yet he seemed to be in a position of authority. As he turned in profile and the fire struck full upon his face, Rory recognized him as that same youthful brave, whose life he had spared in the house of Ware and he wondered if the warrior were now returning good for good?

It would not have been beyond the Apache character, as Rory knew it. Now that he was sure, for the moment, of the safety of Ware, he paid more attention to the progress of the debauch, for that was what it was rapidly degenerating into.

174

They had found some drinking cups among the supplies of the wagon, and these were poured full and emptied down yawning throats until one barbarian, wide-shouldered, fitted with enormous muscles, actually heaved up a whisky barrel and closed his gaping mouth upon the bunghole.

He reeled as he drank, until a fit of coughing overcame him and he dropped the barrel with a crash to the ground.

No harm might have been done—except to the insides of the warrior—but the barrel struck a rock in its fall, a stave was smashed in, and the amber contents gushed out.

Another brave had been standing with hands prepared to take the barrel from the first drinker. When he saw this waste of the firewater, he uttered a yell, snatched out a knife and went for the staggering culprit.

"Strike home!" whispered Rory, grinning to himself.

But the blow did not fall.

That same squat, young brave whom he had set free was instantly in the path of the charge, and skillfully he tripped up the aggressor, who rolled head over heels.

Then the tide of whisky that leaked from the spoiled cask reached the fire, and instantly a tall column of flame was rushing upward, a mute testimonial to the power of that liquor.

Rory took heart as he watched the flame. He could swear that the stuff was almost pure alcohol to blaze so, and, if that were the case, it would be a helpless lot of Apaches who staggered around the wagon, before long.

The young chief, for that seemed to be his position, seemed to be equally aware of the danger. Now he was seen going from this man to that, dragging one brave and then another to some waiting pony, ordering him to mount, in some cases actually heaving the other upon the saddle.

But all of them would not go.

They had the sweet taste of the sugar in their throats, and the strong fire of the whisky in their blood. So off horseback they rumbled and went sprawling back to the sugar barrel and the two remaining whisky butts.

More and more, Rory felt at ease, more and more hope rose in him. Strange things had been accomplished, more than once in the West, by the combination of whisky fire and Indian flame!

The young chief, when he saw that his efforts were useless, drew back and took a place by the prisoner. For his own part, he had not touched the sugar, had not tasted the whiskey. His face was gradually darkening as he looked about at his companions.

He said in Spanish to Ware: "You see? The firewater turns my people into hogs. They roar and shout for a time. Then they fall down. You see that man?"

"I see him," said Ware, and the calm, full strength of his voice pleased Rory Michel.

"That is a great warrior. He had three sons. Two of them died very bravely. The youngest one is going to be great chief some day. This man is a hero. He never turns his back on an enemy. But now you see what is coming to him? Phaugh! It is not with rifles that the white men will beat us out of our land. It is with poison like this!"

Ware nodded his big head, gravely.

"Poison is the word for it," said he. "Poison—the best stuff to drink after a murder!"

"Why do you call it murder?" asked the brave.

Rory was now working his way, snakelike, among the rocks. He encountered the shadow, cast by the shoulders and head of Ware. And so he could hear the dialogue with perfect clearness.

"I never have harmed the Apaches," said Ware, "but they have tried to steal my horses and cattle. They have already killed two of my men. And now they intend to kill me."

"That is true," said the savage, calmly. "But then Black Arrow was killed by your people. Therefore, it was time for us to kill in return."

"The soldiers killed your young chief, not my people. My people were all at the mine, as you very well know."

"You are white. The soldiers are white. They are your people," insisted the Apache. "As for you, we are saving you until we go back to your house. There we will kill you slowly, in front of your people. You will be glad of that, as a brave man should be, because it will give you a chance of dying very bravely, and never making a sound, while your own squaw looks on at you."

Chapter 33

This pleasing picture of a gallant death made Ware turn his head and look up toward his captor, and Rory was amazed and pleased to see that he was smiling at the Apache. There was more in the mine owner than Rory had imagined. That was plain.

A sudden fury seized upon several of the Apaches at the same instant, and with a yowling like so many wild beasts they leaped at one another, while the young chief sprang away to intervene. It was not an easy task that he had before him. Half of the Indians were quite helpless, by this time, staggering about on uncertain legs, chanting, trying vainly to make their numb knees rise in the prancing steps of the war dance.

In a moment, Rory was at the back of Ware, muttering near his ear:

"Sit still—don't move your hand when I cut the thong. It's Rory Michel."

And Dean Ware, sitting rigidly, did not so much as turn his head from left to right, nor even part his lips to answer.

Yes, decided Rory, Ware was the proper father of such a girl as Nancy. There was the same stuff in them both, though it had been hammered into different shapes!

177

One touch of the knife made the hands of the prisoner free.

"Sit to one side and hitch your legs around!" ordered Rory. It was done, and the hand of Rory went out with the knife and freed the legs of Ware as well.

"Are you numb? Can you move?" demanded Rory.

"I don't know. There's some feeling in my feet still. I think that I can move," said Ware, in the faintest of whispers.

"There's a horse straight behind you," said Rory. "Stand up. Stretch. Try to feel your strength. Then turn and jump for the saddle, pull the horse around and ride straight up the hollow. Go straight ahead. I'll be close to you all the while!"

So he said, but he was not so sure.

He could wish, now, that he had not left the stallion so far to the rear, but he was afraid to waste time by going back for it. That young chief was still sober and some of the other braves were sufficiently calm to be efficient in a time of need. It would not do to take too many chances with them and their rifles.

He could only wish that all of the bar silver in the bed of that big covered wagon were its own weight of whisky, and all of that whisky was pouring down the throats of all of those Apaches, the young chief included. Then, and then only, could he really feel that they were safe.

He whispered a final word of caution.

"Count thirty, Ware. Then rise and try to get on your horse. When you're on it, ride like blazes up the hollow. You hear me?"

A faint nod of the head answered him.

"Good luck!" whispered Rory, in return, and he began to work back, snakelike, among the rocks, along the course by which he had come.

It was not nearly so easy to go backward as it had been to come on, but he finally gained the shadow of the cactus which had sheltered him before.

As he did so, he saw the shadow of Ware rise.

Looking closely, he was aware that, at the same

time, the young chief had settled the dispute among his followers. A moment of gravity, almost of silence followed, and Rory wished that Ware would have sufficient sense to see that, of all instants, this was the worst for an escape.

He could almost have shouted a warning, but at that moment he saw Dean Ware turn, grasp the bridle of the pony behind him, and half throw, half drag himself into the saddle.

A yell rose at the same instant; it seemed to Rory that rifle barrels were flashing under the firelight like swords beneath the blazing sun. And then, to his trouble and bewilderment, the pony dashed close to the fire and straight through the excited Apaches!

Guns exploded, but Rory thanked Heaven that there was no gun in the hands of the sober chief. Instead, that young worthy made a leap for the head of the pony, missed his grip and fell, while Ware was borne by the excited horse straight through the tangle of braves, and on into the sheltering shadows of the night beyond.

Had he been wounded? Had a bullet plowed through his body, and were his life and blood ebbing from him now? That could not be ascertained just now.

But Rory, rising, sprinted as hard as he could, back to the spot where he had tethered the stallion.

He had not had all the success he could have wished. But perhaps one life was all that he could have saved among three, even supposing that three had been breathing when he arrived on the spot.

Leaping into the saddle, he saw that half of the Apaches had mastered the fumes of the whisky sufficiently to be rushing at full speed in pursuit of the fugitive.

Well for Ware, then, if he had had the matchless speed of the black stallion beneath him, but he lacked it.

He had, instead, only an ordinary pony beneath him. His weight exceeded that of any of the Apaches. His horsemanship was almost infinitely poorer. He lacked the very language and the manner of riding which would ordinarily get the most out of such a mount.

179

No wonder that Rory put the stallion to full speed and that he dashed in pursuit.

Of all the Indians, there was only one whom he really feared, and that was the one truly sober warrior of the lot, the chief himself.

But that one was enough of a danger to overtake and murder Dean Ware. And thereby all the work of Rory on this night would be more than undone. Desperately he rode.

He could see that a number of the Apaches were still about the fire. Two or three, including the hero who had lifted the barrel to his mouth, had now fallen to the ground, a cheap prey. Others were uncertainly trying to capture their restless ponies and join in the pursuit.

But the entire lot looked to Rory more than nine-tenths incapacitated. Therefore he drove the black horse recklessly on, close past the fire and, turning in the saddle, he shouted to the liquor-stunned ears of the Apache.

They answered him with a whoop of dismay and astonishment. Guns exploded, but he heard not the whistling of a single bullet.

In the meantime, by that short cut, he had gained priceless ground. But he could not simply ride up past the entire party of the Apaches who were galloping in pursuit, racing their ponies. He would have to make some sort of a detour.

Which way would Ware turn, in case he were pressed hard? Which way would he strive to dodge, no matter how vainly?

Toward the mine, perhaps. Instinct might make him veer in that direction, to bring himself a little closer to home, in his time of need.

So to the right Rory sent the flying black and, crossing the first low ridge, he drove headlong up the next hollow, hoping to cut the line of Ware's flight, if the latter actually turned in that direction.

In the hollow to his left, he could hear the pounding of hoofs, the yelling of the maddened Indians. There would be no quarter, now, no pausing to make prisoners, but red death and red scalps taken from all who fell.

Then, just before him and on the left, he saw the silhouette of a horseman streak over the rise closely followed by a second rider.

The first was Ware. His upright carriage in the saddle, the bulk of his body contrasting with the horse, could be no other person. It was Ware, and, behind him, crouched low, as a cat about to spring, was an Indian. The moonlight flowed in dim lights upon his half-naked body; stretched in glistening line upon the barrel of his ready rifle.

Then Rory called, and the black horse answered as only it could. They closed fast. They gained hand over hand, when suddenly Rory saw the Indian sit upright in the saddle and turn toward him.

Had he seen? Had he guessed who that other single rider might be?

At any rate, Rory could risk no delay, for he saw the rifle of the pursuer now raised to his shoulder. Even firing from horseback, the Apache could hardly miss; he was not three lengths of his flying horse from the quarry.

Snap shooting by moonlight is no easy thing. But Rory told himself that his bullet dared not miss. He turned himself into steel. As he pulled the trigger of his revolver, he saw the Indian pony of the pursuer leap frantically, high into the air. He saw the rider unseated, arms and legs sprawling wildly into the air, the rifle falling one way, the Apache pitching headlong another. Then horse and man went down and rolled headlong on the slope.

Over the edge of the rise, a solid body of Indian riders now appeared, riding hard, but not as their leader had ridden. And Rory could shrewdly guess that he had managed to tag the chief whom he had feared so much.

As for the rest, half intoxicated as they were, it hardly mattered if they were on the trail, so long as

181

they could not come to grips, hand to hand with their quarry.

Past the head of them he went, racing the stallion still, and he heard them yelling, in one long, howling cry, the title which they had given to him. Drunk as they were, and even by moonlight, they had recognized the black horse and guessed at the name of the rider.

Past them, like the wind, he blew. And just before him was Ware, the fugitive. He saw him turn in the saddle once; then, again, a gun gleaming in his hand.

Loudly Rory shouted and then again before the leveled weapon that covered him was lowered. A moment later, he was at the side of Nancy's father and, turning, he saw that the Apaches were not gaining ground.

Some of them were actually pulling up, as though, in their whisky stupor, they told themselves that it was a hopeless and helpless matter to attempt to catch this maker of great medicine on his winged horse.

Side by side he rode with Dean Ware.

The giant cacti streamed past them, like gaunt sentinels, uselessly frozen at their posts. The hills moved like waves of the sea, pouring gradually to the rear, settling in their wake.

And Ware never turned his head toward his rescuer, but held his glance straight on, rigidly, like a soldier making a charge.

Yes, there was more to him than Rory had ever guessed before.

Chapter 34

The sharp, clear and pressing questions of Ware began after they had gone on for some distance. "Rory," said he, "those copper-skinned brutes told me that the entire place had been taken and my family murdered. Thank

182

God that you've escaped to let me know exactly what happened!"

"The Indians," answered Rory, "almost got us today. They were in the barn and ripping up the house a good deal with a plunging fire. But we managed to burn the barn. Before long, you'll be seeing the glow of the ruins off yonder."

"I suppose there was a surprise attack that carried everything before it?" asked Ware, cold agony in his voice.

"No," said Rory, "there's not a one at the house, Mexican or white, who has been so much as scratched, not up to the time that I left. And I left the barn burning as a torch to light up the surroundings. The Indians lied to you, Mr. Ware."

The latter pulled up his pony with a jerk. He grasped the high, broad pommel of the saddle and seemed about to fall to the ground.

"You're not breaking bad truth to me easily, Rory?" he pleaded. "You mean this."

"I mean every word. Not a soul at your house has been hurt."

Ware fairly groaned with relief. His head went back and his face was upturned for a moment exactly like a man who is about to fall in a faint.

It was a long moment before he could speak, and then he said in a deep and grave voice:

"I've seen them both dead. I've had the weight of it in my heart every moment since the Apaches told me. They're not men, Rory. They're fiends to have told me that. I saw it all wiped out. Not the mine. I didn't care about that—not about a thousand mines. But the two—"

He had to stop again.

"Tell me," he said, "how you managed to break out?"

"We had to burn the barn," said Rory, "so I made a bolt of it, and chucked in a little incendiary bomb that the captain had made."

"Captain?"

"Burn. He's with us."

"Burn's a good man. God bless him, I know that he'll fight. You, Rory, you rushed the barn, bombed it, and got away, and couldn't get back. I see that now."

"That's about the way of it. So I rambled down the road to see what might be happening to you on your way to the mine. You were a good deal on the mind of your family, Mr. Ware."

"I'm a little dizzy with it all," muttered the other. "The soldiers who were to have been posted there until—"

"Oh, well, Major Talmadge didn't know the country nor the ways of it very well," said Rory. "The result was that when the Apaches came down for a talk, one of them was shot through the head by Terris, a white renegade and ruffian, and Talmadge didn't have wit enough to hang up the rascal. So the Apaches have been doing some hanging and shooting on their own account"

Said Ware: "God knows that you've done enough to make me value you, man, but you talk, actually, as though you approved of those red demons. Yet if anything is proved, it is that I'm right—that I've always been right—they have to be wiped out root and branch, root and branch! The old saying is right: No good Indians except dead ones!"

Rory nodded.

"That's the old saying," he agreed. "And there'll be no peace in the West till it's forgotten. However, there's no use arguing about theories, Mr. Ware. We got our hands filled with trouble, you see. I'd like to know, however, how they happened to scoop you up so quickly that none of you had a chance to do any shooting. The wind covered up any other noise that was made."

"We were making good time," answered Ware. "I had collected nearly everything that was owing to me. I had part of the money in bar silver, and part of it in all sorts of goods. We had gone along very carefully all the way, with at least one man ranging ahead of the team to beat up the country for any possible danger that might be in our way. And there hadn't been so much as

184

a single alarm. Now we were so close to home that we paid no attention to precautions any longer. We went along in a group. I was riding beside the wagon, and poor Blucher was riding the near-leader.

"We got down to the bottom of the hollow, where you saw us, and then the trouble came up around us like a wave of darkness. One moment all was peaceful and easy. The next, I heard a bow twang, and saw Blucher tumble off the mule he was riding. I was pulling out a revolver when I saw a gleam of copper skin beside me, and there was an Indian, reaching for my head with a swing of his war club. I tried to duck, but the club clicked me behind the head and spilled me onto the road. That's the only reason that I'm alive now, that the first stroke just failed to brain me.

"When I came to, a knife was held to my throat, and the Apache had a good grip on my hair with his other hand. I don't know whether he was going to scalp me first and kill me afterward, or what. But I could judge that death was not a step away from me, until the fellow who seemed to be chief, the little bandy-legged man, came up and pushed the brave to one side. He talked Spanish to me and said that he remembered me, and that on one occasion I had him in my power and yet he was still alive. Therefore, he wanted to tell me that he would never permit me to be murdered, so long as I conducted myself as a peaceable prisoner.

"I was glad enough to be peaceful, Rory. And after they'd tied me up, I sat by the fire they'd made and watched them looting the wagon and prancing and dancing, full of whisky and sugar. That was when I heard the lies about the murder of my family. And a little later, I heard you whisper behind me. I never heard singing, Rory, that seemed half as pleasant to me as that whisper of yours. So now you have the story of what happened to me there in the hollow. Two good men were killed, there. And God give me a chance to avenge them, one way or another!"

His voice rose and rang, as he spoke the last words, but Rory Michel shrugged his shoulders.

185

"You know, Ware," said he, "that it's as wrong to blame an Apache for a killing as it is to blame a cat for stealing milk."

"Rory," exclaimed Ware, "you aren't going to defend them, still?"

"Let them rest for a little while," suggested Rory Michel. "It won't be long before they give us trouble enough at your house. We need a plan, Mr. Ware. What have you in mind?"

"There's nothing for it but a sudden rush," said Ware.

"To break through the line to the house, do you mean?"

"Yes. If we try the light of the dawn, Rory. That's a good time, when people are drowsing, and the light is very bad."

"Suppose that we get to the house, then?"

"It seems to me," said Ware, "that once I have a chance to fill my eyes with my wife and Nancy, I'll be ready to die. I don't care what happens, then. It seems to me, Rory, like the end of the world, and the filling of all happiness."

But Rory shook his head.

"It will be a shock to the Apaches," he admitted. "If we manage to get in as easily as we managed to get out, they may begin to think that we have Satan on our side. On the other hand they may be so furious that they'll settle down to starve us out if it takes them forever. They've had you, and they've lost you. At least one of their best warriors is dead, and another one was cut up at the barn. They've collected some loot in this little raid of theirs, but they haven't counted a coup or taken a scalp. And they won't want to look the other tribes in the face unless they can make a better report than they're showing now. You know that!"

"Perhaps that's true," said Ware. "If they sit down to a real siege, of course, they'll win, Rory."

"Of course, they will," agreed Michel. "What's the best plan?"

"I don't know, except to get inside the house and fight as well as we can—as I can, I mean to say, be-

186

cause there's no reason why you should try to squeeze yourself back into that death trap."

Rory shrugged his shoulders.

"Let that go," he suggested. "The way I see it, we won't get rid of the Apaches until we've cut the chief rope that holds them here."

"What chief rope?" asked Ware. "Their love of scalps?"

"No, their love of medicine. Big Horse is the fellow who keeps them pegged in on this spot," answered Rory. "I'll wager that the rest of them would scatter for plunder and scalps fast enough and leave this house of yours in peace. But Big Horse won't let 'em. He's making religion of the thing—the killing of me, you see?"

"But you're not inside the house any longer," protested Ware, "and there's no reason why you should return."

Rory sighed and shook his head.

"I don't know just what to say about it, Ware," said he, "but I'm sure that the Apaches are convinced that I can turn my horse into a hawk, and myself into a sparrow, and ride that horse onto the roof of your house and slip down the chimney—and there become horse and man all over again. You know, Ware, that once a man can make big medicine, he can do just about anything from the Indian viewpoint. When they take that house, they'll be mighty surprised if they don't find me inside the walls, no matter where they've last seen me."

"Magic, eh?" said Ware.

"Yes. Black magic. But Big Horse is the fellow we have to persuade before the tribe will leave this place."

"Very well," replied Ware. "You know a great deal more about the proper course of action than I do. I leave the thing to you, Rory. How can we possibly persuade Big Horse?"

"By putting a bullet or a knife blade under his fifth rib, right through his medicine shirt," said Rory.

"Medicine shirt?"

187

"Yes. His invulnerable medicine shirt, that turns the edge of a knife and laughs at bullets. If I can get rid of Mr. Big Horse, I think that the rest of 'em, chiefs and all, will feel that they're working against pretty important medicine; Big Horse and all his advice will seem several pegs worse than nothing, and inside of twenty-four hours, I'll bet that they'll break up and hit the trail looking for loot."

"You know, Rory," said the major, "you talk about the thing as calmly as though you could walk, invisible, straight into the Apache camp, put a bullet through Big Horse, and walk quietly out again."

"Well," said Rory, "something like that will have to be managed, I take it. That's the problem we have to solve; and all those lives in the houses are apt to depend on its solution."

Chapter 35

They kept straight on until they saw the red glow above the ruins of the barn. The night was wearing late, now, and the silver of the moonlight was being tarnished by the first dull beginnings of dawn. Ware muttered angrily when he saw the destruction of the big barn.

"It was that or else the end for all of us," Rory assured him, rather tartly.

"I know, Rory," said the mine owner. "I don't complain of what you did, man. I only complain of the bad luck and the accursed Apaches. The government will wake up, one of these days, and send out a force to clean them out of the country. Look, Rory, look! We'll have them swarming after us in another minute. There they go, and there, prowling! The infernal wolves!"

For in fact, three riders could be seen moving slowly

against the rim of the sky, humped on their horses. It looked as though they were riding patient rounds about the Ware buildings.

"That's Big Horse," said Rory. "He's a fellow with a brain. He's the sort to know how to blockade the house. They see us, perhaps, since we see them, but they can't tell that we're not Indians. Not at this distance and in this light. Ware, I see what has to be done, now. And you've got to help me."

"You be the general, my lad," said Ware. "You're worth more in a moment, in such business as this, than I am in an entire year! A lot more!"

"I've got to be inside your house, and yet stay outside it."

"Hello!" said Ware. "What's this?"

"The Apaches will have to think that I'm in that house. That's all."

"What sort of medicine are you going to work now?" asked Ware, half smiling through the dusk of the morning.

"This!" said Rory, and slipped to the ground.

He took off his coat, bulked his slicker big, wrapped the coat around it, and tied the coat at the neck and the hips. The stirrups he tied under the belly of the stallion. The coat he lashed into place upon the saddle.

Then he said to Ware:

"This isn't enough to fool a five-year-old child at midday, but it may fool even an Apache in this light. Take the reins of the Doctor and bolt for the house. Somebody inside is sure to be on the watch and you'll be seen and the door jerked open when you get there. Ride straight in. The Indians are sure to see you, but I hope they won't spot you until the last few jumps, and you'll be inside before they can stick you full of arrows. When they see the stallion with something on his back, they'll be sure that it is I."

Ware accepted the reins of the Doctor and stared rather helplessly at Rory Michel.

"And where will you be, my lad?" said he.

Rory lied with a bland face. "I? I'll be as safe as a kernel inside a nutshell. Don't worry about me. You

189

have the hard half of the job—to go in there and take command, and know that you're living in a trap you can't get out of. Because you'll never again be able to bolt through the line as I did. They'll be watching to keep people in; and after this morning, they'll be watching to keep people out, too; and they'll do it. My own plan takes too much time for telling; so let it drop. I'll be doing what I can. That's all I can say."

Ware suddenly reached out his hand.

Rory took it and received a strong grip.

"I'm growing young again," said Ware, "and a little humbler, I think. I'll take my marching orders from you, however. You're a wiser man than I am, Rory, and a braver and a keener. Good-by. Whatever you do, I know that it will be right."

He turned in his saddle, jerked his hat low over his eyes, and without further farewell he spurred his mustang forward. It started with a lunge; the reins of the stallion jerked tight, but in another moment he was galloping lightly at the side of the smaller horse, and Rory was delighted to see the stuffed coat inclining forward under the pull of the lashings to just the angle of a rider going at full speed.

Rory had sunk down behind some rocks, the moment his friend started, and through a cleft he watched the progress. He saw the three Apaches, now well in the distance, rein their mounts suddenly around and rush yelling around the house.

They were coming so fast that it seemed to Rory that they would be able to cut in between Ware and the house, but now a rifle spoke from a side window, and the Indians swerved far out to get safely from the gunfire. Before they could gain a shooting angle from which they could open fire upon Ware, the latter was at the veranda, the front door yawned open, and in went Ware and the stallion.

The Indian pony, however, was not so tractable, and pulling suddenly back, it raced across the open, the reins dangling.

The whole hive of Apaches was now up and stirring. The entire body of them, as it seemed to Rory, poured in a thundering flood around the place, letting off their guns with a roar.

And not a rifle shot answered them!

Rory was delighted by that silent gesture of contempt, but he could not help wishing that the Apaches were making less noise. If so, he could have heard, he was sure, certain sounds of rejoicing from within the house.

The light was brightening; the Apaches began to slacken in their furious rounds and draw back, as though realizing that very soon they would be in serious danger of distance shooting. At the same time, Rory knew that he must prepare to take distance, and he began to slip on hands and knees across the ground, or sometimes, flattened out, he wriggled like a snake from cover to cover. It was half an hour, and the dawn was fairly bright, before he got behind a considerable hummock.

That sheltered him for the moment from observation from the direction of the house, but he could not even dream how long that security might endure. The Indians were likely to be ranging all over the landscape, at any time of the day, and one glance at him would be the signal for his death.

He had with him a good rifle, a revolver, and plenty of ammunition, but he was without shelter. And, without a horse of any sort beneath him, he felt as though he were stripped of clothes, naked and helpless before cruel eyes.

The immensity of his danger flooded about him like a bright light. It was a thing for which, he thought, he had prepared himself but now he realized with a sinking heart that his chances were hardly worth consideration, not even a fool's consideration!

It was the absence of the stallion that stripped him so bare. He had grown accustomed to having the matchless sweep of that galloping stride at his command. To be without it was to be like a hawk without wings, stumbling feebly along the ground.

Whatever happened, however, he must not be seen. They were familiar with him now, so familiar that even a distant glance at his features would enable them to make sure of him. That would undo the thing for which he had given up the stallion.

There was in his pocket a large handkerchief of thin silk, and this he knotted about his face, drawing it up to the bridge of his nose and tying it at the nape of his neck. This secured him well enough from recognition. Until they actually laid hands on him and stripped the mask away, he would simply be an unknown quantity to any Apache observer.

Now that he was masked, he moved on, slowly, with infinite precautions, making so many pauses that it was almost as though he were attempting to deceive the broad, open eye of the heavens above him by the delicacy, the minute-hand slowness of his progress.

But what he was doing was melting from covert to covert, carefully marking out one spot of refuge before he left another.

In this manner, like a starving animal which stalks, and knows that it dies if it fails this day, Rory Michel worked his way to the side of the valley, toward the rougher, higher ground. So infinite were his precautions, that it was almost mid-morning before he arrived there, sun-scalded the length of his body, his brain ringing with heat waves, his eyes darkened, his body badly scratched with thorns and sharp edges of rock.

It was as though he had been swimming rather than crawling over that rough surface.

Now that he was again among good-sized rocks, he could breathe at ease for a few moments. So he lay down with his face in the shadow of a boulder, and groaned with sheer relief.

Above him, he looked up into the pale blue of that desert sky and watched, after a time, an arc of a buzzard's circle in the air, repeated fainter and farther and higher, until at last the whole light circle was distinctly drawn within the vision of Rory.

And he thought, as he looked up there, that there was nothing in the world really worth consideration, really worth preserving, except physical life itself. What mattered those people yonder in the house of Ware?

192

Let them be wiped out. He, Rory Michel, had done enough, and having done enough, it was high time for him to look to himself before he became buzzard food.

After all, his plan was too mad, too perilous. No one could possibly succeed in such an aim as he had. No other man would have conceived it in the first place. It was a child's dream, not the scheme of a grown man!

So said Rory to himself, and then he heard, far off, the neighing of a horse.

The thin, clear, metallic sound trembled through his brain as the whine of a distant trumpet rings in a soldier's ear. He was up at once and, looking down from his height, he saw before him an arm of the main valley and, in that arm, the entire extra horse-herd of the Apaches, easily kept under guard by two or three young warriors who ranged across the mouth of the gap.

The top of this small valley backed into an inaccessible ravine, tangled across with sharp boulders and brash, with small trees and cactus patches more formidable than barbed wire.

It made a convenient walled pasture, this pocket, and one that seemed perfectly secure. But Rory, lying on his stomach, his hands clasped under his chin, looked down into the hollow and told himself that it was as a fish hawk dips a fish from the water of the lake, as the trout skims securely along through the water, so he, Rory Michel, was going to dip down into the great trough of that valley and lay hands upon a horse and make off with it in spite of Apache courage, Apache cunning.

He forgot his love of life, his dread of the future, and the circling of the buzzard high in the pale sky above him. Once more he was only the consummate thief, prowling at a difficult problem, his eyes lighted with a joyous anticipation.

193

Chapter 36

It is said that no thief who is worth his salt can pass the Old Lady of Threadneedle Street without a giddiness of heart and brain. This is caused by a sudden and almost overmastering desire to penetrate through those walls, not for the sake of the treasures hidden within, but because of the glory of doing what no other man ever has accomplished and the joy of so huge a victory.

And so the heart of Rory Michel swelled in his Irish breast as he lay on the verge of the cliff and stared down into the hollow.

The thing was impossible, perhaps; all the more worthy of delightful contemplation, therefore. For what is worthwhile in this world except the accomplishment of the impossible?

So Rory told himself, at least, as he lay there under the white-hot blast of the sun, regardless of it, feeling nothing but his new and keen desire.

But even supposing that he succeeded in the impossible, and even supposing that he managed to capture one of the horses and lift it out of the gap, which horse should he take?

A good horse would hardly do. It must be the best. On the black stallion, he had been able to laugh in the face of pursuit. But when others were mounted as well as he, he could laugh no more. He knew this and, therefore, he studied the herd of horses with a keen eye.

These should be the best. The Indians were now sitting quietly down to a siege, and they would have at hand only their second string mounts. The best would be reserved to strengthen and fatten against the needs of the war trail. So here in the little cup-shaped valley should be the cream of the lot.

They were hard to choose among. Nearly all had fairly good lines, a sweep of mane and tail; wild-caught mustangs, many of them were, of course. Indian handling did not really tame one of the animals to any purpose. They were as wild in their spirits as ever.

Now and again, as they grazed, a sharp squeal rang up from the ravine, and two or three of the herd would form into a sudden twisting knot of fighters.

One of the herdsmen at this would dash in, swinging a whip, and scatter the battlers. And, yet a moment later, more trouble would begin.

It appeared to Rory that one horse was always included in this fighting, a compactly built gray stallion with a longer and scrawnier neck than most, and a lumpish, ugly head. But even from the distance above, Rory could see the flash of its eye and mark the solid proportions of the square quarters. There was the look of solid power, at least, about this animal.

Now, as he watched it closely, he saw that the wicked brute simply went from place to place hunting for trouble, and the instant he had a fair chance, like a beast of prey, he rushed at one of the other horses.

Finally, one of the herdsmen attached himself to the ugly-natured gray and hemmed him off in a corner. Once there, the stallion proceeded to graze calmly, with pricking ears of content, as though all the while his only desire had been to draw all the attention of the man to himself.

"If your feet are as fast as your brain is mean," said Rory, at last, "you're the horse for me, my ugly-headed lump of a gray. But if you're slow, I'm as good as dead before I start down into that draw!"

He meant what he said.

Once he intrusted himself to the back of a horse in the open, it would need wonderful speed, great stamina, or both, to hold off the rush of the Apaches in the pursuit. The Indians had been badgered enough. A little more, and they would be touched upon the raw.

Now that Rory had made his decision, he went down the side of the ravine with care. There were plenty of rocks and shrubs to shield him, but the slope was so great that in most places he was in serious danger of dislodging earth or fragments of rock.

And the least rattling of debris down the hill was sure to attract the attention of the guards.

An old Indian is three times as keen in his senses as a white man; a young Indian is three times as keen as a wolf.

He began to feel better and far more secure, finally, when he found unexpectedly, hidden behind boulders and brush, what looked as though it had once been a regularly used path. Cacti and brush had grown up on it, but there it remained, dimly defined and sloping at a fairly comfortable angle down to the bottom of the valley.

Along this he stole, now.

It was not easy going, even with this advantage of a road to walk on.

The cactus branches continually reached out and stabbed him or caught at him with more than cat-claws. Delicately he put them aside and the varnished branches of the shrubs. But slowly as he moved, he could not help dislodging a small amount of dust which floated upward and hung in the air to mark his passage like a few strands of spider webbing.

It was not much, but he did not want even so much as this to catch the fierce, quick eye of one of those boys.

So he paused, now and then, in the midst of his progress, to let the dust settle. But settle it would not, hanging as though by magic in the thick, hot air of the canyon.

So, cautiously, step by step, he moved on and down the path. The sun burned him and the close, windless air stifled him. Yet the heart of Rory Michel was as light as the heart of a child, running in the open air of the first spring day, after long, dark winter.

For there was danger near him, lying in waiting for

him, breathing about him, and he loved it for its own sake.

He was not far from the bottom of the path, when what seemed a large and safe stone rolled under the pressure of his foot and dissolved into a rattle of falling gravel among the brush.

He sank down to one knee, his upper lip curling back from his teeth, his eyes narrowed to glints of dangerous light. It was not fear that he felt. There were three guards over those horses, and there were more than three bullets in his revolver, alone.

Then that instinct to fight he banished, with difficulty. Once he revealed his position by gunfire, the Apaches would swarm through the hills after him. They would hunt him down by combing the ground, inch by inch. With the first report from one of his own weapons, he was no better than a dead man.

So Rory grew more and more tense as he waited for what result might follow upon the noise that he had made.

And, a moment later, he heard the voice snarling in Spanish: "It was a lizard going through the brush."

Venturing to peer through a tangle of cactus, he could see the reason for the Spanish speech, for it was a young Mexican half-breed who was speaking, a lad he had noted in the Apache camp when he had been working over young South Wind.

Broad-faced, slant-eyed, he was not a pretty picture, but Rory could have blessed the interpretation which the youth was now placing upon the noise in the brush.

With him was a pure-blood Apache of the tribe, one of Rising Bull's special followers, who had attached himself directly to the chief.

He answered, in the same tongue: "How big would a lizard have to be to make such a noise?"

"A lizard," said the half-breed, "that a bird chased —one of those little hawks. I've seen them do it. The lizard is so frightened that it runs blind. It knocks into stones and into twigs and stems of brush, in trying to get away. That's what made the rattling."

197

"Hai?" said the Apache, apparently not at all convinced.

"And why not?" asked the breed.

"Well, then what made the trail of dust there in the air?"

"What trail?"

"There, above the cactus and the tops of the shrubs."

"I don't see anything."

"Look again and rub your eyes, my friend."

"Well, I'm looking again. There is nothing in the air."

"A child could see it or an old woman. There is dust hanging there. There—there—when the wind stirs, it carries the dust away!"

Rory, gritting his teeth, felt the sweat streaming down his face rapidly. Three steps would bring either of those youngsters full upon him, and then it would be a matter of his life or theirs, and a rattle of gun shots.

"Well," said the breed, "you tell me, then, what could be in there?"

"I'll go see," said the Apache.

"Go, go!" exclaimed the other, impatiently. "Go and let the cactus tear your clothes, and your skin, for nothing. Maybe you think that the medicine man is in the house and out of it, too, and hiding here to look at you and me!"

And he laughed in a loud, bawling voice. "Well," said the Apache boy, "I cannot help thinking about him."

"You think he is here, eh?" mocked the breed.

"Who knows where he may be?" answered the Apache. "He is here, and he is there, and he is gone again. There is no other man like him. Big Horse is a child compared to him. He comes and he goes as he pleases. He takes the dying man by the hand and leads him back to life. Is that true?"

"Well, I have heard such things," said the breed.

"You have seen them, too," insisted the Indian.

"Perhaps, I have. What good, then, if he were there? He is here no longer. He has turned himself into thin air. If you saw dust, it was the dust he knocked away before he rose like a sightless bird and sailed away across the hills. Perhaps he is sitting on the roof of the white man's house, now. Perhaps he is tearing a scalp from the head of an Apache. But if he can do all that you say, you would never find him."

"No, that is true," said the Apache, suddenly convinced. "I don't know why I didn't think of that before. I didn't really expect that he would be there in the brush. But I heard the thing; perhaps it was a lizard, after all."

They went away together. Suddenly they began to laugh at something, and young Rory Michel nodded a little grimly to himself. It was a very good thing for all concerned that the Apache had not followed his first keen suspicions.

But what could be done now about the securing of a mount—about the taking of that gray stallion which meant so much to Rory Michel? He began to hum to himself, a far fainter sound than the murmur of a bee on the wing, and the old rioting desire for trouble worked up in him like a rising head of steam.

Chapter 37

It was the half-breed who had under his charge the gray stallion, and now the boy hurried off to prevent the wicked fighter from doing damage to the rest of the herd. But he had delayed too long. The gray had slipped back like a snake, and was already in the midst of a knot of excited, stamping snorting, squealing horses. Rory laughed to himself as he peered through the brush to watch the trouble.

The stallion was, in a sense, after his own heart!

In the meantime, he worked through the shrubbery

until he had come close to the edge of it, where he knew that he would be seen if the Indian boys took their attention from the tangle of fighting horses. But two of them were whooping and laughing with glee, while the breed yelled and raged and struck with his whip.

He did not separate the horses, but he managed to drive the whole herd over to the side of the valley; and down that edge of it they whirled until they were directly in front of Rory's place of concealment. One of them, just before that spot, tripped on its own trailing lariat and fell head over heels, while the others split and raged and struck with his whip.

That was the time for Rory. He waited until the gray was immediately in front of him. Then he slipped from his place of concealment like a wild cat and leaped on the back of the stallion. It was not easy. One hand had to grip his rifle, and the other catch up the lariat as it dangled from the neck of the horse.

But before the startled Indian lads knew what was happening, the gray fighter, with a strange, masked man on his back, was flying at a slant up what they had thought to be a sheer wall!

No wonder that they didn't commence shooting instantly. They were too staggered to see Rory putting the flashing horse through the tangle. Both the gray and Rory got many a deep and stinging scratch during that wild flight, but the horse seemed to think that it was being flogged on its way, flogged more cruelly than it had ever dreamed of being flogged before, and Rory was willing to take deeper excoriations than these for the sake of finding such an animal between his knees.

He was nearing the top of the declivity when the yells of the lads ended and rifles began to crack. But not a bullet came close enough to him in his ears, and in another moment he and the horse were over the high brim of the hill and cantering along the upper level.

A changed man was Rory now. The hawk had regained its lost wings. If they were not quite of the caliber that had borne him successfully away from so many dangers before this, they were at the least a match, he hoped, for nearly anything that the Apaches could bring against him.

He would have a good testing in a moment, he knew. Therefore he did not race the pony on this level. He looped the rope around its muzzle to serve as an effective rein, and kept the horse to an easy canter.

At that slow pace he felt that he could estimate better the strength of the animal, and he was delighted by the easy and supple strength of the hind quarters bearing him up, and he looked down with satisfaction along the slope of the shoulders.

Over the hill's top behind him swept the three herders. They had caught up their riding ponies; they were coming full tilt, yelling like three fiends, and now Rory let out the gray to its full speed.

He was delighted with the result. A poor traveler throws itself high, and the striding is ragged. A horse with a fast pace usually seems simply to pour itself out over the ground, devouring smoothly the road beneath. So did the gray pony pour itself, with its wicked head thrust well forward and its ears flattened until it looked like a cartoon of a flying snake.

Rory looked back, and he saw that the boys were already preparing to unlimber their rifles, sure sign that they considered the chase a lost cause. And so it was, for the gray was adding up distance between them with every stride that he made. Perhaps the three were not the finest horsemen in the tribe, but they would make up for skill with the lightness of weight.

They began to shoot, but they were too eager to slow up to a walk and take careful sight. The minute Rory was certain of that, he gave them no more attention, but devoted himself straight ahead to the riding of the pony. The noise of the explosions grew less and less. Gradually he knew that he was pulling almost out of range, and at last the firing ended altogether.

He could look back and see that the youngsters had halted. One was turning now and whipping away, no doubt to carry word of the theft to the warriors. A hot welcome would those three herders receive from the owner of the gray stallion! The two remaining, after a

201

moment, started forward again more leisurely upon the trail of Rory, not as though they expected to run him down, but merely to trail him for the party of avengers when they finally came up.

So Rory, passing over a rocky knoll, quickly dismounted, took the end of the lariat under his arm, and, lying flat in the rocks, drew careful aim. It was a five-hundred-yard shot, but he felt that he could knock either of the youngsters out of the saddle. However, that was not his desire. He felt no malice against them, but rather a sort of pity when he considered the treatment they were likely to receive at the hands of the older men. What he wanted to do was to scare them off to a greater distance, and he tried to drop a bullet on the ground just under the nose of the one who was nearer to him. He apparently succeeded. He saw the pony fling up its head with a start that almost unseated the rider. Turning his attention to the second boy, Rory taking aim, sent a bullet past his head!

That was enough. The two took to cover—dove for it, as it seemed—and Rory Michel went onto the bare back of the gray again, grinning with satisfaction. It would be a careful stalk before the lads came up to that rocky ridge, he felt. So he allowed himself time for a simple little trail problem to throw them completely off. It was not a difficult thing that he attempted, merely a changing of the angle of march in the midst of a surface of hard rock in the next gully.

Instead of driving straight ahead, he turned to the side and put the active pony into the shrubs that climbed the hillside. So, in another five minutes he was safe and high above the plain, could look as far as the Ware house with ease, could see the two young braves stalking with desperate skill and patience the shelter where they thought he was halted, and could mark the scampering progress of the messenger across the open.

Rory was very pleased with himself and with the horse that he was riding. It was a vicious brute, but its spirit had been thoroughly subdued by the rough treatment it had received. Blood was still trickling down from a hundred little rips and tears that the thorns and the cactus barbs had made as the horse rushed through, and not unnaturally it attributed all of this suffering to the will of its new rider.

It seemed to Rory that he was lifted out of his recent danger. His low position on the plain had been like his peril; his present height among the rocks was like his present safety. And he began to laugh softly, his eyes shining.

Then he saw the messenger disappear into the Indian camp.

It was a revelation to Rory the speed with which the Apaches swarmed out in answer to the appeal. It was like knocking upon a hornet's nest, so suddenly did the warriors pour out in a black cloud and come rushing across the rolling ground, pitching up and down over the rough going like so many reckless, racing ships in dangerous water.

He took off his mask and let it sag down about his throat, ready to be raised again in an instant, and, reining back, he was instantly lost in the thicket of scrub trees and brush behind him. All the world seemed fair to him, and as he went along he took out the big red, square-cut ruby and gloated over it. It was not key-shaped, but it would open many doors, he felt, before the end!

He came to a clearing, and first arranging the slip-knot so that it would not fall off the head of the stallion, he tied an end of the lariat to a small tree, lay down on his back in the shade, and was instantly asleep.

As for the hunting Apaches, perhaps there were two chances out of three that they would pick up his trail, but coming in such numbers, they were sure to make sufficient noise to warn the gray horse, and that wily warrior was almost certain to pass on the warning to him in sufficient time.

At any rate, who can be sure of his fate? Chances must be taken.

But the first thing that troubled Rory was the cool breath of the evening wind. He wakened cold, shivering, and starved with hunger. But when he stood up and shook his head once or twice it seemed to him that his troubles had all passed away.

He removed the sense of hunger by pulling up his belt two notches. He removed the dizziness by finding a runlet of water and bathing his face while the horse drank, then he mounted, and with his rifle balanced across the withers of the animal, he returned to the eminence from which he had overlooked the plain before.

The whole scene was reddened now by the sunset light. And through it he could dimly see the scattering of warriors who moved around the Ware buildings at a safe distance. He could also see the smoke rising above the orderly circles of the tepees which stood at a considerable distance behind the blackened site of the ruins of the barn. By the number of the lodges, he decided that the party must have been considerably recruited during the day. No doubt at this moment councils were under way in the camp of the redskins, and wise minds were being brought to bear upon that important question—was the medicine of Big Horse strong enough ever to counteract the evil power of the white magician?

He laughed as he thought of that. As if in answer to his laughter, he heard the faintest of stirrings in the trees behind him. The gray stallion heard it also, and whirled about to face it with such a suddenness that Rory was almost knocked from his seat. But swiftly as he and the horse had moved, they were far too late, for Rory saw a horseman half screened behind the nearest trees and the long gleam of a rifle barrel pointed steadily toward him.

He was about to throw himself from the back of the gray to the ground and trust to a snap shot with his revolver to solve his trouble when he saw the rifle slowly lowered.

Before he could recover from his amazement, he heard the familiar and pleasant voice of South Wind saying:

"Father, if you have sent for me, see! I am here!"

204

Chapter 38

Out into the open rode the son of Rising Bull, his right hand lifted in greeting, and Rory shook hands with him with a great grip.

"Whether I sent for you or not, I'm glad to see you, South Wind," said he.

"If you had not sent for me," said the boy, "how could I have found you? All the wisest warriors among my tribe have been hunting, and I am the only one who did not wish to find the trail. Therefore you have brought me to you!"

The statement of faith was so calm and sincere that Rory blinked as he listened to it. It was a thing against which he saw that he could not argue. To South Wind it was as clear as day that magic had led him to this spot. He would not tolerate any denial whatsoever of that power.

"Well," said Rory Michel, "I had to talk to you. I wanted to know how it is with you in the tribe and what is happening inside the lodges. Can you tell me, South Wind?"

"There is very much trouble," said South Wind. "Now we have lost several good warriors in a very short time. Black Arrow is dead, and Two Red Feathers is dead, also, and Big Horse is working hard to save the life of Spotted Buck, who was wounded when you threw fire into the big barn."

"But Spotted Buck is weakening, I suppose?" said Rory.

"How did you know that?" asked the boy gloomily. "Have you put a spell upon him? He is a good man, father. Will you lift the spell that you have put on him?"

205

"I have put no spell on him," said Rory, "but the truth is that there is no power in the medicine of Big Horse."

The boy said nothing.

And Rory went on: "Did you ever know Big Horse to make a real cure, South Wind?"

"Yes, yes," said the lad. "He has cured many people. He cannot always bring them back from the edge of death, when the body is already falling, so to speak, but he has done some wonderful things."

"Well, South Wind," said Rory, "I won't argue it with you. But tell me more about the camp. What is your father's place, now? Do the braves still hold it against him that he has tried to be a friend to me?"

"They talk against him a little," said South Wind. "But they don't talk very much. Mostly all of the talk is about you. Since you burned the barn, the strongest warriors are afraid. They say that you can hold lightning in your bare hand. Can you do that, father?"

Rory stared at the boy with wonder and almost with alarm.

Then he held out his hand.

"Look at my hand, South Wind," said he. "Do you think that that skin would hold fire any better than yours?"

South Wind shook his head. "I know that a man cannot tell so easily as that," he said. "It is what the mind does that keeps the fire out or lets it in. I am not a medicine man, father. I cannot explain these things, any more than I can explain how you cured me, only I know that I was saved! But I see that you will not answer questions, and that is not strange. If your secrets were stolen, that would be a sad thing for you. I ask no more."

"Does Big Horse still make medicine against me every day, you say?"

"Every day. Every day he burns sweet grass and herbs, chants, and does a medicine dance. I thought, if I ever saw you again, you would be more than half dead. It is strange to see you looking so strong, father!"

"There are two kinds of medicine making, South

Wind," said Rory. "One is big and strong. The other is little and weak. To make the little medicine, Big Horse is quite capable. But for the other he knows nothing. That is why he cannot hurt me, no matter how hard he tries."

South Wind nodded gravely.

"How long will they stay in that camp?" asked Rory.

"They will stay till they have torn down the walls of the houses stone by stone," said the boy.

"Are you sure?"

"Yes, I am sure. They are very angry—all of the braves."

"A man has to be very angry before he can tear down stone walls."

"Well, father, we have endured a great deal. To the other tribes of our people we will be a thing for laughter if we are beaten away from this place. Do you think that will happen?"

"I know that it will happen," said Rory grimly.

The boy started and sighed.

"Do you prophesy against us, father?" he asked meekly.

"I do."

"Then let me tell my people," said South Wind.

"How can you tell them that you have seen me? How can you say that and come back alive and without my scalp?"

"Why," said the boy, "all the warriors know that I am your friend. They could not expect me to be anything else, could they? Am I to give back knife thrusts and bullets in return for my life?"

"Very well, then," said Rory. "You may go back to the tribe and tell them what I have said."

"That we are bound to fail here?"

"Yes," said Rory.

"I shall tell them," said the boy. "By what sign shall I tell them?"

Rory was rather abashed at this unexpected return. "What sign?" he muttered.

"Yes," said South Wind. "If it is the will of the Sky People, what is the sign that they will send to us? Tell me, so that I may have the minds of my people prepared to see it, even if it is no more than the flying of three buzzards in the sky at a certain hour on a certain day."

Rory looked inside his mind, and he could find nothing on the spur of the moment. He could only find there the purpose which he had long been aware of—the killing of Big Horse.

Suddenly he said: "I will tell you, South Wind. I will tell you the sign that the Sky People will send to you."

"Good," said the boy. "For I know of many people who are able to read the future a little, but not many men have lived, I think, who could foretell the signs which the Sky People send!"

His face shone with curiosity and with pleasure as he waited for Rory Michel to make the revelation. Rory could have laughed had not the matter been far beyond the proper limit of laughter.

Then he said: "South Wind, this is what will happen in the camp of the Apaches. Go back and tell all of the braves. Call the chiefs together and say that you have seen me, and that this is true: the Sky People are angry with the Apaches. The Sky People love Rising Bull, and they, therefore, gave me the power to heal his son. Now they are blackening their faces against the Apaches because the braves listen to the voice of Big Horse. You must tell the warriors that, South Wind."

The boy sighed. "I am my father's son," said he, "and if I say such things, the braves will laugh at me, perhaps."

Rory nodded. "But I told you that I would give you a sign."

"Yes. What is the sign, father, so that I may be able to keep the men from laughing and make them all believe what I say?"

"The death of Big Horse will be the sign," said Rory.

"How?" exclaimed the boy.

"The death of Big Horse will be the sign."

"The death of Big Horse!" repeated young South

Wind, stricken with wonder. "And how will he die, father?"

"No man shall strike him," said Rory, "but the Sky People will."

"With a bullet or with a knife or with a sudden sickness?" asked South Wind, wide-eyed with astonishment.

To be sure, he was offering to Rory a good deal of leeway in making his choice of weapons, but the latter could hardly pitch on the right one on the spur of the moment.

"I see blood on the face of Big Horse," said Rory. "That is all that I can tell you, South Wind. You know that I cannot see every small part of what the Sky People do."

"True," nodded South Wind. "But what you see is very wonderful, father. It is a thing to hear, but hardly to believe. *Hai!*" he cried out. "How the warriors will jump when I tell them what the sign is to be! I can see how the eyes of Big Horse will roll in his head. He will start making medicine at once, and he had better. All of his medicine will not save him, I think!"

"Yes," said Rory surprisingly, "he may be saved."

"He may? And how? I thought that the judgment had gone out against him?"

"You see how the thing goes," answered Michel. "If the Sky People have made up their minds, they can unmake them again when the man they speak against changes his bad ways and takes to good ways."

"What ways must Big Horse take to?" asked the boy, still wide-eyed.

"He must tell all the braves that the way to save themselves from danger is to leave this region at once and go away. He must set them the first example and go himself. If he does these things, then he will not have to die."

"He cannot do that," said South Wind, shaking his head. "He cannot suddenly change his mind when he receives the threat from you, or else the warriors may say that he is afraid."

209

"There is a time to be afraid," declared Rory sternly, "when the Sky People are about to reveal themselves. But if Big Horse is so brave that he is a fool, he will not persuade his people to leave the whites alone and he will continue to make medicine against me, and so the sign of the Sky People will be accomplished upon him. Do you hear me, South Wind?"

"I hear you, father," said the boy, plainly frightened.

"Now go back to your people," said Rory, "and tell them everything that I have said to you."

"I shall," said South Wind.

"And, in the whole tribe, give only your father a good word and my greeting. Say that there is peace between him and me, peace forever."

"That is good," muttered South Wind. "Father, shall I go now?"

"Yes, go now," said Rory. "It is almost the end of the day, and what you have to tell them, the Apaches will want to think of before the darkness comes down on them."

"There is only one thing more," said the boy. "You have told me a great deal. Tell me this, in addition. Tell me, if the Apaches do not leave their camp, when will the sign be given to them and Big Horse be struck dead by the Sky People?"

The very blood in the body of Rory turned to ice.

"This very night!" he shouted, and South Wind, backing his horse, whirled and fled as though pursued.

Chapter 39

When young South Wind left the height and started for the camp, galloping his horse like one possessed until he came near the tepees, he uttered a ringing alarum cry such as the men give when the enemy is about to charge in upon them.

The warriors sprang out of their tepees, gripping weapons, but saw only the single horseman, the son of Rising Bull.

Had he gone mad?

As he passed them, he shouted to all men to come at once to the central circle, before the lodge of the chief, his father. The words whipped from his lips and he was gone. When the first curious listeners came up, South Wind was already kindling a fire in the open—not a big fire for heat, but a little fire for illumination. He wanted to be able to see the faces of his listeners; and he wanted them, above all, to be able to see his own face.

Now, for the first time in his life, he occupied a really important role which proved, more than anything else he had done, that he was worthy to be considered a man. To him the white medicine man had revealed himself and the will of the Sky People—if only he could convince the warriors that what he said was true!

They came hurrying, most of them wrapped in blankets, wide-shouldered and burly fellows who looked deceptively fat under their robes. Wives and children poured behind them. And the smaller of the children dove straight ahead through the forest of legs and elbows, scratched and lunged and fought their way through until they came out in the front rank. These little ones stood up, bare as frogs, brown-bodied, with coppery high lights on the skin, planting their small fists on their hips and looking up at the orator.

Rising Bull, somewhat alarmed at the formality of these preparations, came to the side of his son.

"South Wind," he said, "what has happened? You have not been drinking firewater? You have not decided to make a great, foolish joke?"

South Wind turned his handsome young head and answered in two words: "The father!"

And Rising Bull gasped: "You have seen him?"

"Yes," said the boy.

It was enough to settle any doubts in the mind of the chief about the right of his son to address the assembly of the Apaches. He drew back, rather proud of the new distinction which was to descend upon his family. And now the whole assemblage, except for the outlying scouts who encircled the house of Ware, was packed in close around the fire and the speaker.

It made a wild picture. Their faces, most of them ugly, were picked out and set glistening by the flames, the glow of the fire touching the face of the speaker himself. Here and there, like a spark flying from the fire, the light glinted along the blade of a spear on which some warrior was resting.

When the right time had come, young South Wind said: "I have called you because I have heard of a great word and a great medicine for my people."

"Whose word?" asked the voice of Big Horse as he shouldered his way importantly forward, forcing the warriors to give place to him by the sheer influence of his supposed spiritual power.

"The word of the great magician, the prophet, the white father who brought me back from the dead," said the boy.

There was a derisive muttering from Big Horse. Now he had arrived at the front line of the listeners, and there he looked fully and squarely upon the face of the boy, though South Wind pretended to be ignorant of the sneer which the tribe's greatest medicine man was wearing.

"I was watching the house into which the white man

skulked this morning. I have watched it all day," said Big Horse. "And that is why I know that he is still in there and that you did not go close enough to talk to him. What words are you prepared to say now, South Wind?"

The boy was infuriated; the more so because he saw all heads beginning to turn toward the older man. He knew that his own veracity would be doubted. He knew that attention would be diverted to Big Horse, and instead of having his chance to make a stirring appeal, he would have to submit to a dialogue.

"I am prepared to speak the truth," said South Wind.

"Speak the truth, then," said Big Horse, "so far as you know it, but do not say that you have talked to the white fox who stole back inside the house of the white men this morning."

"I speak truth," insisted the boy, "and I say that I saw him!"

"Today?"

"Yes!"

"And how close?" sneered Big Horse.

"Closer than you stand to me. I held his hand!"

"You held the hand of our enemy!" shouted Big Horse in anger.

"He is my friend. All my people know that. I held his hand. I heard his voice, and he heard mine."

"You heard and held the hand of a foolish ghost!" shouted Big Horse. "With my own eyes I saw that he did not leave the house, where he had entered this morning."

"Your own eyes are dull," said South Wind, panting with excitement. "He turned himself into a mist as thin as the wind, and your medicine was not strong enough to let you see it!"

"What you say?" exclaimed the medicine man. "You say that it was the man?"

"I say that it was."

"Tell me, then," said the medicine man, "some sign that will help us to believe you?"

"I will tell you by describing the horse that he rode."

"What horse, then?" asked Big Horse. "One with the wings of a hawk?"

"No, not with wings, but a good horse," said the boy. "You, of all people, should know. It was your own gray horse that was stolen away today!"

The effect was instantaneous; a universal grunt showed the decisiveness of the hit, and the medicine man actually rose once or twice upon the tips of his toes and seemed about to shout an insult, his face was so convulsed with his anger.

But Big Horse, being intensely angered, and by no means yet convinced, still refused to let the speech go on smoothly, and insisted, by the force of his more eminent position, in reducing it to a dialogue. He next asked:

"Did he tell you wise things, this ghost of a white man, South Wind? What did he tell you that we should hear?"

"He told me that we must leave this place."

"Ah, ha!" cried the medicine man. "That I could have suspected. We know that he would be glad to drive us away. He would be glad to see us gone, so that he could have much glory, and the red eye, as well. So he sent you to come and lie to us and whine to us, did he?"

The whole body of South Wind quivered with rage, but he knew that if he lost his temper in the presence of the older men of the tribe, he would lose caste, since lack of self-control is despised among all red men.

So South Wind simply said: "He did not send me to whine to you and beg of you. He sent me to give you a good warning that may save many lives."

"We can take care of our own lives!" said the medicine man.

There was a deep, growling assent to this.

"Come, come!" urged Big Horse. "We have been standing here for a long time, and you have told us almost nothing!"

"Because your own words fill the whole lodge," answered the boy with dignity.

There was a sudden shout of laughter at the truth

214

and the aptness of this hit. Even Big Horse could not find a retort for the moment, and swayed heavily from side to side against the shoulders of the neighboring braves, breathing hard.

In this slight pause the lad went on:

"Now the braves hear me. I tell them that I have heard from the true speaker, the great healer whose work you have seen, and he tells me that there will be disasters for the Apaches unless they leave this camp."

"Ha!" cried out Big Horse. "And what signs will be sent if he is a true speaker?"

"They will not be birds in the sky," answered the boy grimly.

"No? When will they come, whatever they may be?"

"At night," said the boy.

"A good time for sending signs," said the medicine man, looking around him with a triumphant sneer. "The Sky People do not send signs at such a time unless it be lightning in the sky."

"It will not be lightning in the sky. It will be blood on the ground," said the boy.

"Ha!" exclaimed Big Horse, impressed in spite of himself by the solemn dignity and assurance of the boy. "Did you say that the sign will be blood on the ground?"

"Yes," said South Wind.

"And at night?"

"Yes, this night!"

"Whose blood, then!" exclaimed the medicine man.

And he pointed a challenging hand at the boy.

"Yours!" shouted South Wind, half mad with excitement.

A roar of excitement went up. Heads tossed like waves. As for Big Horse, he was so completely thunderstruck that he could only gape and stagger like one drunk.

Young South Wind went on, his voice ringing:

"You are to die tonight! That is the sign to this people, unless you change your ways and work hard to persuade everyone to leave, set them the good example and lead the way from this camp, far off!"

Then Big Horse, recovering his breath, roared in a voice of thunder:

"I, Big Horse, now defy that bad prophet. I will show everyone that his medicine is weak. I shall be alive in the morning, and then who will believe in the white liar? South Wind, too; you will be laughed at all your life. You have had a dream, like a sick boy or an old woman! But I, Big Horse, will be living when the morning dawns. Let everyone know that that is what I am saying. I, Big Horse, shall live through this night and prove who are fools and who are wise men. Friends, listen to me! I am talking, now!"

But no one paid very much attention to him. When they looked at Big Horse, it was as at one already sick to death.

Chapter 40

What was happening inside the village, Rory Michel could not know. He was only aware that he was taking on himself the most perilous adventure of his whole existence when he approached the lodges of the Apaches.

He had no plan really. The whole affair was so much a matter of chance that he could only make one step after another, hoping that he would reach a goal.

Two hundred yards from the gleam of the fires among the tents he could see dim forms passing between him and the lodges, so in a little swale of ground he tethered the tough gray mustang which had meant so much to him on this day. It had finished serving him for the moment, at least.

As nearly as he could calculate, the distance from the hollow where the horse was left to the verge of the camp was about two hundred yards. And unless he finished his business before moonrise, the bright little gray would then stand out to the eye like a piece of polished silver or a patch of water. Two hundred yards was not far. It was, however, some twenty-odd seconds in actual time, and in twenty seconds an Apache could catch a horse and race farther than a furlong. However, if he had a start of two breaths over any pursuers, he would have to run and hope.

No matter how well affairs went for him in the village, he was well aware that the most perilous part of his task was almost sure to be his attempt to get out of it after his dealings with Big Horse.

It was the thick, smoky darkness that comes just at the end of twilight when the night seems as dark as it can be, yet constantly grows blacker, the stars increasing in fire and in brilliance; and now he was close enough to make out that a steady procession of men moved around and around the camp. They were mounted, and each followed the other at a distance so close that the man next behind always could make out clearly the form of his leader. It seemed to Rory that there must be at least a dozen riders promenading in this fashion around and around the tepees.

If he could see them, it would not be long before they could see him, though to be sure he had the advantage of marking them out against the scattering points of fire within the camp and the common glow of the entire place, dim and uncertain as it was. However, he was of a mind to take every precaution.

He abandoned his rifle, well marking the place where he left it. If he came out of the camp again in this direction, he would not want to be bothered with a weapon of its weight until he was close to his horse, if even then. He had with him, as he forged ahead, one Colt revolver and a hunting knife as sharp as a razor blade.

He went on his hands and knees, and even in this position he did not go steadily, but flattened out on the ground from time to time. There was nothing to aid him except the dimness of the light. There was no sign of cover. There were only the stones scattered around the ground. When he paused, he stopped, flattening

217

out, and curled himself up to resemble a boulder as well as he could.

That small trick, the starlight, and his prayers, were all that could see him through the line.

When he came nearer to the path along which the mounted sentinels moved, he went very slowly. He chose for his moment of locomotion the instant that a leading rider had gone by; then he moved cautiously ahead for a little, until the rider behind was coming up.

By slow spurts of this sort he was enabled to draw up to the path of the riders and then to work his way onto it.

That was the moment of greatest peril, he well knew. If he paused, lying straight in the path, they were almost certain to find him. If he tried to cross the path too quickly, then he would draw attention even more surely, as it is well known that a moving form is ten times as conspicuous in any light as one crawling or motionless.

So he lay, one moment, with the feet of the horses stamping dust into his very face, and the next in expectation of receiving a lance thrust through his ribs.

As each horse went on, he crawled forward once more, looking back and aside toward the next rider in the procession. He could have laughed at his own folly in dreaming that he might escape in this manner. Of course, he could not get clear! He could see that next rider too clearly now. So, as he slipped over on his side and rolled into a ball again, he was ready with his revolver to make a death struggle against hopeless odds.

There was a sudden shout from the Indian behind, the rush of hoofs, and then a pony vaulted over Rory. He had not moved. He had seen the Apache coming at full lunge, with spear lowered, body bent behind it. And he had not moved the gun in his hand because terror simply froze his limbs and made him incapable of action.

And the lance had not gone home with its thrust!

The Apache would turn about. His fellows would come. They would play with the foolish white man as cats with a mouse!

But no! There was a brief interruption for the riders, a guttural calling back and forth. Then the rounds of the guards were resumed!

Rory, weak and sick, recovered himself a little and began to move off once more with the same pulsations which he had used in approaching. But he was even more careful now.

For now they had him between them and the lights of the village, and therefore his visibility was increased tenfold!

As he moved he wondered what had happened in the mind of the Indian who had rushed up with the leveled lance.

Perhaps the fellow had thought that he saw a movement in one of the supposed stones and had charged it, but at the last instant refrained from shattering the fine point of his lance upon solid rock only to gain the scorn of his mates. The darkness was very thick indeed, and the immobility of Rory had perhaps saved him in the desperate pinch.

He was drawing up to the verge of the village now when a new and unexpected danger came straight upon him. It was a solitary warrior, wrapped in his robe, who came stepping out into the darkness. Perhaps he was more than half dazed by the completeness of the dark. At any rate, he suddenly stubbed his toe against the ribs of Rory and went down.

The Apache fell with a sound that Rory would never forget, a soft, whining noise, and even while he dropped through the air, Rory saw the glistening of a bared knife, as ready as the teeth of any wolf.

To pull the trigger of the revolver would be to sign his own death warrant. Instead, Rory struck hard, upward, with the heel of the gun, and he felt it smash heavily into the face of the man. The head of the Apache sagged back, and he lay twisted and misshapen along the ground.

There might be a grimmer ending to this meeting. It was life or death for Rory, as he well knew, and thrusting the revolver back into his clothes, he pulled out his knife and kneeled above the Indian.

His left hand felt above the heart of the unconscious victim. His ear he inclined to listen to the breathing. But he was both horrified and relieved to find neither pulse nor breath, as it seemed to him—horrified to think that life had been smashed out of the brain of the brave by that unexpected stroke in the dark, and relieved to know that he would not have to drive home the knife in a senseless body.

He would let him lie in peace until they found him in the morning or later on in the night. In the meantime, that robe was exactly to the taste of Rory.

He picked it up and swept it about his body. From head to foot he was now covered in it, and he moved on as he had seen certain of the Indians walking in the camp from time to time, when they did not wish to speak to others of the tribe, when they wished to show that their thoughts were like a wall between them and the rest of the world. So Rory arose, and, swathed in that robe, he walked slowly, but straight into the maelstrom perils of that Indian encampment.

Now a word, a look, a single false gesture would reveal him to the keenest eyes in the world, and he would die more hideously than the brains of white men could conceive of, even.

He told himself, once more, that there was no gain in straining his mind for a plan. He could only put one foot ahead of another and trust that fate would bring him to an end of some sort.

Under the muffling hood of the robe, he made sure that the entire camp was in a state of busy preparation. By firelight here and there he saw weapons being prepared, and busy men and women. The little boys were out, prancing even at this late hour through the mazes of the war dance, leaping, letting out bloodcurdling whoops.

Then a heavy hand fell upon the shoulder of Rory, and he glanced aside to see the burly form of one of the lesser chiefs, a veritable Hercules of strength. He muttered something in the harsh Apache tongue, which was totally unknown to Rory, and jerked a thumb over his shoulder as though calling the attention of the promenader to other business. But Rory, because he could think of nothing else to do, moved on with a measured step.

The chief followed angrily, gripped at his shoulder again, and seemed on the verge of taking a strong hand with the silent warrior. Then Rory tried a trick which he had learned when he was a child and in a hard school. He pivoted on one heel, and without throwing off the robe, he raised his right hand and brought it down, opened, the edge of the palm like the edge of a cleaver, right upon the tensed cords in the middle of the Apache's arm. The blow was like the fall of an iron rod. The chief, with a grunt that was half a groan, started back, and then, with a shout, would have rushed upon Rory.

But he checked himself. His right arm was hanging helpless at his side, and would continue to hang there helpless for some moments. With his left hand, the warrior did not choose to close with such a dangerous and crafty foeman in the stroke of whose hand there was paralysis.

So the chief paused, and Rory moved on, slowly, step by step.

He had already passed through three separate dangers where his life had hung precariously in the balance. And now there was a great surge of relief and belief in him. A feeling arose that if he had been permitted to go this far by tyrant fortune, he would not be thwarted again at the door of success.

There was now a new and annoying feature. At sight of the manner in which he had foiled the chief a dozen delighted youngsters came prancing after him. He might avoid the eyes of a ferret; he would not avoid detection from these bright scamps!

Chapter 41

They thronged about him with the impudence of all boys, of all ages, of all nations. Your Indian youngster is proverbially spoiled and pampered and given his way among men. And now these lads scampered around Rory closely and began to reach out their hand and pluck at his blanket.

He could think of only one thing to do, and he did it: a piece of acting that might scatter them with superstitious awe, to which all Indians are so susceptible. Gathering part of the robe around his hand, he turned and slowly raised his right arm above his head, at the same time drawing the upper flap of the robe closely across his face.

He was like a scarecrow, or a stuffed, lifeless figure rather than a man. There was only the lofty gesture to suggest actual flesh and blood.

Not a sound came from the youngsters. He remained for half a minute in this posture, and then suddenly slipped the flap enough to permit himself to look out.

They had taken that gesture, no doubt, to be a heavily impending curse if they did not remove themselves from his path, and they had gone like so many scampering rabbits.

Rory, faintly smiling, turned and went on his way.

He knew well enough the general direction he would have to take, which was toward the center of the camp, where the medicine man was sure to have his lodge. And there he would find a very alert Big Horse waiting. The carefully circling line of watchers outside of the camp was proof enough of the lengths to which Big Horse was going in order to ward off his fate.

Now, as he came still nearer to the center of the camp, he was aware of a voice chanting, then wailing in a sort of broken dirge. Next he heard the sound of rattles shaken, and occasionally a heavy stroke falling with a boom upon a drum. Could that be the medine man?

It was he, and perhaps others with him, for now Rory came in sight of the lodge, well known to him by the ornaments and cabalistic signs painted all over the skins. And out of that tepee poured the chanting and the clash of rattles which he had heard.

Before the face of the tent there were at least a score of warriors gathered, and each of them, Rory noted with surprise, was muffled in a robe very much as he was. Perhaps when they came so close as to hear the making of a potent medicine they did not wish to have their faces seen by the spirits which Big Horse was summoning!

At any rate, they stood very quietly, listening though now and then one of them would start and mutter something as if surprised or interested.

Rory melted for a moment into the rear of that waiting group, and presently he heard a voice—was it not the voice of that same half-breed whom he had despoiled of the gray horse and much reputation that same day?—saying to another figure softly:

"This is a very great medicine. This is strong enough to cover the sky with clouds."

"It is strong enough to put out the stars!" said the other who had been addressed.

"What will the white man do against it?"

"He has done many things before. He can make himself invisible. He may be standing here among us this moment!"

The hit was so close to home that Rory could hardly keep back an exclamation. And the boy who had spoken first actually turned around and looked sharply toward him.

"I," said the boy, who was plainly the herdsman, "saw him make the gray pony fly today over the hill. No horse could have run as the gray horse ran."

"Big Horse will put a spell on you for losing that stallion," replied the other.

Rory did not wait to hear any more of this, but drifted back into the darkness; and then, gradually, moved off behind the other tepees until he had come, in a half circle, right up behind the lodge of the medicine man.

There was no sign of another person here. The audience which had gathered confined itself strictly to the region just in front of the lodge. Inside of this a fire glimmered through the semitranslucent hides. Above the lodge a thick column of white smoke was ascending, rising straight as a pillar through the windless air. The odor of aromatic herbs was heavy about the place.

Rory was instantly kneeling beside the ground flap of the lodge, which was furled up or let down according to the state of the weather. He examined the thongs which bound the nearest section of it, and then cut them rapidly until he felt this portion of the flap ready to come away in his hands. But still he paused, for he could see the shadow of the medicine man prancing around inside the tepee with a great shouting and clashing of rattles.

He waited until the shadow swung out of view to his right, then he dropped the section of skin and slipped quickly under.

Before him there stood a number of those packages of goods of which Big Horse was so proud, a part of his wealth, and these still concealed Rory as he watched the worker of magic make another round of the place.

Big Horse had donned his best regalia for controlling the spirits, which must have been a wolfish lot in his estimation. A bearskin was drawn over his shoulders, and the gaping, grinning head was mounted above the head of Big Horse, making his seem a giant of strength and of ugliness. The arms and paws of the skin hung dangling about the body of the medicine man.

As if the bear's head were not enough, there was a hideously painted mask to conceal his face; he shook a

224

great rattle in either hand, and about each ankle there was a thick circle of the rattles of snakes.

This nightmare Rory saw as through a mist, for the dense white smoke now was rolling through the lodge as a fog rolls in from the sea. A part of it only was able to rise through the vent, and the rest steamed out to the sides and closely filled the place.

But yet there was light enough for Rory's revolver!

He drew his aim, and then found that he could not curl his forefinger about the trigger!

He tried to remember now all the evil that he ever had heard about Big Horse. There was plenty of it. Covetous, cruel, vicious in every way, the medicine man retained his position in the tribe only because he was strong in war and kept a hold upon the superstitious fears of the braves. He was generally hated as much as he was feared.

But to shoot down this worker of miracles in cold blood was too much for the Nordic blood of Rory.

He knew that he was more than half mad to attempt what now came into his mind, but there was something in the idea that appealed irresistibly to his impish imagination.

He stood up, dropped the robe from him, and was revealed before the medicine man!

Big Horse, stopping short, staggered heavily, seemed about to fall forward into the red blink of the fire, and then mastered himself and drew himself erect. Over the hollow of his left arm he threw the length of a rifle. The hands of Rory were empty. And how could Big Horse guess with what lightning speed the white man could summon a revolver into his hand!

The first shock of surprise having passed, the medicine man seemed to swell and expand with pride.

Suddenly he shouted loudly in Spanish: "See! I have drawn you in. I hold you here helpless. I have drawn you here, where the Apaches will be able to see you die!"

And Rory answered with an equal loudness:

"I have come to laugh at you, Big Horse. My spirit

has come here and floated through the Apache camp. It is not my body that is here, Big Horse. It is only my spirit, which the Sky People have drawn out of my body and sent here to kill you!"

All of these words were apparently audible to the Apaches outside the tent, and there was a sudden outbreak of exclamations beyond the lodge, though these were instantly muffled and controlled.

"Your spirit?" exclaimed Big Horse. "I see the smoke curl about you. You are as solid as the trunk of a tree, and I shall soon send a deadly bullet tearing through your body."

"You will see, Big Horse," said Rory. "Your rifle cannot hurt me any more than it could hurt the bodiless air. The bullet will turn and strike back through your own body. All of this has been promised to me by the Sky People. For you have been a bad man, Big Horse, and they are not pleased with you!"

"The Sky People," said the medicine man, "are all my friends. They speak to me. They have been speaking to me tonight. I asked them to bring you here, so that I could count my coup on you and take your scalp, and now I see you standing here."

"It is only my ghost that you see," said Rory. "My body is lying far away in the hills. It would be an unhappy thing for me if an Apache were to find it there, stretched on the ground, seeming to sleep. Then the coups would be counted and the scalp would be taken, but never by you, for my ghost has the power to kill you, and you must die. Do you hear me, Big Horse? The last day of your life has come to you!"

Big Horse tried to laugh, but the sound seemed to choke him. He swayed his body, as though striving to work up a passion through physical gestures.

"You have come among my people and tried to steal my name and my strength from me," he shouted. "But now you will see that all your magic is not equal to the magic that is in this rifle. It is your last day which has come. And my hunting knife will have your scalp. Because of your death, I shall be more famous and stronger than ever! It is the end—and the red eye shall come back to me!"

"Look!" said Rory with a sudden gesture. "It is here only to dazzle and blind you!"

Snatching the ruby from his pocket, he held it up where the firelight winked and glimmered through it.

Big Horse uttered a faint cry of rage and jerked up the rifle to his shoulder, but the right hand of Rory Michel was already on the butt of his revolver. He barely drew it clear from his clothes and fired, hip-high.

The heavier clang of the rifle answered him at once, but the bullet flicked high above the head of Rory through the wall of the lodge, and Big Horse, dead before he struck the ground, leaned and fell forward heavily, straight into the fire that burned in the center of the lodge.

Chapter 42

Rory, slipping back through the gap in the flap of the lodge, pulled after him enough of the wrapped packages to block the way by which he had come, and he had hardly done so when he heard a number of men rush into the lodge, and instantly there was a wild uproar of alarm, many voices shouting together.

Rory did not wait. If this were not a convincing bit of magic, if they did not believe that the big-caliber revolver bullet which had smashed home between the eyes of the magician had really come from the rifle of Big Horse himself, and been turned back against him by the direct intervention of the Sky People, then, it seemed to Rory, all the power of credence had been removed from the souls of the Apaches.

For his own part, he muffled himself once more in the stolen robe and walked straight through the camp.

He was not hindered this time. Neither woman, man, nor child gave him word or look or so much as the touch of a finger, for the terrible news had spread through the encampment more rapidly than a ripple spreads from the dropped pebble and soon washes the shore of the pool all round.

So did terror spread through the lodges of the Apaches. A sign had been promised them, a prodigious sign, that very night, in the dead person of their chief medicine man. And behold! The sign had been performed exactly as foretold.

It was hardly a wonder that Rory met with no interruption. For there was now only a single thought remaining in all the brains of those savages, and that was the urgent necessity of getting away from the accursed spot as soon as possible. Before Rory came to the outermost lodges, he saw the women already frantically at work striking the tepees, all shouting to one another, each urging the next to greater effort.

The tumult of the encampment was like smoke rising from many fires. And out of that smother of sound and confusion, Rory stepped calmly on to the spot where he had left the Apache "dead."

He had been wrong. There was no body on the spot!

He was glad of that. He had had enough of midnight killings to last him for a long time.

He continued to the place where he had left the rifle, found it in due course, reached the hollow, and there mounted the gray stallion.

Now he was on the horse, gathering the rope which served him as reins, and he could say that he was safe enough. If he were seen, mounted on the familiar silver silhouette of that horse, it would be a brave man among the Apaches who dared to approach or fire a shot at a ghost!

So Rory, looking on at the encampment which was being leveled as though before the blast of a storm, laughed to himself a little and then turned toward the house of Ware.

So far as he knew, the indiscretion of Major Talmadge of the cavalry had cost the whites the lives of Blucher and the bookkeeper, and the value of the big barn, together with all the livestock on the Ware place. It had cost the Apaches, first and last, four or five of their best men, and pretty badly smashed the reputation of that section of the tribe. This was not all. They would not be in haste to go on the warpath against the white again—not for a considerable time.

And Rory felt that the work was all his!

He turned the gray stallion straight back toward the house of Ware, and coming close to it, pulled the mustang down to a slow walk and went on with his right hand raised above his head.

As he came within twenty paces he heard a suddenly excited voice calling out, and after this a sharper and a higher cry:

"Rory Michel!"

Then the front door was jerked open, but though he dismounted, he did not enter.

"Come out, every one!" called Rory. "Come out and watch the moon rise!" He laughed as he called.

"Get in here, man!" exclaimed Ware impatiently. "They'll be filling you full of bullets in another moment or so!"

"Not they," answered Rory. "They've done with shooting for tonight. They'll not be interested in the warpath for quite a while to come. Come out here and see for yourselves!"

As he spoke, he turned and pointed, and from the house came the others, hurrying.

The word passed to the rear of the house. The Mexicans also came out in a sudden tumult.

And then the entire group was struck silent. Eastward, where the pale fire of the moonrise was appearing, moved an endless chain of figures, printed black against the radiance. Woman and warrior, the aged and the infant, some on horseback, some trudging, bent under loads, on foot, the Apaches were making back toward the mountains from which they had swept down in the raid.

The only person to speak, for some time, was Ware

himself, who kept muttering: "They're beaten! By heavens, they're beaten! It's not possible, but there they go."

The Mexicans got back their tongues first and used them for a tremendous outburst of enthusiasm and shouting. They danced. They embraced one another. They lifted that hardy rascal, Miguel, upon their shoulders. And Rory Michel, drawing back a little into the shadows that fell across the veranda of the house, looked out upon the others as at fantastic forms gibbering and moving in another world, outside the realities which he had known.

He slipped inside the house, and the instant his step was heard, the black stallion whinnied. A moment later Rory was sleeking the satin of that long and graceful neck.

But he felt greatly, vaguely troubled; he hardly knew why. There was no sense of triumph in his heart. There was only an odd feeling of loss and of impending disaster.

Yet the bright face of success was ready to shine on him. In a short half hour everyone in the place was feasting. Into the moonlit yard behind the house the Mexicans were gathered, with all the delicacies their hearts could desire. And around the long table in the Ware dining room, with Ware himself at one end of it, and his dazed wife at the other, sat the garrison—honest Captain Burn looking very red and pleased, young Rory next to him, and pretty Nancy Ware opposite them.

Ware made speeches. Nobody wanted to listen to them, but he felt words rising in his throat like water in a fountain's neck, and they had to be poured abroad. Well, it hardly mattered. He could not spoil happiness which was so complete.

Then Captain Burn said: "I want to ask a few questions. We all are still wearing our scalps, and I want to know why. Who'll answer that mystery for me?"

"Rory Mitchel!" said a chorus.

"Ware, you're sitting here as big as life, and looking pretty pleased with yourself. Why aren't you dead?"

230

"Rory Michel!" shouted Ware cheerfully, and beamed upon the youngster.

"The barn had to be burned, or we would all have been swept away the first night of the siege. Who burned the barn?"

"Rory Michel!" came the resounding chorus.

"Hush!" said Nancy Ware. "We'll be driving him away if we keep up."

They looked at Rory and saw that his expression was dark and that he was staring straight before him.

"Rory," said the girl, "will you do something for me?"

"Yes," said Rory absently, gloomily.

"Promise me?"

"Yes, I promise."

"Then tell us why the Apaches decided to move away tonight."

He glared at her.

"I can't tell you that," he insisted, with color rising in his face.

"You've promised," she repeated stubbornly.

He pushed back his chair a little, as though he were about to spring up in his anger. But she met his eye steadily.

"Are you going to hold me to that promise?" he asked her.

"Of course I am,"

He bit his lip.

"Well, it was all magic," said he. "You see, I'm a medicine man."

"What sort of magic?" she went on, pressing him hard.

"I met South Wind," said Rory, "and sent in word by him that the Apaches had better scamper or trouble wou'd be coming to them. And if they wanted a sign, it would be the death of Big Horse this same night. So that's why you saw them trooping across the hills."

"Wait!" cried the girl. "Was the sign accomplished? Was Big Horse killed—in the middle of that Indian cam ?"

He was silent, redder than ever, glaring at her.

231

"Big Horse was killed," he confessed.

"And you did it, Rory?" said she.

He looked about him uncomfortably.

If he was red, the others were pale, almost ghastly of eye as they stared at him. For each one was listing in his mind the incredible dangers to be surmounted in the stalking of that camp filled with wolfish, keen-eyed humans.

"Let it go, Nancy, will you?" he said to her.

She nodded finally in answer to this.

"Yes, I'll let it go," said Nancy. "Great heavens, Rory! I can't even think about such a thing. I don't know what stuff you can be made of. I'm bewildered!"

But that ended the pleasure of the dinner for Rory.

It was no longer a feast of triumph; it was an embarrassment that forced him back into himself, and he began to stare blackly down at the table before him, and would not speak a word to anyone.

He was glad to seize on the first excuse to leave the others to coffee. For his part, he went out with the black stallion, not not for a ride, but to walk quietly along, the big horse following, now cropping the grass, now frolicking like a dog around its master.

Chapter 43

Walking very slowly, Rory went on until he came to a hilltop, where he sat down on a rock and watched the progress of the silver moonlight flowing down the dim length of the valley.

A step came up behind him. Without turning his head, he knew who was there.

"Nancy?" said he.

"How did you know it was I?" said the girl as she sat down beside him.

"Well, it wouldn't be anybody else," he answered. "Would it?"

"I suppose not," said she. "And if you know that, tell me why I am here."

"I'd find it easy to do that," he replied.

"Go on, then."

"You saw me looking glum. You felt that I ought to be happy. That's the answer. You came out here just to make me happy," said Rory.

"Ha? Did I?" said she, as abrupt in her intonation as a man could ever be.

"Yes," he said.

"Go on," she said. "You haven't finished, Rory."

"No, I haven't finished. I'm going to talk a little. You want to hear me say it?"

"What are you going to say?"

"Oh, you know. That I'm pretty fond of you, and all that."

"Hold on, Rory," said she. "Is this a love scene?"

"No, because it takes two to make a love scene."

"Keep on," said Nancy Ware. "I like to hear it, anyway."

"I guess you do," said he. "You take my scalp and tuck it away. That's all right, too, I suppose!"

"Rory," said the girl, "you're feeling blue."

"A little bit. Yes."

"Tell me why, will you?"

"You know why."

"No. I don't."

"The truth is, Nancy, that I want you and I know that I can't have you."

"Can't you?" said she, turning suddenly toward him.

"Don't do that," protested Rory.

"Don't draw your conclusions with too long a bow," she replied.

"I'm not. I'm looking the facts in the face, and they make me absolutely sick."

"What makes you sick?"

"Oh, I know. If I talked about things to you now, you might say 'yes,' " said he. "Because you're grateful.

Because I've saved the hides of your family. But you wou'd n't mean it."

"Don't be so sure," said she.

"Don't talk like that," he urged again. "You get me all excited."

"You know what's the matter with you, Rory?" she asked.

"Tell me."

"It's this. You take yourself too seriously."

"Well, that's a new way of looking at it. But go on and tell me how I take myself too seriously."

"You do. You take yourself too seriously. You think you're the only man who's ever done anything wrong."

He started violently.

"That's interesting," he said. "And what do you think I've done that's so wrong?"

"Broken most of the ten commandments," she replied.

"Have I?"

"Haven't you?"

"Listen to me, Nancy. You're all right. You're the real thing. But do you mean that?"

"Yes, I mean that."

"Nancy, the fact is that I've fallen in love with you. So much that it hurts. I've got to get away."

"You wouldn't want to take me with you, Rory?" she asked in a grave and thoughtful tone.

He sighed.

"There you go again," said he. "In another minute I'm apt to lay hands on you, Nancy. But that's no good, and I know it. Putting hands on you, touching you, that won't help. You'll still remain a thousand miles away from me."

"Rory," said she, "what are you making out of me? An angel?"

"No, not that."

"No, don't make me an angel. I'm just like you. Full of the old Nick, if you want to know."

He laughed and made no answer.

"You're thinking how bad you've been?" she suggested.

234

"Well, perhaps."

"You've killed men who are not Indians, Rory?"

He straightened.

Then he answered soberly: "Yes!"

"Well, I knew that before," she said. "You have the way of a man who has done that."

He nodded.

"You've looked pretty far into me," he said.

"Pretty far," she agreed.

"And what about it?"

"Where are you going?"

"Oh, just away."

"That's what you've always been doing, isn't it?" said she.

"What makes you say that?" he asked.

"I asked a question first. Haven't you always been dodging about?" was her reply.

"Pretty much. Yes."

"Since you were a boy?"

"Yes."

"Ever stayed six months in one place since you were your own master?"

"No, I suppose not."

"Well, Rory, why not begin now?"

"And stay here?"

"No, but let me be the place. Stay with me."

"Hold on, Nancy. You don't know what you're leading up to, I'm sure."

"I know all about it. I say stay with me."

"You'd marry me to save me, eh?"

"I'd marry you because I love you."

He was silent.

He lifted his head and looked at the moonshine flooding the valley.

"It's a funny world," said he. "I know that it wouldn't be right, though. You'd never be happy with me. I'm not your kind."

"You're above my kind. You're outside my kind," she replied quietly. "You've walked half a year to get a horse. You've saved the lives of all the people who are dear to me. You've saved that house back there. You've smashed a whole tribe of Indians."

"By tricks," said he.

"No. By using your brain and risking your neck."

"Nancy," said he.

"Well?"

"Do you mean this?"

Suddenly she laughed.

"You're making me do all the leading, Rory," said she. He stood up with his back almost turned upon her.

"I'm trying to take hold of myself," said he.

"Why try so hard?"

"Nancy, I've been a waster, a drifter, a no-good fellow all my life."

"You've been another thing, too," said she.

"What's that?"

"A boy," she replied. "Why, Rory, in spite of all your man-killings, you've never grown up. Don't you see that? Take me and grow old along with me!"

He turned sharply round upon her.

"Did you speak to your father and mother?"

"About what?"

"About me."

"Yes, I asked them both if I could ask you to marry me."

"Hold on, Nancy!"

"Because I knew," said she, "that you'd never do the asking for yourself."

He did not sit down. He kneeled before her and said: "Nancy, I feel a little weak, as though it were the end of the world."

"It isn't the end of the world," she told him, "but it's the end of a lot of things for you."

He took her hands.

"I see what it means, Nancy," said he.

"Tell me about it, then," said she. "Does it mean happiness, Rory?"

"It means the end of me as a medicine man, thank God!" said he happily.

BOOKS OF DISTINCTION
FROM WARNER BOOKS

A CIVIL TONGUE
by Edwin Newman   (81-435, $2.50)

"Newman's second book is as salutory as his first, wrenching and amusing in turn. Like a miner who has struck a vein of richest gold, he has opening up before him an endless series of entertaining, educative and minatory volumes."   —*The New York Post*

STRICTLY SPEAKING
by Edwin Newman   (82-542, $2.25)

"A mighty important book is STRICTLY SPEAKING . . . Author Edwin Newman, the broadcaster, feels that the sorry state of the English language is a reflection of the sorry state of society. He spares no one in criticizing the poor way we speak and write."   —*Philadelphia Bulletin*

MODERN AMERICAN USAGE
by Wilson Follett
Edited and completed by Jacques Barzun

(81-529, $2.50)

Avoid common errors and increase your effectiveness in speech and writing with this handy detailed desk reference. Learn exactly how to use the correct terms to express yourself. This is the standard reference guide to complete, clear and correct communication, "a book that everyone should have."   —*Rex Stout*

TOLL-FREE DIGEST
by Toll-Free Digest Co., Inc.   (91-338, $2.50)

Contains over 17,000 listings of numbers across the country that you call at no charge. The money you save on your first toll-free call will pay for this directory. . . . Then it's welcome to the land of the free!

THE COMPLETE UNABRIDGED SUPER TRIVIA ENCYCLOPEDIA
by Fred L. Worth   (83-882, $2.95)

864 pages of pure entertainment. A panoply of sports, movies, comics, television, radio, rock 'n' roll, you-name-it, at your fingertips. The biggest, the best, the most comprehensive trivia book ever created!

THE BEST OF THE BESTSELLERS FROM WARNER BOOKS

REELING
by Pauline Kael   (83-420, $2.95)
Rich, varied, 720 pages containing 74 brilliant pieces covering the period between 1972-75, this is the fifth collection of movie criticism by the film critic *Newsday* calls "the most accomplished practitioner of film criticism in America today, and possibly the most important film critic this country has ever produced."

P.S. YOUR CAT IS DEAD
by James Kirkwood   (82-934, $2.25)
It's New Year's Eve. Your best friend died in September. You've been robbed twice. Your girlfriend is leaving you. You've just lost your job. And the only one left to talk to is a gay burglar you've got tied up in the kitchen.

ELVIS
by Jerry Hopkins   (81-665, $2.50)
More than 2 million copies sold! It's Elvis as he really was, from his humble beginnings to fame and fortune. It's Elvis the man and Elvis the performer, with a complete listing of his records, his films, a thorough astrological profile, and 32 pages of rare, early photographs!

A STRANGER IN THE MIRROR
by Sidney Sheldon   (81-940, $2.50)
Toby Temple is a lonely, desperate superstar. Jill Castle is a disillusioned girl, still dreaming of stardom and carrying a terrible secret. This is their love story. A brilliant, compulsive tale of emotions, ambitions, and machinations in that vast underworld called Hollywood.

STAINED GLASS
by William F. Buckley, Jr.   (82-323, $2.25)
The United States must stop a war with one man and one man alone. His name: Blackford Oakes, super agent. His mission: Kill his friend for the good of the world. This is Buckley at his spy thriller best, with the most daring, seductive, and charming hero since 007.

THE UNSHAKABLE, UNSTOPPABLE, UNKILLABLE CAPTAIN GRINGO IS BACK IN:

RENEGADE #2, BLOOD RUNNER
by Ramsay Thorne   (98-160, $1.50)

They're waiting for a man like Captain Gringo in Panama! In this soggy, green hell where the French have lost a fortune in lives and francs trying to build a canal, the scum of the earth — and their scams — flourish. Every adventurer with a scheme, every rebel with a cause wants a man like Captain Gringo — running guns, unloosing a rain of death from his Maxim, fighting Yellow Jack, Indians, army ants, even the Devil himself if he stands in the way!

BE SURE TO WATCH FOR MORE EXCITING ADVENTURES WITH THE LEGEND OF THE BORDER — CAPTAIN GRINGO, COMING SOON!

"THE KING OF THE WESTERN NOVEL" is MAX BRAND

____ **DRIFTER'S VENGEANCE** (84-783, $1.75)
____ **PLEASANT JIM** (86-286, $1.25)
____ **GUNMAN'S GOLD** (88-337, $1.50)
____ **FIRE BRAIN** (88-629, $1.50)
____ **TRAILIN'** (88-717, $1.50)
____ **MIGHTY LOBO** (88-829, $1.50)
____ **BORDER GUNS** (88-892, $1.50)
____ **WAR PARTY** (88-933, $1.50)
____ **SILVERTIP** (88-685, $1.50)
____ **MAN FROM SAVAGE CREEK** (88-883, $1.50)
____ **CHEYENNE GOLD** (88-966, $1.50)
____ **FRONTIER FEUD** (98-002, $1.50)
____ **RIDER OF THE HIGH HILL** (88-884, $1.50)
____ **FLAMING IRONS** (98-019, $1.50)
____ **SILVERTIP'S CHASE** (98-048, $1.50)
____ **SILVERTIP'S STRIKE** (98-096, $1.50)